RISING

a novel by

Regina McIntyre

"Rising" by Regina McIntyre

© Regina McIntyre, 2024

Published by DAMTE Associates Publishing LLC

This novel is a work of fiction based on the events that took place in Warsaw during World War II. Names of the important leaders and historical data of the time are used as a foundation and scaffold to build the structure of the story. Any dialogue attributed to real historic persons is fictitious, unless annotated and referenced.

All other characters and events are purely fictional, and no reference is intended to any person living or dead.

The opinions expressed in this manuscript are solely the opinions of the author and do not represent the opinions or thoughts of the publisher. The author has represented and warranted full ownership and/or legal right to publish all the materials in this book.

This book may not be reproduced, transmitted, or stored in whole or in part by any means, including graphic, electronic, or mechanical without the express written consent of the publisher except in the case of brief quotations embodied in critical articles and reviews.

Sequel to RESISTANCE, Copyright 2022 by Regina McIntyre.

ISBN: Softcover   978-1-6698-1399-6
          eBook   978-1-6698-1398-9

The Author Wishes to Recognize

Her Reliance on the Following

Historical Reference Works

For the Basis of the Chronological Facts

Underlying Her Tale

Of Historical Fiction:

"RISING 44: The Battle for Warsaw" by Norman Davies, 2004,
Penguin Group, 375 Hudson Street, New York, NY 10014

"NOWAK: Courier from Warsaw" by Jan Nowak, 1982,
Wayne State University Press, Detroit, Michigan, 48202

"THE SECRET ARMY: The memoirs of General Bór-Komorowski"
by Tadeusz Bór-Komorowski, 2011, Pen & Sword, Limited,
47 Church Street, Barnsley, S. Yorkshire 270 2AS

"FIGHTING WARSAW" by Stefan Korbonski, 2004, Hippocrene Books,
171 Madison Avenue, New York, NY 10016

"THE SECOND WORLD WAR: A Complete History" by Martin Gilbert,
1989, Henry Holt and Company, Inc., 115 West 18th Street,
New York, NY 10011

"Warsaw Airlift—4 August to 28 September 1944"
WIKIPEDIA The Free Encyclopedia,
Wikimedia Foundation, Inc.
www.wikipedia.org

*This book is dedicated to the
unknown RAF pilot, who, during the
Warsaw Airlift of August 1944,
saw his wing in flames
and knew he would crash.*

*Before the plane burst into flames on the
outskirts of the suburb of Praga,*

*he dropped the much needed supplies over
the devastated city of Warsaw, Poland.*

<u>As described in:</u>
"THE SECRET ARMY:
The memoirs of General Bór-Komorowski"
by Tadeusz Bór-Komorowski, Copyright 2011

"At the end of the war, when the Third Reich
was facing defeat and occupation, the Nazi leaders
turned to the head of German army intelligence
in the east, Reinhard Gehlen, and asked him in
desperation to advise on how to form
a German Resistance movement
against the allies.

Gehlen, who was not a Nazi,
advised that they follow the model of
the Polish Home Army."

Excerpt from:
RISING '44: THE BATTLE FOR WARSAW
By Norman Davies, Copyright 2004.

POLISH HISTORIC CHARACTERS (Nom de Guerre)

Government-in-Exile Premier Stanisław Mikołajczyk (Mik)

Government-in-Exile Commander-in-Chief,
General Kazimierz Sosnkowski

Jan Stanisław Jankowski, Chief Delegate in Warsaw (Prezes)

General Tadeusz Bór-Komorowski, Commander Home Army
(Bór)

Deputy General Antoni Chruściel, Commander Warsaw District
(Monter)

General Tadeusz Pełczyński, (Grzegorz), Bór's Chief of Staff

General Leopold Okulicki (Niedźwiadek "Bear Cub," Cobra)

Colonel Karol Ziemski Wachnowski, Organizer under Monter

Kazimierz Puzak, Chairman of Council of National Unity

Sowa, Mayor of Warsaw

Ignatz Walczak, Secretary Treasury

Janek Kaplinsky, Under Secretary Treasury

Anonymous sixty-year-old Polish man who initiated the
Telephone Building Siege (appearing in the story under the
fictional name of Albert Kryzostanski)

Countess Zofia Tarnowska, Red Cross Representative

Manya Wachowiak, Red Cross Representative

Lieutenant Colonel "Zyndram"

Władysław Czajkowski, Director of Underground Office
of Recovered Provinces

BRITISH HISTORIC CHARACTERS

Prime Minister, Winston S. Churchill
War Correspondent, Alexander Werth
British Air Marshal Wilson
Secretary of Air Archibald Sinclair

SOVIET HISTORIC CHARACTERS

Premier, Marshal Josef V. Stalin
Minister of Foreign Affairs Vyacheslav Molotov
General Konstantin Rokossovsky
General Zygmunt Berling

GERMAN HISTORIC CHARACTERS

Der Führer of Germany, Adolf Hitler
Reichsführer of Germany, Heinrich Himmler
Governor-General of Poland, Hans Frank
SA Gruppenführer Ludwig Fischer
Brigadeführer Franz Kutschera
SS-Ogruführer Erich von dem Bach-Zelewski

INTRODUCTION

Russia and the Third Reich signed the secret Nazi-Soviet Pact just days before the September 1, 1939, invasion of Poland. On 28 September, the German-Soviet Treaty of Friendship was signed; this document superseded the original 'secret pact' and firmed the alliance by setting the protocol for cooperation and demarcation of territory. The map of Poland was divided into two parts, Germany claimed the land west of the River Bug and the land east of the river was marked as the Soviet Zone, agreed upon as the 'Peace Boundary.' Vyacheslav Molotov, Russia's Commissar of Foreign Affairs declared, 'Poland has ceased to exist.' Soviet Premier Jozef Stalin would lay claim to Russia's part of the territory throughout the Second World War.

This Treaty of Friendship, Cooperation, and Demarcation ended abruptly when Hitler invaded Russia in June of 1941, forcing Stalin to seek a union with the Grand Alliance. The USSR was forced to recognize the Polish Government-in-Exile and sign the Atlantic Charter which outlawed the principle of territorial aggrandizement.

During the Big Three meeting at Tehran in November of 1943, code name 'Eureka', the former 'Peace Boundary' appeared under a new label. Molotov presented a copy of a British telegram dated 25 July 1920 describing the 'Curzon Line'. The British staff had no knowledge of the enigmatic boundary, a configuration that was designed by Lord Curzon. After the First World War, the division of territories was administered by the Supreme War Council. Britain's Foreign Secretary Lord Curzon of Kedleston designed the demarcation line to serve as a future border between the Second Polish Republic and Bolshevik Russia. Stalin looked upon this as an infraction upon Soviet soil and perceived the line as an added incentive to conquer Poland.

PROLOGUE

Just before noon, on Christmas Eve, Michal Bednarek, newly appointed interim-editor of the underground *Polish Journal,* was treated to an unexpected visit. Zygmunt Kaminski, founder and publisher of the clandestine newspaper showed up at Michal's office in Napoleon Square.

"Come, I'll treat you to lunch at the Nectar."

Stille Nacht was being caroled at the Nectar, it served as background music while the two friends enjoyed a convivial chat over beer and *Schmorgericht.* There was no talk of war or reprisals. The dining room was regaled in Holly and Evergreen branches; the servers actually carried a warm glow about them as they loaded and unloaded their trays.

Out on the street, Kaminski reached out for a handshake. "Michal, I'm leaving for Blizna to get a first-hand account of the new Nazi weapon they've been exploding over the marshes. The villagers are trying to get an intact specimen for the Home Army. I'd love to be there when they do. Also, the Germans are being routed by the Russians and bombarded by the Western Allies. It's important that Poles be apprised of current events. The Allies are committed to opening a second front, and if they do, we Poles will be responsible for dealing with the exiting Germans from our country. Meanwhile, I depend on you and Jerzy to keep the Journal going. Maintain communication with the Resistance for copy. We will continue to work together via radio messages. I'm like the Holy Spirit, I'll never leave you on your own."

Michal tightened his grip on Kaminski's hand. He did not respond, an image of total destruction flashed across his mind's eye. The next year would see the decisive end of the war. Would Poland achieve her long-awaited Independence?

Chapter One

Cold winds snarled through the stark landscape of Warsaw in January of 1944. The destruction had been thorough. The devastating *blitzkrieg* of August 1, 1939, left a graveyard of buildings that dotted the landscape of an entire neighborhood in a section of Warsaw. The occasional wall that was left standing stood as sentinel and specter, a testament to the havoc imposed on the territory by Hitler's *Luftwaffe*. A new construction was abandoned. No one knew or cared what purpose the building would have served. Five years later, the ruble remained uncleared.

A shadowy figure moved in a crouched silhouette amongst the ghostly ruins of the past towards the unfinished building. At twenty-three, Zygmunt Kaminski was forced to give up his ambition to become an influential politician. His master's degree in political science and his plans to run for office in the Polish Parliament were brought to an abrupt halt after Hitler's invasion, and subsequent occupation of Poland. He had recently moved from Poznań to Warsaw to be where the action was, the seat of the Sejm Complex. Instead, he was confronted by the onset of World War II.

Zygmunt Kaminski had, in fact, been born in Poznań, the Polish city just across the border of Berlin, Germany. Kaminski's mother, Professor Madeline Bergman, a German citizen, taught German in the University of Poznań. His father, Stefan Kaminski, an engineer, took her German 101 class to improve his communication skills. He took her 102 class to pursue the instructor. Both goals were gratified.

In June of 1915, they were wed. Under Nazi diktat, the fact that his mother was German allowed Zygmunt to be considered a *Volksdeutscher,* which duly extended to him the same privileges as a German citizen. German was his second language; he spoke it like a native.

He managed to escape conscription in the *Wehrmacht* because of an irregular heartbeat. This gave him the opportunity to re-invent himself. His uncle, Gustav, was a printer and Zygmunt was familiar with the process. He had acquired a basic knowledge of the craft of printing and the distinctive features of the types of paper that was used. With this rudimentary background he invested his life's savings, and some money that he borrowed from his father, to rent office space in Centre City. He stocked the shelves with the varied textures and types of paper used in the commercial world and set himself up with a thriving business in Warsaw. Kaminski was a born salesman. His official *Ausbeis,* work permit, from the labor office of the German General Government listed his occupation as Purveyor of Paper Products. He directed his knowledge of printing and his talent for writing into the publication of a subversive underground newspaper. Kaminski became the founder, publisher, and editor of *Poland's Journal.* This information was not included in his *Ausbeis.*

It was in his role of journalist that Kaminski approached the battered, unfinished building, which currently housed the administrative offices of K-Division, the highly secretive Intelligence operation of the Polish Underground militia, the Home Army. He rapped out the signal knock that had been assigned to him. An officer opened the door and respectfully escorted him to the secretary, she rendered him a half-hearted smile as she directed him to a chair outside of Colonel Kumor's office.

Several coal-burning braziers were set about the premises to offset the bitter cold of January 1944. The staff of K-Division made a valiant effort to cope with the frigid conditions; they layered their clothing with sweaters and scarfs and struggled to perform their tasks efficiently while their hands were muffled in warm, woolen gloves. Kaminski stood up from the chair and flailed his arms about him to build up body heat against the icy chill that bounced off the walls of the drafty building. The cold served to fuel his resentment. He had been ordered to the compound to give a report on the conditions in Blizna.

After what seemed an interminable length of time, the secretary re-appeared and ushered him into the colonel's office. Kumor pointed to the chair that faced his desk; Kaminski did his best to soothe his angst and appear to be compliant. Kumor was a formidable character; he stood six feet, four inches tall, lean but brawny, an athletic type; his facial features were rugged and irregular, a conspicuous scar followed a diagonal line across his left cheek. He had proven his courage and resourcefulness in espionage during the Soviet-Polish war of 1920, by escaping from a Russian prison camp with some of their highly classified military strategies, which the Polish Army put to good use.

The vigorous frame of the Colonel seemed out of place in the chair behind his desk; he'd be better suited in the field, leading his men in an offensive against the enemy. In his usual brusque manner, without any attempt to offer a greeting or the time of day, he began the session with the limited information he had on hand.

"Agent Markay has alerted us of the fact that the German's are manufacturing an impressive weapon in their new experimental station. He reports that he observed a freight train, out of Blizna, carrying an object covered by a tarpaulin, which he discerned to be a monstrous torpedo." Kumor eyeballed the journalist, "What can you add?"

Kaminski maintained the snappy pattern, "Markay's observation fits the description of the object that is wreaking havoc on the community. Testing of the explosives being detonated in the area of Blizna are causing considerable property damage. The villagers live close to the bone, and these disturbances have galvanized them to act on behalf of the Home Army. They rush to the scene of every explosion to retrieve the fragments of the missiles before the Nazis come to fetch the parts. So far, the fragments only reveal that they are metal; not enough remains to suggest exactly what these weapons are capable of."

"We know they are flying bombs, thanks to the gutsy action of the two prisoners on Peenemunde, who were able to get their hands on the blueprints and design, but you're right, we don't know how devastating this missile can be. We need an intact specimen." There was a brief pause, Kumor lowered his chin and placed a penetrating eye on Kaminski.

"Will you be going back? I must be kept apprised of events as they occur down there."

"I have to conduct business here in town, to validate my position and not be held suspect. You'll have to rely on your Home Army sources."

The sharp look of annoyance that Kumor shot his way caused Kaminski to flinch, he hastily added, "I have engaged a reliable villager, code name of *Woda*, he will wire me of any new development that takes place in my absence." He rose from his chair, and in a gentler tone, added, "I will gladly share any information that I receive with you."

Kaminski squeezed into his German built Adler; there was little room to accommodate his portly frame. Reams of paper and boxes of notebooks and tablets filled the seats, products of his latest purchasing trip to the printer in Kraków where the official Nazi seals, insignias, and logos of the varied administrations were imprinted on specific types of paper, to ensure against forgery. The trip served two purposes; he needed to replenish his stock, and the authorized trip provided a cover up for the investigative journalism he was conducting in Blizna.

Initially, the weapon was being developed in Peenemunde, on the Island of Usedom in the Baltic, under the direction of Wernher von Braun. Two Polish prisoners of war, who served as janitors at the German Army Research Center, came across the plans of a new weapon the Germans were working on. They managed to gather sketches, maps, and reports of a rocket launching site on the island. Somehow, they were able to smuggle the contents to the Polish Information Bureau. The Bureau, in turn, dispatched the information to Prime Minister Churchill in London, where the facts were verified and direct action against the project was taken. In August of 1943 five-hundred-ninety-six RAF heavy bombers attacked the German Army Research Center in Peenemunde targeting the living quarters of the scientists, the factory workshop, and the experimental station.

The Germans then moved the operation to the village of Blizna, in the Pipet Marshes of southeast Poland, out of range of British aircraft.

Kaminski caught wind of the operation when he accidentally learned that the local villagers were being bombarded with flying objects that were destroying their property. Some journalistic snooping gave him enough information to discern there was a story in Blizna. He arranged for an interim editor, Michal Bednarek, along with his assistant printer, Jerzy Gruber, to maintain *Poland's Journal* while he investigated the story.

Chapter Two

itler had closed the universities and secondary schools in
October of 1940, leaving only the elementary schools,
grades one to four, to provide rudimentary lessons that
would ensure a population of lower-level workers to perform in the
German labor market. Governor General Hans Frank appraised the
situation, *"The Poles are to supply only labor and it will suffice if
they can simply read and write…"*

Professor of history, Leona Bednarek lost her position and
the university that had employed her for sixteen years. The
university was closed, and the professors went into hiding to
escape being executed as members of the elite. She quickly
arranged to conduct clandestine meetings in her home to a group of
dedicated students who were working toward their degrees.

There was an entire network of underground university
studies. Professors risked their lives to teach their subjects in
established hide outs located throughout the city and its suburbs.
Forged certificates and diplomas were dated 1938 and 1939, to
present authenticity to the documents. As a result, several hundred
students received their degrees during the German occupation.

Leona Bednarek stretched her arms above her head and
emitted a resounding yawn. The final draft of her curriculum for
the new semester was completed to her satisfaction, and she had
the rest of the day before her. She no longer conducted classes in
her home.

Leona's husband, Michal had insisted that she give up teaching after a venerable neighbor of theirs was betrayed by a collaborator and carted away by the Nazis.

Leona strategically mapped out a plan, contrary to her husband's wishes, and used her bargaining skills to gain admittance into the catacomb atmosphere of the basement of the church. Her Wednesday night history class was made tenable under the auspices of Father Jan Lipinski, pastor of St. Anthony of Padua. Lipinski offered to lecture a weekly scriptural lesson in the chapel upstairs as a coverup activity.

Once inside the church, the history students separated from the crowd, and discreetly made their way down the stairs to the northwest corner of the basement.

Lunch with a friend would serve to relax and refresh the professor's spirits. She gave a cursory review of her list of possible candidates and decided that Father Lipinski was the most likely candidate. Not only was he bright and witty, but there were several issues on her mind that he might help clarify. She made a phone call to firm up an appointment and then selected an outfit that was warm and conservative.

The cold, damp weather bestowed a mind of its own to her dark brown hair, and she tussled with the brush to come to some arrangement. There were no cosmetics, her rouge and lipstick tubes were long since depleted; she would have to rely on some cheek pinching and the thick, dark eyelashes that showcased her green eyes. In mid-life, Leona Bednarek was still a very attractive woman.

The remnants of a recent snow left a residue of icy patches on the streets and Leona had to carefully navigate her way to the church. A lacy covering of ice had settled on the bare branches of the trees providing them with a shimmering curtain to address the bright cerulean sky above. She marveled at the natural beauty still available despite the atrocities occurring in the daily lives of a people at war.

Pani Trypka, the rectory housemaid, answered the front door and led Leona to the sitting room where a fireplace was glowing under a fresh supply of wood. "Father has had an unexpected visitor. He apologizes and asks that you make yourself comfortable. May I offer you a glass of sherry?"

"Thank you, Magda," she handed her a package, "and here is another bottle to add to the wine-rack."

Porcelain place settings in a delicate pattern of pink roses were neatly arranged on the round tea table, two comfortable fireside chairs completed the convivial scene. Leona removed her coat and gloves and gave them to the housekeeper. She pulled her chair closer to the fire to rub her hands while she waited for the sherry to warm her body. Unaccustomed to idle moments, she hoped the priest would not be too long with his unexpected visitor. Meanwhile, the crackle and sizzle of fresh wood in the fireplace, accompanied by the rhythmic spikes of colorful flames that danced along the logs radiated a mesmerizing effect. Perhaps it was the double sherry that Trypka poured; she relaxed and allowed her mind to wander.

Irena, her daughter, had become engaged over the Christmas holiday to a young man with a questionable background. Jerzy Gruber was employed by the *Nowy Kourier*, a German propaganda newspaper. His appearance suited an SS agent. Tall and very well built, there was an Aryan quality reflected in his blonde hair and cool blue eyes that expressed an unflappable, intelligent nature. He conveyed an attitude that commanded respect. His uncle, Heinrich Gruber, was employed as a foreman in a German leather factory. A card-carrying Nazi, Heinrich professed to be the leader of a cell of German citizens, alleged insurgents, who held no allegiance to Hitler's Nazi Party. Purportedly they were working in league with the Polish Underground. Leona wouldn't admit it to anyone, but she had difficulty accepting these facts at face value.

In fact, Heinrich Gruber had recently implanted two of his best operatives into the Wednesday scriptural lessons of Father Lipinski to observe any on toward behavior among the participants that might suggest a collaborator operating in their midst. Lipinski and Leona were the only ones to know about the protective measure; the identity of the planted observers was known only to the priest.

Leona was on her second glass of sherry when the tall, gaunt figure of the priest entered the living room.

"Forgive me, my dear, I had to attend to some unfinished business." He settled his long and lean frame into the seat across from her.

"No need to apologize, Father, I have been most comfortable. Actually, I can't remember a time when I was this relaxed. The interlude has allowed me time to gloss over some issues of concern."

Pani Trypka brought in a tray of sandwiches and coffee and interrupted the flow of conversation. Lipinski said the blessing and waited until his housekeeper left the room before opening a serious dialogue.

"And what are these issues of concern that you are dealing with, Leona?"

"I have yet to recover from Heinrich Gruber's revelation of Michal's involvement in the underground newspaper. It cast a heavy shadow over the remnants of a pleasant Christmas dinner."

"Leona, that was inadvertent; he had no way of knowing that Michal was hiding this information from you."

"We've discussed it, Father. It seems Michal felt that I had enough intrigue on my plate with the covert history classes. He wanted to spare me any additional worry."

"I'm curious, Leona; when does he find time to write for *Poland's Journal*, in addition to his official duties with the Schindlerites, and his *pro-bono* work in civil court?"

"Father, he's a master juggler. You mention his role as magistrate in the civil court for Polish citizens; did you know that he is also a participating lawyer in the Secret Court of the underground?"

"No, of this I was unaware," the priest vented a heavy sigh and shook his head, "Not only is he spreading himself too thin, Leona, he is placing himself, as well as you, at grave risk."

She leaned back in her chair as she allowed a reminiscent thought to interrupt their conversation. "I remember his initial stance on covert activity, 'I am a professional lawyer, I do not involve myself in intrigue.' That was before Kaminski grabbed a stranglehold on Michal's conscience."

"Now that Kaminski is back at the helm, perhaps that is one less hat for Michal to wear."

"It's one of my prayers Father."

The housemaid came in to clear away the dishes, and Lipinski busied himself at the fireplace, poking aside the ashes to add another log.

"Is there another pot of coffee for us, Magda?"

"Yes, and I have some *pączki* for you to dunk."

While they waited for desert, Leona ventured, "May I inquire as to the visitor you met with earlier, Father?"

"But, of course, Leona; I was about to tell you. It was one of Gruber's security officers, reporting on the suspicious behavior of a new member to the scripture study. Unfortunately, this member will not be attending future sermons. He met with a tragic accident on his way home, last night."

The priest lowered his head and muttered a prayer, "God rest his soul." He looked up at his guest, the usual benign smile was replaced with a grim set of his lips. "I shall offer mass this week for the indulgence of his soul."

Chapter Three

Former Attorney Michal Bednarek was having lunch at the Nectar with Herr Berghan, one of his Schindlerite clients. Bednarek's dress and carriage were a testament to his conservative approach to life. A handsome man, his blonde hair and fair skin belied his twenty-odd years of service on the bar.

The judicial system of Poland had been radically curtailed under the German occupation, and Bednarek could no longer function as a lawyer. His current means of obtaining a living was as a Public Accountant, a position he held while he was working his way through law school. He went about his new endeavor with the same professional zeal that he employed in his career as an attorney. As a result, he managed to gain a significant reputation among the invading horde of Schindlerites, German entrepreneurs who bought up the confiscated Polish enterprises at a fraction of the cost. Bednarek was considered to be trustworthy and reliable.

Bednarek glanced up over the booth and caught a glimpse of Kaminski walking toward their table. In lieu of his usual carnation, Kaminski displayed a deep red rose nestled in the buttonhole of his snappily tailored suit jacket. Short and portly, he carried his weight in a robust manner; his congenial nature and quick wit, along with his impeccable German, won him many friends among the German citizens of Warsaw.

"Herr Berghan, how are things in the leather industry?" he offered this in German.

Kaminski nodded toward Michal, "Pan Bednarek, how convenient. Gentlemen, may I join you? I see you have not yet ordered." This was rendered in Polish.

Michal managed an automatic nod. He had no idea that the underground journalist had returned from his secret mission in *Blizna*.

Berghan beamed a smile, "Where have you been, Kaminski?"

"Kraków. The paper industry is constantly re-designing the official products to stay ahead of the war against forgery, so I've been on a buying spree to stay *au currant*."

"And when may I expect you to drop by the office?"

Kaminski pulled out his pocket calendar. "Tomorrow at nine?"

"Good, we don't want to be caught using unofficial stock."

He held on to the calendar, "Pan Bednarek, you're not on my list of patrons."

"No, I shop the Stationery Store for my needs. Ledgers and journals are not apt to be used in forgery."

"Oh, I have that stop this afternoon," he glanced at his watch, "three o'clock." He emphasized the time.

The waitress appeared and they placed their order, three luncheon specials—*Rheinsalm*, Rhine salmon, with white wine from the same region.

"Herr Berghan, you'd be interested to know, I had lunch with Governor Frank at the Castle."

The comfortably upholstered Berghan beamed again, *"Und, was is loss?"*

"He is proud of the industrial and commercial enterprises that the Schindlerites are maintaining here in Warsaw. He says we do better than Kraków in our revenue to add to the German coffers."

"Ah!" Berghan rubbed his hands together with a satisfied smile. Kaminski wasn't sure if the gesture was in response to his comment or the dish of salmon the server had placed before him

Buxom Street was home to several covert buildings closely guarded by the partisans living nearby. The basement of one of the apartment houses neatly stored the ammunitions and guns obtained from the Western Allies. British and Polish pilots, flying out of London, risked their lives to parachute weapons, as well as cash, into carefully selected areas around Warsaw to supply the Home Army's underground militia.

The Stationery Store, which sat on the corner, was a haven for subversive activities of both Civil Resistance and the Home Army. Edward Potopski's family had owned and operated the shop for generations. Herr Gruffman, a wealthy Schindlerite bought the property as an investment. Potopski received an estimated one month's revenue along with an offer to stay on as manager of the shop. During negotiations for the sale of the confiscated property, Gruffman had been assured by the Gestapo that Potopski was a reliable collaborator who had proven his ability to inform on persons of interest and could be trusted. Potopski's reputation had been earned by the secret disclosures he sporadically made to the SS regarding known Polish collaborators.

The Secret Court held dossiers on these traitors and provided Potopski with fictitious accounts of their disloyalty to the General Government. The SS wasted no time in responding to these alleged reports. The collaborators were arraigned, prosecuted, and executed under the Nazi rule of retribution. The Secret Court was thereby relieved of the disposition of these traitors, and Potopski was able to maintain his reputation with the SS as a trustworthy collaborator operating within the Polish community.

Edward Potopski had only one reason to stay alive. He had no family, his wife and children were murdered during the *blitzkrieg*, while he was on Marszałkowska Street throwing flaming oil-soaked rags under the approaching German tanks. Potopski was dedicated to the eventual destruction of the Nazis. The store became a refuge for traveling insurgents and a secure hideout for covert meetings.

Bednarek arrived at the shop a little after three; he picked up a packet of legal pads and took them to the register. Potopski smiled as he looked out the two windows that offered a view of the intersecting streets. He then turned his attention to his customer and gave a go-ahead nod. Michal walked to the back of the store and opened the door to a closet. Behind a rack of heavy coats was a sliding panel that led to the basement. He switched on the light; the expected warning pings of a bell sounded as he made his way down the stairs.

Sparse furnishings of cots, a table and chairs, dinnerware and a cabinet of canned and dry food products offered the rudimentary requirements for a short stop-over for traveling insurgents. Michal sat down at the table and went over his report for Kaminski. He glanced at his watch, three-twenty, Kaminski was running late. Michal had a five o'clock appointment with a jeweler, Wagner, who always ended his visits with a cash payment. He'd allow himself fifteen more minutes.

Kaminski's affable voice announced his presence upstairs, the conversation had something to do with the new shipment of paper products. Finally, the sound of the door closing at the top of the stairs and three pings of the bell signaled a visitor's approach.

"You're late!"

"Too many errands on my list. I apologize." He walked over to the table and took a seat facing Michal, "Jerzy tells me you are embroiled in judicial activities."

"The Resistance has initiated a new program called Operation Heads. The officers of the SS and the local Blue Police who are involved in brutality against the citizens of Warsaw are to be held accountable through due process." He cast a discerning eye Kaminski's way, "You'll need to keep this bit of information on ice, Zygmunt. The Secret Court, in alliance with K-Division, has collected evidence and depositions against the new SS Police, Chief Franz Kutschera. His daily roundups of innocent Poles for public executions have far exceeded that of Stroop's, his predecessor. Kutschera was at the top of the Operation Heads list."

"Has a date been assigned?"

"I will keep you posted. So far, one of the top surveillance experts in K-Division has, through a stroke of luck, observed an Opel Admiral limousine entering the drive of the building at Aleje Ujazdówska, number 22, SS Headquarters. He watched while the passenger alighted from the car, the officer wore the insignia of a general. The operative began to monitor the comings and goings of the general and identified him as Kutschera. He also uncovered the general's home located at Aleja Róż number 2, only one-hundred and fifty meters away from headquarters. The limousine is used as a precaution, it's armor-plated.""I just met with Kumor, who never mentioned a word."

Michal snickered, "He would disclose this information to you, a journalist?"

Kaminski let the jibe ride, "Anything else going on that I missed?'

"Yes, had you accepted our invitation to dine with us at Christmas, you'd have heard Jerzy's Uncle Heinrich inform us that several officers of the Home Army had been murdered by leaders of the Red forces in the area of Volhynia. I haven't had the time, or the inclination to confront Kumor about this."

He shot an admiring glance Kaminski's way, "Did you really have lunch with General Frank in Kraków?"

"Of course, not," he scoffed.

"But your proud announcement to Berger?"

"Oh, that," he laughed, "That was just to puff him up. No doubt he's been bragging about the remark to all of his friends," the glint in his eyes matched the grin on his face, "I like to maintain good customer relations."

Chapter Four

The sealed order had come directly from the desk of General 'Nile,' Commander of K-Division. It was hand-delivered to Judge Peter Butkowski, Chief Justice of the Secret State's judiciary system; due process of the case against the commander of the SS troops became official. Valid depositions had been signed by eyewitnesses and family members who had suffered the loss of loved ones under *SS-Brigadeführer* Franz Kutschera's public executions. The daily carnage of these 'round-ups,' *lapankas,* was draining the civilian population of the city and generating widespread psychological fear among those who had to live under the oppressive occupation of the German General Government. The vicious reprisals were conducted against innocent civilians, as an ongoing fear tactic in order to maintain control over the population.

Justice Butkowski had Kutschera's death sentence inscribed in the legal terminology as dictated during the Secret Court's trial, which was duly completed with Kutschera in absentia. It was signed under the seal of Chief Delegate, Jan Stanisław Jankowski, a.k.a. 'Prezes.' The use of a *nom de guerre* was meant to ensure the anonymity of those in command of the underground, "no identification upwards."

Civil Resistance agent, Mateusz Nowacki, a.k.a. 'Virski,' carried the official document, carefully glued between the pages of a German magazine, to its final destination, the desk of Colonel Kumor of K-Division.

The recent Christmas holiday had cast a heavy gray shadow over Virski; he marked the occasion by remembering that this was the fifth Christmas he had endured life without a family. His aging mother and his young wife were killed during the *blitzkrieg* in 1939 when their apartment building was demolished. He tried to convince himself that death had come quickly, and they were not subjected to the brutal existence of life under Nazi rule. That thought enabled him to sift through the trauma and depression, one day at a time.

There was a vague blandness about Virski's appearance, which no doubt allowed him to engage in his daily activities with relative obscurity. There was no outstanding or bold facial feature that could describe him; his hair was a dull brown, and it was thinning. The only unique feature about the man was his voice, a raspy monotone, possibly due to his habit of whispering in a covert fashion.

Virski sat shivering outside Colonel Kumor's office. Inactivity brought the demons to the foreground; he used the time to focus on the careful peeling of the glued pages of the magazine to expose the official death certificate. Once he had liberated the document, he held it plainly in his hand as he was being ushered into the office to present it to Kumor.

"Here is your next assignment."

"Have a seat." Kumor adjusted his spectacles and carefully read the diktat. He laid the document down on his desk and centered his attention on Virski. "We will hold on to this. We have mapped out a strategy and a tentative date to perform the assassination, necessary details continue to be refined."

Virski was familiar with Kumor's brusque manner of communication and knew he should be on his way, but he pressed the colonel further on an issue he was concerned with, "I hear there are lives lost due to the devious Soviet exploitation of Home Army officers."

"Yes, true. We have eye-witness verification from a sergeant who recently escaped conscription in a Soviet division that was engaged in re-capturing Polish territory in Volhynia."

"I need to meet with this officer."

The first day of February 1944 was windless and chilly. Aleje Ujazdowskie, or Ujazdów Boulevard, was strangely silent, an almost surreal atmosphere hovered over the scene as the customary early morning procession began. The steel-grey Opel Admiral limousine, the official transport of *SS-Brigadeführer* Franz Kutschera, pulled out of the drive of Aleja Róż number 2 and turned onto the Boulevard, flanked by SS men. Closely following the vehicle was an open truck, loaded with German soldiers. As the entourage approached the corner of Pious XI Street, an Adler-Triumpf barreled around the corner; two other vehicles straddled the street on either side of the Adler to provide cover-up protection. The Adler tore onto the wrong side of the street and smashed head-on into the convoy. A passenger jumped out of the Adler, rushed toward the limousine, and emptied a Sten sub-machine gun through the Opel's window, while his accomplice repeated the very same action on the other side of the car. *SS-Brigadeführer* Kutschera lay dying in a pool of blood that was rapidly covering his seat.

Franz Kutschera had assumed the office of Commander of the SS and Police of the Warsaw District on October 25, 1943, with orders from Governor General Frank to "Crush the will of the citizens of Warsaw." Kutschera had earned the reputation of a mass murderer of civilians during his earlier posts throughout Europe. Reportedly, his mistress was none other than Himmler's sister. He was held in high regard among the military elite. In absolute obedience, Kutschera intensified the arbitrary roundups, *lapanka,* of the Polish citizens who were chosen at random for street shootings. Poles never knew when they left their homes if they would be pulled into a roundup and never see their home again.

The day after the assassination of Kutschera, three hundred civilian hostages were shot in a public execution. The Germans demanded a monetary retribution of one-million zloty, a charge of thirty zloty per resident.

On Friday, February 4, 1944, whole sections of the city were closed for security purposes during the Kutschera funeral ceremony. Extra guards were posted throughout the city and citizens had to undergo heightened screening to go about their business. The psychological terror foisted upon the Poles had become a two-edged sword. The Germans found themselves dealing with covert killers who did not hesitate to assassinate high ranking officials. Russian roulette had become a competitive sport.

Seats in the Napoleon Café were plentiful. The Polish citizenry was recovering from the Kutschera reprisals. Only necessary tasks were undertaken by the civilian population; people went about their business in marked silence. They shuffled along the streets in a defensive manner, keenly cautious of the imminent danger surrounding them. There was none of the usual conversation aboard the trams during the peak hours of the day.

A lone figure, Albert Świątek, was seated at his usual table up front in the Napoleon Cafe; he had yet to put his fork to the eggs that sat cooling on his plate. The *Nowy Kourier's* full-page account of the Kutschera assassination held his interest. As a Swiss citizen, he operated under total impunity throughout Warsaw and had no concern about reprisals. However, the Nazis had no way of detecting his thoughts.

The only other diners that morning were Kaminski and his assistant reporter and printer Jerzy Gruber; they sat huddled in a cozy nook at the rear of the dining room. As registered *Volksdeutscher*, they too were able to move about the city with relative impunity. The local Blue Police paid them no mind; their *Ausbeis* had long since been checked and accepted. Jerzy Gruber's *Ausbeis* listed him as a reporter for the *Nowy Kourier*, a Nazi newspaper printed in the Polish language to spread propaganda and also to report on the most recent disruptive activities perpetrated by the insurrectionists. A daily list of reprisals was posted to address the heavy cost of retribution that these acts would incur.

Zygmunt Kaminski was accepted as a well-known salesman of government issued paper products; the two of them seemed to have a lot in common.

Jerzy referred to his notes on a post-Kutschera article for the *Kourier*. Much of the information would be shared with the underground, *Poland's Journal*, with a decidedly different spin.

"The first assassin and two of the cover agents were seriously wounded."

"Did they get away?"

"They were shoved into one of the cover cars and transported for emergency care. The driver tried to get help at three hospitals where they were refused admittance. When they were finally accepted as patients, there wasn't much that could be done for them."

"Well, we have the facts. Reports of the second cover car have swept throughout Warsaw. The two operatives got as far as the Kierbedź Bridge. When the Nazis caught up with them, they made a dash for the river. One was shot as he straddled the balustrade, and the other drowned; he couldn't swim."

Chapter Five

T he many documents of his next client were neatly arranged in rows on Michal Bednarek's desk while he awaited the arrival of Albert Świątek. The stocks and holdings were numerous and old; they were also secure under the protection of the Swiss Government.

In 1772, Poland fell under the rule of Austria, Prussia, and Russia. They redesigned the map of the nation into three parts and took possession of the land nearest their respective borders. The aristocratic Świątek family took flight before the foreign rule had time to re-establish the laws of their country. They fully recognized the potential destructive measures that their neighbor to the east might inflict on them. They abandoned their home in Warsaw and immigrated to Switzerland before the Russians confiscated their land. Established in the *laissez-faire* atmosphere of Swiss economics, the Świąteks increased their capital and secured their stance in the social fabric of Zurich.

Albert Świątek hopped off his bike, unfastened the lock from the frame to secure it on the grate under the window of the building on Napoleon Square. He was not a heavy man, but he was fond of good food and beer, and he was developing a healthy paunch. His thinning blond hair was yielding to patches of gray at the temples and crown; the few lines on his face were at the corners of his eyes and gave testimony of a man who possessed a gentle nature, one who smiled a lot.

He arrived early for his appointment and presented Michal with an expensive Turkish cigar. In turn, Michal offered black-market coffee laced with vodka. Świątek sat in the client's chair that faced the intricately carved oak desk, which had previously served the legal necessities of the *Schlacta,* the privileged of Warsaw.

"Pan Świątek, you arrive by bicycle? Where is that expensive auto of yours?"

"I generally pedal my way about town. It keeps me trim and healthy so that I can indulge in the pleasures of the table and the vine."

"Pan Świątek, I don't want to invade your privacy, but why have you returned to Poland?"

"Please, Michal, Albert—Pan Świątek makes me feel like an outsider."

Bednarek settled back in his chair and chortled, "Albert."

"Well, after Poland won the war against Russia in 1920, I was still young enough to be adventurous, and I was all alone. My wife died in childbirth leaving me not only childless but widowed as well. I was intrigued by the new Second Republic of Poland that Pilsudski had instituted and the fact that commerce had been re-energized under his administration. I confess that I had a visceral hunger to know something of my Polish ancestry. My family maintained the Polish language; I was taught my prayers in Polish. So far, I've been very happy here. I gave some thought to returning to Switzerland after the invasion, but I'm seventy-six years old; how many years have I got left?"

"But you maintain your Swiss citizenship."

"Ah, yes, Michal, Warsaw is too close to Russia and Russia has never forgiven us for our victory over them in 1920. I'm not foolish enough to risk my neck."

"Well, I've gone over your portfolio, and I must say that I'm impressed with the astuteness you display in your selection of stocks."

"Ah, that's a result of my father's insistence that I study finance and economics."

"I've written some suggestions regarding several stocks that are not producing enough revenue to hold on to, and recommendations of replacements that are showing a good profit."

"Thank you, Michal, I am most appreciative."

"Before you leave, join me in another cup of coffee."

Michal poured the coffee and laced the brew with vodka.

As Świątek sipped his coffee he was reminded of the strange setting at the Napoleon. "I saw Kaminski and Jerzy at the Napoleon. Their two heads close together over an article; I presume it was in regard to the Kutschera assassination."

"I believe you're right." Michal puffed on the stub of his cigar in an effort to savor what was left, "They were tipped off prior to the event, so they were on top of the story from the beginning."

Świątek paused to consider the situation, "Perhaps the daily roundups will ease a bit—until the next *Brigadeführer* takes the seat of command."

Michal leaned back in his seat and fixed his gaze on his client, "What new developments are coming up from the front?"

"The Russians have taken Rovno and Lusk, without the knowledge of the Home Army. It came over the short-wave this morning."

"Does Bór know this?"

"I bumped into Virski at the Napoleon this morning and apprised him of the situation. I don't know if Bór's communication system is as rapid as my uncensored radio."

"Be very careful. The German's are not likely to withhold your rights as a Swiss Citizen, but should they learn of your complicity with the Resistance there might be serious repercussions."

In London, things were simmering, and the fire was ignited by Stalin's insistence on the acquisition of Polish territory set by the illusive Curzon Line of 1920. The demarcation line was set by the Supreme War Council after World War I by British Foreign Minister, Lord Curzon. The borders were designed to incorporate the eastern city of Lwów within the Polish border. Later, and unbeknownst to Curzon, the document was tampered with by a clerk in the Foreign Office, Lewis Namier. During this time there were communist sympathizers in Britain who were not averse to slanting issues in the direction of the Soviets. Through this clerk's intervention, Lwów became a part of the Soviet Union. The ensuing battle between Stalin and Polish Premier Stanisław Mikołajczyk over the territory was disrupting the more important issues confronting the British War Office.

The balance of power, within the exiled Polish government in London, left Premier Mikołajczyk, with little wiggle room. The leader of the nation found himself constrained by the opposing views of his cabinet. His contention was that it was necessary to comply with the western powers regarding the territory sought after by Stalin, because he felt a hard-nosed approach may lead to suspension of allied aid to Poland. Damned if he did and damned if he didn't. The opposing faction held that ceding any territory to the Soviets was tantamount to treason. Also, Poland's Second Corp, under General Anders, which was currently fighting with the allies in Italy, had suffered greatly in Soviet labor camps and jails after the entire unit had been deported to Russia in 1939.

They had been expelled from their home in the eastern territories that the Soviet Union had recently invaded and laid claim to. To allow their homeland to be ceded to Russia would be an abomination. Premier Mik straddled a thin line of compromise which impeded his decision-making process.

Chapter Six

In a camouflaged bunker, outside of Warsaw, a cadre of middle-aged people drew near the entrance in ten minute intervals. The directors of the various organizations under the umbrella of the Council of National Unity were summoned to a mandated meeting. They were responsible for their means of transport, no one would be excused. Chief Delegate Jankowski, *'Prezes,'* opened the meeting, "We have important new developments coming from London which we must address as soon as possible." He waited while the audience settled down, "I have received a telegram from Prime Minister Churchill."

There was instant silence at the mention of Churchill's name.

"The Government-in-Exile has not been forthcoming in their commitment to the office of the Chief Delegate. General Bór and I are appalled that a territorial dispute has been an on-going issue that we have not been apprised of."

Premier Mikołajczyk, in London, kept the issue of the Curzon Line a secret until he could resolve the claim in favor of Poland. Churchill caught wind of this concealment. As arbitrator between Stalin and Mikołajczyk, he decided to play the devil's advocate and sent a message to Jankowski in Warsaw regarding the current demands being made by Stalin. He labeled the demands, 'proposals.'

Jankowski continued, "The issues addressed in the telegram are critical; they demand an immediate response. First on the agenda is an agreement to accept the Curzon Line, leaving the cities of Lwów and Wilno on the Soviet side, thus compromising the Polish eastern frontier. Second, the Polish Government should agree to dismiss the Commander-in-Chief, General Sosnkowski, who is a constant advocate for the maintenance of Polish territories and an independent Poland. Finally, a bone thrown to the dog; the Russian acknowledgement to Poland's future independence is to offer an area that would include part of East Prussia, Dantzig, Upper Silesia, and territories up to the Oder River. The territory that had previously been a part of the map of Poland."

The Red Army's advances over Poland served to complicate the issue even more. Churchill was concerned that Stalin would insist on claiming those territories for the Soviet Union. In that case, the post-war landscape would be drastically changed. Churchill was bent on achieving a compromise between the two nations. If he could get them to resume diplomatic relations, he would be free to focus his energy on the major battles involved in a world war. He wired Stalin apprising him of the heroic advances being made in Italy by the Polish Second Division, under General Anders. His troops had already entered the line against the German held territory. Churchill went a step further by adding that a newly formed Polish division was being trained in Britain to engage in the upcoming Cross-Channel Invasion. It was up to Stalin to interpret the report.

The representatives of the newly formed Council of National Unity were apprised of the 'proposals' and were irate over the demands made by the Soviets. They had voiced their independent opinions; it was up to Jankowski, and Bór, the Commander of the Home Army, to work out the precise language for the text of the document that would be sent to Churchill in response to his 'proposals.' In brief, Poland would be unyielding in its rights to property and an independent state. The western territories offered by the Russians in compensation, could not be considered as an equivalent to the Curzon Line since they were lands formerly held by Poland before they were taken away by the Germans. In addition, hope for a resumption of diplomatic relations with the Soviets and aid from the Allies would prove beneficial, *if* Poland's full sovereign rights were respected, without outside meddling in the nation's internal affairs. The document categorically opposed any discussion with the Soviets on the issue of the Eastern Frontiers. The 1921 Treaty of Riga would be upheld. Finally, the principles of the Atlantic Charter should prevail. Along with this clause, a suggestion was offered. "Matters of future serious impact should be delayed until a more favorable climate is in view."

The Atlantic Charter, which outlawed the principle of territorial aggrandizement, was grudgingly agreed upon by Stalin after the surprise invasion by the Germans on Soviet soil in June of 1941. The Soviet leader's representatives were forced to sign the agreement and to recognize the Polish Government.

The completed document of response was read to the representatives of the Council of National Unity and unanimously approved. Chief Delegate Jankowski placed his signature on the reply, along with an ultimatum.

"We shall not bend or break on these conditions. Anarchy would reign in Poland."

The issue regarding the dismissal of Sosnkowski was not addressed. This was something for the Government-in-Exile in London to resolve.

Chapter Seven

The blustery winds of March kept Father Lipinski safely ensconced in the spacious lobby of the church as his parishioners filed past him after mass. Pan Albert Świątek smiled respectfully and bowed his head slightly as he took the priest's hand, "An interesting sermon, as usual."

Father Lipinski held on to the hand; a gesture that suggested an invitation to linger. Several parishioners gave a quick nod in the direction of the priest and moved on without the anticipated parting word. Świątek read the gesture as a cue that the priest had something on his mind; he excused himself and allowed the queue of church members to pass on as they offered their thanks and goodbyes to the venerable pastor. Świątek walked over to a corner of the lobby and waited for a private moment with the priest.

The last parishioner closed the heavy linden door behind him, and Lipinski gave his friend that benevolent smile of his. "Albert, what are you up to at this hour?"

"My usual pattern after church is to breakfast at the Napoleon."

"Come, break your fast with me. I assure you Magda will produce a magnificent breakfast with the same coffee that is served at the Napoleon."

Pani Trypka outdid herself. Father Lipinski's eyebrows raised when he saw the large portion of *"kiska,"* a liver sausage that contains barley, spread out on the serving platter that took center stage on the breakfast table.

"It's not from the black market," she offered in defense, "Olga put some aside for me at the market, yesterday."

An appreciative grin spread across Świątek's face.

"Good for Olga," he blew a kiss to the cook, "Thank you, Magda, your shopping skills complement your culinary skills."

Father Lipinski brushed his usual reserve aside; his angst would not sit in reserve until coffee was served in the parlor. He busied himself with the buttering of his slice of black bread.

"So, Albert, what is the latest you have heard on the radio?" He raised his head and searched his friend's eyes for the anticipated bit of news.

"It's not good, Jan. Have you not been apprised by the Cardinal?"

"No, unfortunately the church does not rank in the privileged security that is offered to a Swiss citizen. Our radio contacts are severely limited."

There was no point in skirting the issue; Świątek let him have it full on, "The abbey is gone, the Bishop is dead."

Lipinski swallowed hard; he allowed his body to absorb the shock before he replied, "What happened?"

Świątek deferred a direct answer by deflecting to a background scenario.

"The Germans did observe the protected historic zone provision. *Generalfeldmarschal* Kesselring informed the Vatican and the Allies of this fact in December of last year."

"Then why the destruction?"

"Allied troops were suffering casualties in their attempt to take the hill. The Germans maintained posts along the steep ridges under the monastery; their impressive defensive tactics led the allied officers in command to suspect the abbey had become an outpost for the Germans."

Father Lipinski was incredulous, "The abbey of Monte Casino has stood undisturbed for almost fifteen hundred years," his tone was wooden, devoid of pitch.

The genial priest shook his head, as though he was ready to take on the significance of a deed perpetrated, and therefore must be accepted; as it could not be undone.

"What has been the response from the Vatican?"

"There has been no response from Pope Pius the Twelfth; however, the Cardinal Secretary of State, Maglione, was unable to adhere to the pope's restraint. It is reported that he told the United States' diplomat to the Vatican, Harold Tittman, that the bombing was "a colossal blunder," and went on to call it "a piece of gross stupidity.""

"Was there any benefit from this tragic destruction?"

"Ironically, no. German paratroopers occupied the obliterated site and the exposure from the rubble proved to be an advantage that the enclosed structure of the abbey would never have afforded."

"So, capturing the mountain becomes more difficult?"

"I'm afraid so."

"Perhaps that is a matter of retributional justice."

Chapter Eight

Things were becoming increasingly complicated, as well as dangerous, for the Secret State, and Virski was buckling under the strain. The Communist faction of the Polish Underground was initiating a subversive propaganda campaign against the Home Army to discredit them to the Western Allies. Meanwhile, the Soviets were independently breaking through the occupied territories of Poland, in what was meant to be a mutually aligned campaign with the Home Army in their fight against the Germans.

Tucked beneath his vest was the latest copy of *Poland's Journal*. The headline read, "Russians 27 miles from Poland". The article covered the Soviet advances into the occupied territory of Poland by General Berling's Army, a Polish military unit formed by the Soviets in Russia. Berling's forces were politically and militarily subordinate to Moscow. At the same time, the Red Army was renewing its offensive to regain Leningrad. The Soviets had become the leading players in the war against the Reich.

Shortly after the Exiled Government of Poland settled in London, a quasi-government was established in Warsaw. As the Government Plenipotentiary, it operated under the authority of the exiled government. Completely structured in the fashion of a bureaucratic administration, it contained, Departments of Justice, Sabotage and Diversion, Registration of German Crimes, Radio Information, Armaments, Chemicals, and Legalization. The diverse offices operated in the capacity of hierarchic dependence throughout the districts of Poland under the umbrella of the District Director of Civil Resistance. Virski was an administrator of Sabotage and Diversion in the Warsaw District.

On this cold winter morning, Virski felt the need to escape his own company. A change of scene, along with a good breakfast, might clear his head and offer an insight into the problems at hand. He looked around the dining room for an empty table.

Huddled in a corner at the back of the Napoleon Cafe were Kaminski and his assistant, Jerzy Gruber, conducting their early morning press briefing. Jerzy looked up and caught Virski's eye; he rose from his seat to extend a greeting. Through clenched teeth, masked by a broad smile, he muttered, "Zygmunt, this is our opportunity to verify Uncle Heinrich's Christmas story," He remained standing until Virski neared the table. "*Dzień dobry,* join us Mateusz."

"Yes, yes, *dziękuję*" Virski took the hand extended to him and settled in the seat across from Jerzy. The waiter placed a cup of coffee before him and took his order.

"Things are not looking too well," Kaminski came right to the point, "We've heard that fifteen or sixteen officers of the Home Army have disappeared. Is this a valid story?"

"Yes." Virski eyed him over the rim of his cup, "How did you get the story?"

"Jerzy's uncle, Heinrich, dropped the news like a hot potato during Christmas dinner at the Bednarek's."

Jerzy pushed in, "If it's suitable, we'd like information on the missing soldiers."

"Exactly, it should be revealed. I must pick up some paper products from Potopski. Perhaps we could discuss this later in the day; say around three this afternoon?"

Virski finished the last dregs of his coffee and brought the napkin to his mouth; he offered a rueful smile. "I have to leave. I'll see you later?" He counted out his coins and left them on the table.

Kaminski grabbed a hold of some unofficial paper goods, legal pads and journals, the stuff familiar to Bednarek. He dumped the load on the front seat, climbed into his Adler and made his way to the Stationery Store. Edward saw him approaching the shop and ran to the door to help tote some of the bundles he had loaded in his arms. They dumped the products on the counter. Kaminski tipped his hat and smiled at Edward; he then proceeded to the basement where he was surprised to find Virski already sitting there. Virski was drumming his fingers on the table in the presence of an unknown man sitting across from him. Kaminski judged the man to be in his fifties. Determining the age of a person during war was challenging. The hardships and hunger endured by the Poles during the occupation of the Nazis left its mark on the psyche as well as the physical appearance of an individual.

Kaminski unbuttoned his top coat and removed his *Hamburg.* He bowed his head in the direction of the stranger and offered a warm smile. It was obvious that the man had been through some trying times.

Virski followed through with an introduction, "This is Corporal Janek Slota of the Home Army; he was at Volhynia, on the other side of the River Bug in early November. He was one of fifteen soldiers selected to accompany their unit commander to a meeting that was initiated by the commander of the Soviet partisan unit." Virski paused before revealing the atrocious outcome, "He is the only one of sixteen members of the group to come away with his life."

Kaminski took a seat facing Slota and pulled a notebook from his pocket, "What can you tell me of the abduction of the other members of your group?"

The response was delivered slowly, in a deep voice. "The purpose of the meeting was to discuss the coordination of mutual action against the retreating Germans. We were offered vodka as the meeting went on between our commander and two Russian officers. They seemed to be pumping our commander for information about his knowledge of the Home Army, our numbers, units, the amount, and types of ammunition. The commander told them that the Home Army was well equipped and was aided by airdrops from the west. Then, the older of the two asked if we would consider fighting in General Bering's communist Polish Army. The commander flatly refused, saying that we were pledged to fight with the Home Army."

He paused, as if to hurdle the emotions of re-living the story. He covered his mouth as he produced a cough, as if to strengthen his voice that had become increasingly weak.

"The light in the room was switched off, soldiers rushed in and seized the company. Our commander and his deputy were shot, and we were conscripted to the communist partisan troops." He breathed deeply; he had managed to get through the worst of it. "I was familiar with the route from Lublin to Warsaw; my grandparents had a farm there that I visited as a boy. The first chance I had, I escaped and followed the river. I've been back in Warsaw one month, now."

Kaminski rose from his seat, "Why is there no *wodka* on the table?" He walked over to a cabinet that held staples for visiting insurgents and pulled out a bottle and three coffee cups which he filled to the brim. Slota's hand shook as he grasped the handle and downed a long swig.

Virski continued where Slota left off, "The incident was repeated a short time later, at another invitation, to discuss mutual action with yet another Soviet partisan commander. This time the commander took along his adjutant. These Soviet receptions have cost the Home Army seventeen good men."

"Have the Allies been apprised of these events?"

"Yes, but not to our benefit. Ironically, the Polish communist radio station, Kosciusko, is sending out radio messages falsely accusing the non-communist partisans of murdering members of the communist Resistance groups."

"So, Heinrich's report was well founded."

"For the record, Zygmunt, you can always count on Gruber; he never reacts to a situation until he is sure of the source."

Chapter Nine

In the town of Czerniaków, the Germans had transformed a pre-war auto parts industrial unit into a state of the arts manufacturing site. The building had been stripped, leaving only the bare walls of the structure. New generators, engines and machinery replaced the outmoded models of the former industry. The German *zeitgeist* of precision and attention to detail soon had the factory accelerating its productivity, and Governor Ludwig Fischer seized upon this opportunity as a propaganda tool to elicit pride among the German citizens of Warsaw. A front-page article of the factories contribution to the war effort would surely boost morale. Things were not going that well in Italy. The *Wehrmacht* was losing ground daily to the advancing offensive action of the allies. German lives and conquered territory were being lost at an unsustainable rate. Citizens of Berlin were scattering pamphlets of protest against the war. Hitler was feeling the heat.

Czerniaków, a rundown suburb of Warsaw, also offered a secure hideout for the subversive *Poland's Journal*. The printing press, documents and necessary paraphernalia were safely ensconced in a modest dwelling that was deeded to Jerzy's Uncle Heinrich, a card-carrying member of the NSDAP, National Socialist German Workers' Party.

Formerly a thriving industrial community, Czerniaków had lost its manufacturing luster; homes that had once been maintained with pride by the workers of the foundry and factories were falling to decay as the area took on the appearance of a ghetto. Surveillance was at a minimum, and Heinrich's NSDAP credentials offered additional security to the property.

On Marszałkowska Street, the main thoroughfare of Warsaw, a tobacco shop was insignificantly tucked between a luxury department store and an upscale furniture storeroom. Lukasz, the owner, had just switched on the lights, unlocked the door, picked up the latest edition of the *Nowy Kourier,* settled the forty copies into the bin that announced its label and logo, turned the key of the cash register, and was on his way to the back room to finish his coffee and read the latest edicts and reprisals printed in black and white in the German propaganda tabloid; his sharp intellect would reveal the veiled gray areas. A customer approached the old shop and set off a ping of the bell that hung over the door. Lukasz turned around and was pleased to find that his coffee break was interrupted by a favorite customer.

"*Dzień dobry!*"

Jerzy Gruber removed his cap and walked up to the counter, "Good morning, Lukasz, I need a pack of cigarettes. I'm on my way to Czerniaków to cover a story for the *Kourier.*"

Lukasz read the smile on his face. "You have a bounce in your step," he noted; he turned to the shelves of tobacco behind him and selected a package of Turkish cigarettes that were a favorite of Jerzy's, "would there be anything else?"

"Yes, a package of sweet mints, if you please."

Lukasz offered a knowing smile, "Just as I thought; enjoy your visit to Czerniaków."

He handed Lukasz a bill and waited for his change; embedded in the transaction was a note that Jerzy had slipped in for Irena.

The code of behavior for the "Liaison Girls" who carried encrypted messages to members of the Secret State was written in stone. The procedures were simple enough but had to be followed to the letter. The structure had so far been proven fail-safe. There were four sectors allocated to the city where "drop-off" boxes for communication throughout the network were secured. The Tobacco Shop was one of the deposit sites.

Irena Bednarek was one of the few messengers trusted to deliver "Rush" messages. These were the urgent communiques that warned of imminent danger. Only those women who proved to be efficient and fearless were considered for this post. The other entity within the network was tagged, "Normal," though no less important, there was no urgency attached to their delivery. The procedure required a good deal of caution, both for the Liaison Girl and the proprietor of the drop-off site.

Irena held a "Normal" delivery in her pouch, destined for the Tobacco Shop. She had developed a friendly relationship with Lukasz and trusted him to be just as discreet with her personal life as he was with her messages.

"Dzień dobry, Pan."

"Dzień dobry, Panienka Irena." He stood at wait behind the counter while his customer walked over to the bin that held the *Kourier*, she glanced over the front-page headlines and then deftly slipped her Normal message in the fold. She placed it on the counter while she feigned to be looking for something else that she might purchase, she then turned her attention to Lukasz.

"How may I help, *Panienka?*"

"I'd like a package of sweet mints, if you please."

"Of course!" He slipped the newspaper into a bag and hung it on a hook behind the counter that served the purpose of holding the customers items.

"Will there be anything else?"

Irena took one last look at the shelves, paused for a thought, "No, that will do, thank you."

Lukasz placed the package of sweet mints in a small brown paper bag; he lowered his chin and raised his eyebrows. Irena paid for the purchase with downcast eyes; she was still a novice at romantic assignations. Lukasz tendered an affable, "Go with God."

Irena stammered, "Remain with God."

The newspaper was left hanging on the hook.

The cryptic message within the package of mints from Jerzy was merely two digits, "2-5," indicating the window of time for a proposed tryst. It was just about noon; she would have more than enough time to bathe and change before she caught the tram to Czerniaków.

Janina threw a knowing look at Irena as she walked past her carrying her robe and bath salts on her way to the bathroom. The maid had become quite familiar with these afternoon baths.

Unperturbed by Janina's self-righteous smirk, she added an extra scoop of Gardenia scented salts to the water and allowed herself the luxury of stretching her body to the length of the tub. Immersed in a lather of suds, she fancied, *I'll borrow Mama's black satin blouse, the neckline is perfect, Jerzy will love it.*

The water was growing cold, and she should be on her way. She sat up and pulled the plug. A shudder of apprehension came over her at the sight of all those helpless suds being pulled into the vortex of water on its way to the drain. Making love and traveling to Czerniaków for a rendezvous seemed out of sync with the reality of life in the constricted environment of a cruel and vicious German General Government.

Chapter Ten

A sudden spring frost had crept in during the night and there was growing concern about sowing new seed on Good Friday. The unyielding turf, still bearing the frost of a hard winter could definitely hamper the farmers who furrowed their rows with hand plows. The Furtak farm might be in jeopardy. The weather was erratic, providing sun and warm temperatures one day and onion snow the next.

Pola Gudzynska was wide awake; the movement and kicks within her womb were relentless. The room was cold, the small cabin that became their honeymoon home had been converted from a fodder shed, and the small wood burning stove held little sway against the winds of an erratic spring. She would have loved to stay in bed and catch a little extra sleep before the cock crowed, but Dysthmus had a busy and dangerous day ahead of him, and he needed his sleep. She pushed off the warm quilt and stepped onto the cold floor. She glanced at his face, peaceful and relaxed; he squirmed ever so slightly, and she stood where she was until he tugged at the covers and snuggled in tightly.

She pulled the heavy, worn shawl from the chair and threw it around her shoulders and slipped her cold feet into a pair of thick woolen slippers. Out on the porch, she drew strength from the last stars before the sky began to flicker shafts of pale light.

Somewhere, deep in the orchard, rose the silvery twitter of a lark. Pola leaned heavily against the rail to lower herself to her knees for a morning prayer. Her first thought was of the baby, Felix, named for her brother, if it was a boy; Ludwiga, for her grandmother, if it was a girl.

Felix Duzat had been shot in a busy street in Warsaw. A group of boy scouts were defiantly engaged in posting around town the emblem of the *Kotwica,* an anchor symbol of the Resistance organization by the Polish Underground and Home Army. Felix, an innocent bystander, was shot in the head by the patrolling gendarme who raced to the scene of the disturbance.

Felix was merely twenty-two years old.

Ludwiga was killed when the Gestapo raided the Duzat farm after her sons spearheaded a devastating disturbance against the Germans.

The Nazis levied an exorbitant tariff on the farmers and the documents of imposed quota were retained in the offices of the village managers. The Duzat brothers were involved in a resistance operation of document burning in their village of Sochaczew. In retribution, the Nazis slaughtered the entire Duzat family and confiscated the farm. At the time, Pola was living in Warsaw, employed as a waitress at the Nectar, a cover for her role as Liaison Girl. She was the only member of the Duzat family to escape the massacre.

Kneeling against the porch rail for support, Pola offered her daily prayer, "Please God, the delivery will be easy, and the baby strong and hearty to face this harsh world and this war that is raging through Poland."

She was never able to go beyond this point; there might not be a Poland for the next generation. The honk from Furtak's truck announced the start of the day; soon the sun would rise, and the cock would crow.

It was Furtak's unit that organized the drive against the Nazi quota mandate. He assumed responsibility for Pola and took her into his home. Dysthmus was a frequent visitor to the farm where he hid his contraband material. During his frequent visits, a love affair developed, and they were dangerously close to engaging in a physical relationship. Rather than have Pola succumb to the inevitable compromise, Dysthmus proposed marriage.

Furtak and Dysthmus had been involved with the resistance movement and shared the bond that develops during the life and death encounters of war. When the wedding plans were announced, Furtak cleared away the tools and debris that filled one of his barns and offered it as a home for the young couple. The barn walls received a new coat of paint and Furtak offered the furniture from his sons' rooms, who were serving in the Home Army. The barn sat nestled pleasantly in the grove of apple trees that sat upon a hillock and offered a good view of the surrounding fields.

Pola continued to help on the farm and when her pregnancy made it difficult for her to work the fields, she helped Furtak's wife, Bianca, around the house and employed her skills as a seamstress in the fashioning of uniform shirts for the Home Army.

Dysthmus opened the door and stood on the threshold shivering in his long johns. "Pola, why are you out here in the cold? Come inside; you'll catch cold!" He walked over and helped her up from her knees. "You hop back into bed, and I'll make breakfast."

She shook her head, "Furtak has signaled for work to begin."

"Since when do I dance to Furtak's tune?" He gave a soft tap to her bottom, "Get back in bed."

She managed to doze a bit before he brought in a tray of bacon and eggs with dark bread and butter.

She turned up her nose, "Barley coffee?"

"I beg your pardon, *Pani Shlachta!"* He ruffled her hair, "We're all out of black-market coffee. When you were praying, did the good Lord tell you what the people in the city were having for breakfast?"

She reacted so sharply, he cursed himself for tossing such a cloud of guilt on her. "*Laleczka,* forgive me. That was a low blow. Please, eat and enjoy—for the baby's sake. We don't know what price ours is yet to pay. Thank God for this goodness he has given us."

There was a knock on the door and when Dysthmus opened it, the room was flooded in sunlight. "Kurt, you're early!"

"I caught the milk train, and I found Wojtek rattling around in the store; he gave me a ride."

"Come in and see how I indulge my wife, so when it's your turn you'll know how to behave."

Kurt delivered a warm smile, "How are you little one?"

"Pampered and pregnant. And how is Lucisia?"

"Pampered by me, and thankfully, not pregnant."

Kurt Schraft's *Ausbeis* identified his position as Representative Sales Person; he was office assistant to Kaminski's paper product business. His undercover activity was to aid Dysthmus in the disposition of contraband material.

"Enough of this talk," Dysthmus picked up the tray, "come into the kitchen and have a hot cup of barley."

"*Dziękuję,* no, Wojtek treated me to some quality coffee, along with a nice big *pączki.* "

"Well, then let's get started!" Dysthmus pulled on his jacket and reached for his cap from the peg. Pola stood by the door, affecting a brave pose, she smiled to encourage him on his risky mission. He reached for her hand to kiss, "Stay warm, *laleczka,* " he cuddled her in his arms. He never knew if this would be the last time he would hold her. She rubbed her head on his chest and tightened her grip around him. It was always hard to let go.

Burlap sacks, neatly tied with rope, were lined up along the left wall of the Furtak grain barn. Within the sacks were items of clothing; factory new boots, hand-grenades, and ammunition that were fabricated at covert underground factories around Warsaw. Dysthmus drove the ramshackle truck inside the barn, and he and Kurt began to load the sacks onto the truck.

Out on the road a flashing light beamed them onto the shoulder as the gendarme pulled up alongside of the truck. Dysthmus flashed a smile in their direction, *"Guten Tag,"* he responded lightly in his thickly accented Polish, "I know I'm not speeding; this truck barely moves."

Two officers got out of the car and stood side by side, ready to show their force. "What is it that you are transporting in that truck that barely moves?"

Dysthmus jumped out of the cab, "Come, I'll show you."

He climbed over the rails that held the sacks in place on the flatbed. Pulling at the corner of one of the sacks he extracted a handful of hay from the narrow opening. "Left over hay to distribute to the other farmers before the herds go out to feed on new grass."

One of the officers turned to go back to the car. The other officer waved him on his way.

Chapter Eleven

According to tradition that dated back to the early tenth century, a time when Poland worshipped Pagan rites and practiced witchcraft to beseech the icons of nature for blessings on the seeds they had planted, peas were the first product to be sown. When the moon was full and the spring weather had stabilized, the first seeds would be planted and songs to the forces of nature would be chanted. Once the nation had converted to Christianity, the first planting was offered on Good Friday; that was also the day when the cows and sheep were led to pasture. Good Friday of April 1944 established the beginning of the agriculture production in Poland.

Zygmunt Kaminski carefully pocketed the receipt the agent from the Centre Office of Agriculture had issued him for the amount of quota forms to be distributed throughout the local farm units. The German Government mandated precise amounts of farm produce, down to the last seed. The livestock that each individual farm was required to produce was determined according to the size of the farm. To maintain accurate records of production, official documents and quota forms, were printed and delivered to the farm areas surrounding Warsaw. Each village was under the surveillance of the local farm manager, who issued the documents to the farmers under his jurisdiction and kept a duplicate copy on file. Reprisals for under production were most severe.

Kaminski drove his Adler-Triumpf into the rural area of Sochaczew. Neatly piled on the passenger seat were reams of newly printed forms that he was required to deliver to the surrounding offices of the village farm managers. Safely tucked within his jacket pocket was the receipt for his cargo issued by the supervising agent in Warsaw. This legal document would guarantee safe passage in the event that a vigilante gendarme might accost him and decide to detain him on the road. He was en-route to Sochaczew to attend a meeting of the local unit of the Peasant Battalion and representatives of Civil Resistance.

Stretched across the back wall of Piotr Zaczynski's barn, was the banner displaying the Battalion's slogan:

AS LITTLE-AS LATE-AS BAD AS POSSIBLE

Kaminski chose a seat in the middle of the room; it was his practice to observe the audience as well as the presenter. Occasionally, the reaction from the on-lookers betrayed an opposing view to the rhetoric coming from the stage, and this bit of ambience would lend texture to his articles. He noticed Bórza, chief of the messenger group, known as the "Liaison Girls," sitting up front. Short and squat, she was never out of uniform; her weight was distributed compactly, emphasizing her appearance of strength. The most prominent feature on her square face was a set of piercing blue eyes that peered out from under thick brown eyebrows. No one could recall seeing her in a skirt or dress, she was regularly seen wearing pants and shirts. Her old leather boots maintained their vigor under the spit-and-polish routine they received daily. Her approach to leadership was much like that of a drill sergeant; she was strictly by-the-book.

Dysthmus, a.k.a. Marek Gudzinski, distributor of contraband goods throughout the underground, was seated next to her. Dysthmus, casually wore several hats atop his roguish head. He was duly registered as the delivery man Victor Dielinski, by the

Schultz Sewing Machine Company, an old established German industry in Warsaw that now manufactured weapons and ammunition for the *Wehrmacht*. The administrators of the factory considered Pan Dielinski to be a reliable employee. He delivered the munitions promptly and efficiently for the German Government. In his alternate role as insurgent, he managed to use Schultz' truck for diversionary pursuits as well.

The Peasant Battalion provided him with yet another truck for the legitimate delivery of produce to the restaurants the Germans frequented in Warsaw. Its undercover use was the transportation of ammunition and military supplies to the forest warehouses where they would be kept in readiness for Operation Tempest, the long-awaited uprising.

Dysthmus had a genius for juggling the items he distributed; however, his demanding activities, both legitimate, and the prohibited trafficking of contraband goods, left him with little time to spend with his young pregnant bride, Pola.

Kaminski viewed the distributor's presence at the meeting as commonplace. However, Bórza's appearance was most unusual; she rarely attended any meetings of Civil Resistance. Her attendance at the Peasant Battalion seemed inconsistent with her typical pattern.

Furtak, the unit commander, was the first to address the group. "You will soon be planting your peas and potatoes, as you do every Good Friday. This year you will make provisions to hide as much of your produce as you can, so that the starving people in the city can be fed. Request additional seed from the manager with the excuse that last year's production yielded less than usual, and the high quota demands left little produce for the harvest of seeds. Your careful preparations of hidden foods from last year kept many citizens from starving over the winter. This year we will try to supply the city with food at a low cost to help them survive."

The foreman of the Sochaczew-Warsaw railway line, Bolchek, a staunch member of the communist faction of the underground, lumbered his way to the front of the room. The Socialist Armed Organization focused on railway sabotage. Veterans of rail service discipline and the regulation of time schedules, they were every bit as meticulous as the Germans in their approach to duty.

The large plug of tobacco pocketed in Bolchek's left cheek did not encumber his speech. "The SOA continues to hinder delivery of farm products. Berliners can never be sure if the beef or cheese they eat is safe, after all, it is we who set the temperature in the refrigerated vans. We have emptied cattle cars at isolated areas along the line where the cows are free to roam about the country until they wind-up on some villager's table. Grain cars continue to be dumped. We have been most fortunate in our ability to arrange these incidents at various times and places to ensure minimal capture and reprisal of our agents."

Piotr called out, "What about Kujescki who was shot last week?"

"The Secret Court has a death sentence out for the railway official who shot Kujescki, without provocation. There was no diversionary operation going on. Kujescki was just doing his job."

Diversion and deception had become an art form for the members of the battalion; they bribed minor officials, forged receipts for alleged delivery of food and livestock, and concealed calves before the necessary branding and registration imposed by the village manager. The Germans were aware that they were being robbed from under their noses, but they had no way to prove their suspicions.

During the break, Kaminski made his way to Bórza, who handed him a donut and a cup of barley coffee.

"Have you come to serve refreshments?"

"And are you here to annoy me? Dunk your *pączki* and fill your mouth."

"Please, accept my apology" he took her hand and offered an obsequious bow, "But what are you doing here? I don't often get to see you. You've made your life a secret mission."

"Dysthmus brought me. I wanted to see Pola, my ex-liaison girl; she is just a few months away from motherhood; this meeting offered a perfect opportunity for a visit."

"You came with Dysthmus in that rickety truck of his? How little you value your life. I can do better than that; allow me to take you back to town in the comfort of an Adler."

She licked the remaining donut crumbs from her finger tips, "Only if you allow me to buy you a proper meal."

The conversation in the Adler on the way into town centered on the Gudzynskis.

"Pola was a favorite of mine, although she almost didn't make it as a Liaison Girl. She forgot the address of the secret stop where she was to drop off her first message. I never assign anything of importance to novice messengers the first few times they are sent on a delivery. These errands are merely practice measures and the girls are judged on their ability to perform their duty in an inconspicuous manner. Pola failed the test, and the administration rejected her. To her credit, she refused to accept their decision and made a survey of every building in Warsaw that had a front and rear entrance; she traveled the trams to plot out their routes and destination, and then re-applied for certification. We were all impressed with her tenacity dund had her re-instated. Her code name was Kwiatek. Need I tell you that she remains among my favorite girls?"

The Chestnut Café was owned and operated by a former musical comedy star, Doretka Stasczu, her other outstanding talent was that of a gourmet cook. She had traveled extensively and dined in some of the world's finest restaurants where she used her charm and celebrity status to persuade the chefs to share their prize recipes. Kaminski had a gourmet palate and took most of his meals there.

They arrived at the café at the busiest hour; diners knew to come early. Doretka's menu was meant to be savored, and curfew severely limited the time her devotees could dedicate to indulge their palates. All of the tables were filled; there were two seats available at the bar.

"Do you mind sitting at the bar for your dinner?" Kaminski asked, after he scanned the dining room.

"Of course not."

Kaminski took her arm and led her in that direction. Jacek, the bar-tender, brought them a bottle of vodka—on the house, "Here, look over the menu, I have to get back to my bar-flies." Bórza pulled out her cigarette case and they were momentarily appeased as they viewed their options. Kaminski felt a tap on his shoulder and turned to face Virski standing behind him.

"Virski, I didn't see you at the meeting today."

"No, other things occupied my time. Are you dining or drinking?"

Kaminski disregarded the question while he observed decorum, "You know Pani Bórza?"

Bórza turned and nodded a smile, "How have you been Virski?" They shook hands.

"I wonder if I might join you; are you ordering?"

Kaminski noticed an empty stool at the other end of the bar, "Let's get that stool and set you up proper."

Virski raised his hand, "Sit, I'll get it."

They were waiting their order when Doretka came their way for a little social bantering. She noticed the silver at their places, "Kaminski, you dine with your friends at the bar?" She did not wait for a reply. "Jacek, hold their order while a get a table for them."

She cajoled a party of four to relinquish their table and take coffee at the bar where they could continue to linger; she added an incentive, "Have a drink on me."

Close to curfew, Doretka brought a bottle of cognac to the table, "Forgive my inattention, I tried to get here earlier to chat with you." She took the empty seat at the table set for four and poured the noble brandy into their empty vodka glasses, *"Na zdrowie!"*

"Na zdrowie," was the reply, along with an appreciative, *"Dziękuję."*

"Virski," she gave him a quizzical look, "are you ready to take me up on my proposal?"

He blushed at her probe but did not respond.

She took it on herself to explain to the others, "He comes in here with that interminable long-face, and I know what is his trouble; however, he obviously does not appreciate the attentions of an older woman, no matter what her qualifications and experience."

Kaminski lifted his glass to Virski, a roguish smirk on his lips.

Bórza stood up from her seat and went around the table to take hold of his face in her hands; she fixed a firm kiss on his lips.

"Virski, I'm your age, and we have a lot in common. We could discuss under-cover activities under the covers."

He pulled away from her grasp, a befuddled expression gave way to a rare smile that could be considered appreciative.

Kaminski came to his rescue, "You ladies ought to develop an act together; you could call it the Bawdy Girls."

Jacek called from behind the bar, "All out—curfew!"

Chapter Twelve

The traditional sunrise mass of Easter Sunday drew a hefty crowd. The congregation was an aggregate of Poles, *Volksdeutsche,* and Germans. Father Lipinski's sermon was weightily crafted around the barbaric cruelty of the Romans during the occupation of Israel. He was careful not to mention the Jews, but his homily made its mark.

Irena shuddered in her seat; she grabbed her mother's hand and held it tightly throughout the homily. Leona eyed the congregation surreptitiously; how were the Germans reacting to the obvious comparison? The German officers were all of one countenance, tight-jawed and stiff-lipped. The last blessing couldn't come soon enough. *Deiu Gratia!*

Janina had baked the bread and a large cheese *babka.* The meal would be simple; there was no reason to celebrate with items available at a price from the black market, when the citizens of Warsaw were forced to live on starvation rations from the Gestapo administration. Vegetables from the Open Market, and chicken from a nearby farm would serve the holiday table.

Father Lipinski, Jerzy, and Kaminski were expected to dine with the Bednareks this Easter Sunday.

Lipinski offered the blessing at table, "Dear Lord, this is the fifth year that our citizens suffer from lack of food during this, your time of Resurrection. Deign to look upon your children with compassion. You, who allowed your son to suffer a crucifixion before resurrecting him to your kingdom, redeem us from the heinous hands of the Germans, also your children, who have lost their way by practicing barbaric cruelty. Offer relief to all who suffer during this glorious holy day."

"Kurt and Lucisia will not go hungry today," Kaminski informed the table, "Furtak's wife presented him with a basket full of food, duly blessed during *Święconka* at Father Pawil's church."

Leona let the remark pass, she was not privy of the couple; she assumed they were a part of his news gathering network in Sochaczew.

Father Lipinski's benign smile tugged at his lips, "Sadly, Pawil's health is deteriorating. His constant fasting, and long hours spent in administering to his parishioners have caught up with him. With God's blessing, he has found a young priest to aid him in his duties."

"Where was he able to find him?" Michal hesitated to accept the remark at face value. There were no young priests lingering about Poland waiting for positions. The church was in serious need of clergy.

"Out of Poznań?" Kaminski appeared to be looking for a confirmation.

"Yes, yes, as I understand, he is recently ordained under the auspices of the underground seminary of Poznań. It was safer to send him into a parish in the German General Government than to keep him in the territory of the Reich where he would be known and revealed."

Kaminski leaned back in his chair; his hands folded on his stomach; a satisfied grin appeared on his face. On a recent trip home to visit with his parents, Zygmunt had held an engaging conversation with a boyhood friend, Ludwig Carsten, who had entered the priesthood. Kaminski was an agnostic, but he appreciated the value of comfort that religion seemed to bring to believers. Therefore, he was disappointed when Ludwig could not assure him that the Catholic Church of Poznań was involved in an underground seminary to ensure an ongoing priesthood to offset the shrinking resources caused by aging clerics. Either the church was subservient to the Gestapo, or Ludwig would not take the risk of commenting.

Father went on, "His name is Albert Chiemienski, one of the brightest to come out of seminary in quite a while. His family has given several members to religious orders; uncles and aunts on both sides have become priests or entered the convent. A lovely young man."

Kaminski lifted his drink in the gesture of a toast, "I look forward to meeting him at mass next Sunday."

Father Lipinski bit his lips to avoid a smirk, "You go to Sochaczew for mass, when I have yet to see you at mass here in Warsaw?"

"Curiosity sometimes prompts redemption."

Chapter Thirteen

Adolf Hitler did not have much to celebrate on his fifty-fifth birthday. The Allied forces were trampling aggressively through Italy, and an announcement from the nation of Turkey was a harbinger of what the Nazis had yet to face. The Russians were preparing to drive the *Wehrmacht* out of Crimea and the situation did not bode well for the nation of Turkey. The neutral stance maintained by Turkey during the war, simply was no longer feasible. The Soviet re-conquest of Crimea heralded the need for a drastic policy change—Turkey announced that it was no longer neutral but a "pro-allied nation, though not belligerent". This meant that Turkey would no longer supply Hitler with the necessary chrome used in the manufacture of those veritably indestructible Panzer tanks. Germany was left with a year and a half's supply of chrome on stock.

The weather was turning mild, Małachowski Square was an extravaganza of lavender and yellow; the oaks, the lindens, and the birches presented an artist's palette of shades of green, the rhododendrons had reached their full height and full bloom, a profusion of tulips lined the pathways; nature would not yield to Nazi rule.

Janina had set about the apartment to open every window, making sure that the screens were set in tight. The rooms were cool and wafts of the fragrance of spring lifted her spirit. She set about with her vacuum and feather duster softly humming the tunes she remembered from her childhood, a soft smile to her lips.

Late in the afternoon, Irena Bednarek sheepishly entered the kitchen, "Janina, is it possible for Jerzy and Ryszard to stay for dinner? It's getting late and we're not quite finished with our project," she planted a persuasive kiss on the maid's cheek, "please, Janina?"

"Go, finish what you're doing. You'll eat like peasants tonight."

Janina had come as a teen to serve the Mieleski household, Leona's parents; it was her first job. When the wedding knot was tied between Michal and Leona, she became part of the dowry; she entered the Bednarek household as their cook. The initial staff included a housekeeper and eventually a nursemaid for Irena, the new arrival. That all changed once the country was occupied by the Germans. Janina remained with the Bednareks; by this time, she had become a member of the family, she was not about to leave— and where would she go? She had no family, and she was well past middle age. In addition to shopping and cooking, Janina took on the added burden of housekeeper. She was content with the arrangement which included a small stipend and a secure place within the family. The elderly maid was every bit the wise and honest peasant, and although she appreciated the familial environment, she never took advantage of the situation; she kept her opinions and thoughts to herself.

This request by Irena wasn't unusual. Her two young men never missed an opportunity to be in her presence. Irena was tall and willowy; her movements and gestures revealed a seductive feminine demeanor. A subtle glint of green flecks caste an illusion of turquoise to the blue of her eyes; her skin was pale, and her hair was dark. There was a naïve intensity to her nature that men found most appealing.

There was no set pattern to these 'impromptu' meetings. They were conducted in a hushed, secretive manner by the trio of friends, and Janina suspected that they were plotting some underground intrigue. Why not? The Bednarek's were steeped in conspiracy. She knew about Ryszard's involvement in the looting of the Royal Palace and Jerzy's part in Kaminski's newspaper. She added Irena's name to every rosary she said, there was no evidence, but she strongly suspected that Irena was involved with the Liaison Girls that served the underground as messengers. Of one thing she was certain, she was not blessed with the courage and boldness of these young people. She would never be involved in conspiracy.

Janina made use of what was available in her larder. Barley soup, eggs, and a few strips of bacon, supplied a hearty meal for a table of five. Some flavored gelatin and fresh baked apples would serve as a desert.

Leona passed on the sweets and made a quick exit to attend her Wednesday night history class at the church.

A cool breeze filled the apartment through the open windows, and the company lingered at the table while Chopin's Piano Sonata No. 2 played on the gramophone. Michal excused himself and withdrew to his study to finish an article. The communist Polish Worker's Party was using their radio station, Kosciusko, to spread negative propaganda against the Home Army, placing them in league with the Nazis. Michal's article was intended as a rebuttal to the vicious slurs.

Just as the Chopin recording was entering the final movement, the Funeral March, the raucous sound of sirens echoed through the streets. Janina ran into the room wiping her hands in her apron. "Quickly, shut the windows and pull the drapes."

The loud speakers attached to the lampposts in the street were blaring orders for everyone to take cover. Anyone found in the streets would be arrested.

The residents of the apartments rushed to the stairs on their way to the basement. Michal's entourage joined them. Along the walls of the basement was a fenced off storage space, for the convenience of the residents. The tenants sat on the floor within this barricade. Unconcerned of the dirt and discomfort, they united in prayer. Their collective hope was that the old building would make it through another night of fury. Michal pulled at the chain attached to the light bulb hanging from the ceiling and moved about in the dark to the tiny window that looked out onto the street. He pushed the curtain aside to watch for the "all clear" signal.

The Russians had spread their invasive tentacles over occupied Poland's air space. The drone of the Soviet bombers signaled their approach as the crisscross movements of the powerful Nazi searchlights lit up the sky to flush out the planes. The heavy bombers had difficulty maneuvering around the bright beams. The horrendous sound of explosions nearby foreshadowed the flames of burning buildings as the incendiaries landed on the ground.

Michal uttered one desperate word, "Leona!"

As soon as the sirens began their wailing, the parishioners of Father Lipinski's scriptural study filed down the staircase to the basement. Spiritual and secular history mingled as the two groups huddled together in the room at the northwest corner of the basement. In his steady measured tone, the priest began a rosary.

Leona looked up from her beads and made eye-contact with a young man who obviously was studying her reactions. His gaze was intense, and she found it difficult to look away. At the 'Amen,' the gentleman made his way to her seat.

"Good evening, Pani, I am Kurt Schraft, I am…"

"I know who you are, and I thank you for being here."

"I shall escort you home. There will be no difficulty, I have my NSDAP identification card." This was whispered under his breath.

Kurt walked her to her door and once she had turned the key, he tipped his hat and turned back into the hall to exit the building.

Janina prepared an early breakfast to accommodate the over-night guests. Ryszard was employed as a clerk in the Labor Office and Jerzy had to be at the press office of the *Nowy Kourier*.

Michal reached across the table to take Leona's hand, "Thank God Heinrich's security agent was there to escort you home."

"Yes, he introduced himself while we were cornered in the basement. His name is Kurt Schraft."

A grin spread across Jerzy's face, "Kurt is Kaminski's new associate at the paper office. I call them K and K. Kurt manages the office whenever Kaminski is off on one of his jaunts."

Chapter Fourteen

Dysthmus had arranged a covert meeting to be held in an established insurgent apartment building on Poznań Street. The building had proved to be a safe haven due to the heavy traffic and the reliability of the tenants, most of whom were known insurgents. Approaching warm weather would require a change in uniforms for the Home Army, and a recent ammunition drop from the Allies would have to be transported to the military headquarters that was securely sequestered in the forest. The meeting would center on the necessary items that were stored in Furtak's barn. Dysthmus' partner in contraband, Kurt Schraft, and Ryszard Borowski, a possible second assistant who was recommended by Jerzy, would develop the plans and strategies necessary to transport the merchandise and the logistics involved. It was essential that the instructions, issued by Dysthmus, be followed to the letter to avoid any encounter with the gendarmes.

The bookish and wiry Ryszard was brought on board by Jerzy, who was aware of the university student's involvement in the looting of the Royal Castle in Olde Town. Ryszard was a student of architecture, his zeal for designing buildings was brought about by his boyhood admiration of the Royal Castle, built in the 16th century. The *blitzkrieg* of 'thirty-nine' had destroyed the roof and turrets of the building and laid waste to the ceiling fresco painted on the Ballroom ceiling by the Polish-Italian painter, Marcello Bacciarelli.

Devastated by the malicious destruction of an historical site, the dedicated student, Ryszard, became a committed member of the underground. He joined in with the Castle's staff members and art experts to save whatever they could of the building for reconstruction after a newly Independent Poland was restored.

Dysthmus arrived at the second floor back apartment ten minutes early to set things up. He gave his signal knock and was admitted by the tenant, a fellow conspirator. Jerzy was the next to be admitted; he arrived unexpectedly.

"I'm here to lend a little moral support to Ryszard, this being his first attempt at the distribution process."

"Should I be concerned?"

"Not at all. Ryszard will give his life as surely as you would. I'm just being the mother-hen."

Another knock, this time Kurt, "Where's Ryszard?"

A commotion on Poznań Street drew them into the hallway where they could look out of a window overlooking the street. The Blue Police were conducting a roundup of pedestrians, a *lapanka*. Lined up against the wall of a corner building was an assortment of *Warszawians,* the elderly, the working class, and a few children, who stood facing the wall as instructed, except for one: a slender young man with slicked-back hair and horn-rimmed spectacles who stared defiantly into the guns pointed his way.

There was a rapid knock on the door of the Bednarek apartment. Janina leaned her ear against it, apparently in an effort to intuit who the visitor might be. The quick knock was repeated, drawing Irena into the hall where she found the maid wringing her hands while she leaned against the door.

"Janina…" her sharp tone startled the woman who stood there looking sheepishly afraid.

Irena pushed her way up front and opened the door; Jerzy pushed his way in. He had a queer look on his face, fear—mingled with pain?

"Ryszard has been killed in a roundup!"

"How do you know all this?"

"We were involved in a distribution meeting with Dysthmus at our usual cover place, an apartment building on Poznań Street. The landlord is a partisan. I ran over and interviewed him to see if he could identify the perpetrators for our on-going campaign against the SS. He gave me the information, but he doesn't know where they took the body."

"Ryszard's mother lives in Praga; we'll go there," she ran in the direction of the closet to get her coat.

"Wait a minute. Irena, the gendarme could be stalking his home to compile a list of possible partisans. With your father involved in all his underground exploits, your presence could trigger an investigation of him as a suspect. We can't put his life in jeopardy."

Janina moved forward from her corner in the room to offer a suggestion. "Irena, I have potatoes peeled; I will prepare some potato pancakes for you and Jerzy." She walked over to the tall commode and filled a snifter with sherry, "Here, take this and go lie down until I have your *Placki* ready," she looked over to Jerzy, "May I pour you something?"

"No, thank you, Janina. I'll have a drink with my lunch."

Irena managed the walk through the hall under her own steam, with Jerzy hovering close by, in case she wobbled. He walked over to the two windows that lit up her room and drew the curtains. Between the sherry and the dimly lit room, she might fall asleep, or at least relax a bit.

She went to her desk and began to root through the drawers. She pulled out a folder and a binder. "These are Ryszard's drawings and notes he was making on the restoration plans for the Palace, after the war." She affectionately ran her hand over a page that displayed a sketch of the finished product. "He was very good, you know; he could have been another Wiadek."

"Sh…sh," he gently wiped the tears that ran down her cheeks, "it's alright."

"Mamma and I are responsible," she would not let the matter rest. "We should never have persuaded Professor Wiadek to offer an underground class. If it weren't for us, Ryszard would still be alive."

"Come, Irena, sip your sherry and lie back on your bed. I'll sing to you if you like."

Finally, a weak smile, "No, I can do without that."

Jerzy adjusted the pillows, and she sat on the bed. "Jerzy, you will keep me posted on any developments you learn of his funeral?"

"Of course."

"We don't know the hour or day when the same fate will happen to us. You and Tata are so involved in underground intrigue…"

"Irena, don't add to your grief; we're still here!" He took her in his arms. She kissed his cheek and he turned to kiss her lips. The deep emotions that had filled her with grief suddenly took on another hue. Her breathing became more rapid, her lips parted, and she tightened her arms around Jerzy's neck. The kiss turned into an urgent response that had nothing to do with the time of day and the constant fear of repression and retribution under a Nazi regime.

She pressed her body against him and tightened her grip around his neck, "Jerzy, Jerzy," she murmured as she pulled at his shirt, trying to lift it from the confines of his pants.

He caught her hands in a weak effort to avoid the inevitable, his heavy breathing made his whisper barely audible, "Irena… Irena…Janina is in the kitchen making lunch!"

Chapter Fifteen

Elsa Jurgen was a registered *Volksdeutscher.* Her family had lived in Poland for years. She was still unable to get her national identity straight. For the present, she was secretary to Jozef Adamski, supervisor of the Office of Labor. She had been watching the clock. At 8:20, she laid down her pencil and got up from her seat. She was uneasy about it, but she felt it was her duty to report it. She gave a soft rap on Adamski's door before she entered.

"Yes, Elsa?"

"Sir, the Borowskis are not at their posts."

A pause, "Yes…ah, can you reach them by phone?"

"I've already looked sir; I do not have a number on file."

Adamski sat back in his chair and folded his hands, a pensive look on his face. He could not remember hearing their names in the underground; could they have fallen victims to the SS?

"Well, Elsa, we'll simply have to wait until we get some news."

"Very well, sir."

"And Elsa, check my calendar if there is an appointment for lunch, let me know. I have some personal shopping to do."

"You are free at lunch."

He smiled; Elsa was super-efficient. When she had gone, he picked up the receiver to his private phone line and rang Kaminski.

He and Kaminski had been anxious by-standers during the devastating final hours of the Ghetto Rising. Samuel Tannenbaum, former attorney of the Court of Poland, a.k.a. Adamski, operated under forged Aryan documents. As 'Aaron,' he was an operative of the Home Army where he functioned as the facilitator of the project *Zegota*, code name for the Council of Aid to the Jews. The project was funded by the Government-in-Exile in London; it provided financial, military, and medical aid to the Jews in Warsaw. Impeccable forged identity cards were issued to the few who managed to escape the surveillance of the Gestapo and set up a new persona. After the obliteration of the Ghetto by the Nazis, in May of 1943, they were the only Jews left in Warsaw.

The venue for the impromptu lunch appointment was the Nectar, a restaurant that served German cuisine and was staffed by members of the underground, probably the safest place in town.

Kaminski was entertaining his Schindlerite friends at the bar when he noticed Aaron walking through the door.

"Excuse me, I see the director of the labor office, and I am looking for a part-time clerk."

"Pan Adamski," he extended his hand, "are you meeting someone?"

"Pan Kaminski, *Dzień dobry*. No, I've been doing some shopping and realized it was lunch. Can you join me?"

Kaminski romanced the waitress, and they placed their order. While they waited for their stein of beer, Adamski initiated the conversation, "Does the name Borowski mean anything to you?"

Kaminski sat back and nodded; he knew what the invitation to lunch was all about.

"Ryszard got caught in a street-shooting—Poznań Street, yesterday. The father, Vitzek, is obviously in shock."

"Will you be in contact with him?"

"I'm in on the funeral arrangements."

"Please, offer my condolences and tell him that I will somehow cover for him for the next few days."

A former haberdasher, with his shop in the center of the Warsaw business district, Vitzek Borowski provided a middle-class income for his wife, Wanda, and their son, Ryszard. After the dust of the *blitzkrieg* settled, he was forced to sell his shop, and came away with a month's income to adjust to the new regime. One of his former clients, a wealthy *Volksdeutscher*, with close ties to the General Government, got him the position as head clerk at the Office of Labor. Once Ryszard turned sixteen, Vitzek made a place for him as stock-boy. The daily routine of riding the tram and sharing lunch together enriched the father-son relationship. The sudden loss of his son could very well break Vitzek Borowski.

Leon Waratski arrived at Szucha Street headquarters in the 1935 funeral limousine, driven by his chauffeur. He walked up the steps and was greeted by the guard at the door.

"*Guten Tag*, Herr Waratski," he offered a weak, patronizing smile as he opened the door to admit the visitor into the building.

Waratski removed his hat and walked along the corridor; he entered the office marked, Bureau of License. An officer with the rank of sergeant stood behind a long counter, processing documents for people lined up before him. There were eight people standing in the queue, number nine would have a long wait. Waratski cleared his throat with a loud, "Ah-hem!." The sergeant looked up, made eye-contact, and then lowered his head; Waratski took this as a 'go-ahead' nod. He walked around the counter and presented himself to another officer seated at one of the desks in the large room.

"*Guten Tag*, Ernst, I need a death certificate." He unbuttoned his topcoat and took a seat. Ernst acknowledged the greeting and pulled a printed form from a basket on his desk. Waratski produced a pen from his vest pocket and proceeded to fill in the blanks on the document, affixing his signature to the bottom. Ernst gave it a quick glance, removed the sheets of carbon, tore the original copy along the perforated line, handed it to the undertaker, and accepted the correct payment for the service. Waratski replaced the pen in his vest pocket, along with the death certificate, and stealthily removed a sealed, blank envelope from the inside pocket of his jacket. He placed the envelope on the desk, stood up and buttoned his topcoat.

"*Gut, danke*," he said in parting.

"*Bitte schön.*"

The flora in Warsaw was undaunted by the Nazi oppression. The variety of delicate greens and mauves that abound in spring were evident on every street of the city and suburbs. Wanda Borowski's favorite lilac bush sat in the garden outside her kitchen bursting with blooms. This year, she would not cut bouquets to place in the living room window and decorate the dining table. There would be no tantalizing fragrance from the outdoors to celebrate the season of re-birth. Wanda was unaware of the season; she was far removed from the reality of life on any level.

The old limousine was shined up for the occasion. Vitzek and Wanda Borowski were seated behind the driver. Vitzek stared at the back of the driver's head. Wanda occupied her hands by twisting her tear drenched handkerchief and alternately wiping her eyes. There was no exchange of conversation; the car drove the length from Praga to the church in Warsaw in silence. The driver heard only sobs coming from the back seat of the hearse.

Several people were standing on the pavement in front of the church. They nodded in respect to the couple as they walked towards the steps. A woman, clutching at a handkerchief to wipe her tears, reached out to touch Wanda's arm, but received no response to her conciliatory gesture. The Borowskis made the lengthy climb up the steps to the church; the others followed at a respectful distance behind them.

Kaminski and Jerzy joined the Bednareks in a pew up front. The organ sounded the funeral dirge, and the casket was rolled down the aisle by two of Ryszard's friends on one side and Kurt and Dysthmus on the other. It was the two distributors who had managed to lay claim to Ryszard's body immediately after the shooting just before the sanitation trucks arrived to clear away the deteriorating evidence of the carnage.

Bórza took a seat in the back pew to wait for Virski. They had greeted each other out on the pavement, and she was looking forward to extending an invitation to lunch. They hadn't run into one another since they dined at the Chestnut Café, and she was determined to follow up on the last invitation she had offered him.

Father Lipinski came down the aisle flicking the Censer with incense, accompanied by the altar boys. Bórza waited until the procession reached the casket before she rushed to the door and bolted down the steps. She could see the retreating figure of the man, head lowered between his shoulders, wandering at a slow and steady pace. Toward the river?

She was about to break into a run to catch up with him. She caught herself. No, better to follow at a distance and find out where he was headed; it may be unwise to interfere at this point.

Virski climbed down the embankment and sat down on a bench. The early morning swells of the Vistula were still engaged in the down-stream current. Mateusz Nowacki watched the slow, strong force of water carry debris to an unknown destination. Anger and an overwhelming feeling of despair took hold of him. The swift current paralleled the external influences in his life that had abruptly set his goals and agenda on an entirely different course than the one he was prepared to navigate. He put his face in his hands and vented his frustration in tears. So many lives lost, and now, this young and innocent boy with dreams of becoming an architect.

Bórza stood by and let the scene unfold. It would be a violation to interfere in his emotional turmoil. He would have every right to sever the feeble bond that was taking root between them. She turned to go. She looked back, one more time—he was removing his coat.

She scrambled down the embankment, "Virski!"

He turned sharply in her direction, "*Cholera*!" He reached down to slip out of his shoes…

"Virski," her voice became soft and low, "don't do this— oh, God, how I need you in my life."

He looked up at her from his bent position; his face reflecting the desperation tearing away within him.

She moved in on him and grabbed him into her arms. "Come home with me, Mateusz. I have a pot of *borscht* and *kluski* waiting for us. Don't die until you've tasted my cooking."

He pulled away, still holding on to her arm, an affectionate smile gently pulled at his lips. He drew her closer to him and sobbed until his pain was spent.

Chapter Sixteen

Wyzek, the maintenance man, was at his post at the entrance of the apartment building, he viewed the approaching couple with considerable suspicion. The tone of his "Good evening," was marked with a quizzical note.

Bórza gave a gruff response to his obvious curiosity as she ushered Virski through the gate. He marched behind her in a submissive manner and offered no resistance as he allowed her to guide him past the manager and up the three flights of stairs that led to her apartment. She unlocked the door and helped him off with his coat and hung it on the hook alongside of hers on the back of the door. She took hold of his arm and led him across the room to the one large stuffed chair that sat by the window.

"Sit, I'll just be a minute." She proceeded to the kitchen and lit a flame under a large pot that she pulled from the refrigerator, along with a covered bowl of *kluski,* which she placed in the oven.

Virski had not changed his position in the chair, he seemed to be examining his hands which were folded in his lap.

Bórza pulled a small end table in front of him and placed a large glass of vodka in his hand. *"Na zdrowie,"* she saluted, as she downed her glass of the pervasive liquor.

His lips twisted into a weak wry smile, *"Na zdrowie."*

"You relax, I'll have dinner on the table in a few minutes."

The kitchen window was open, and the adjustable screen was securely held in place by the lifted sash. Bórza had placed a freshly baked plum pie on the wide sill and the flies were in a frenzy in their effort to breach the tightly woven screen. The kitchen was small and compact, the living quarters were tight but comfortable in the apartment that Bórza had maintained since she came to Warsaw from her family's farm in Łódź. She took a job in the telephone company and determinedly worked her way to the position of nighttime supervisor of the long-distance operators. After the dust and ruble settled from the *blitzkrieg,* the German General Government quickly established the necessary communications network. Bórza had an impressive work record, and the Nazis kept her on, although at a marked decrease in salary. Nonetheless, she was fruitfully employed in the second shift which allowed her to operate during the daylight hours to engage in her role of Commander of the Liaison Girls.

By the time dinner was set on the table, Virski was slumped in his chair, head on his chest, the empty glass tilted in his hand. Bórza had never seen him this relaxed, and she hesitated to wake him. He stirred a bit in his uncomfortable position.

"Virski," she whispered, "come, dinner is ready, you must be hungry."

He opened his eyes to stare blankly into her face. She repeated, "Come, I have *borscht and kluski* waiting for you."

He shook his head, "No." He seemed disoriented and visibly fatigued.

She put her hands under his armpits and pulled him from the chair, "Come, you need rest more than food." She managed him through the hall to her bed and sat him down, removed his shoes and tucked him in, "Sweet dreams, Mateusz."

She made a cross with her thumb on his forehead and kissed his lips before she left the room.

Virski had no difficulty relinquishing his bunk at the hideout in Mokotów. He had been sharing the space with several other bachelors from Civil Resistance, who came and went at all hours of the day and night. There was no proper distribution of housekeeping tasks; chaos and disorder prevailed.

He gratefully accepted Bórza's invitation to share her comfortable apartment. For the first time in five years, he was enjoying creature comforts that he had considered lost to him.

Irregular hours continued to be a part of the daily life of the two insurgents, and the conversation between them was limited to the mundane experiences of daily life. Neither one of them divulged the secret intrigues of their covert operations.

Chapter Seventeen

May 20, 1944, a wireless was sent from Blizna to the secret radio station at its current location in Grokow. The staff of the Resistance station had become a mobile unit, constantly in search of new and out of the way locations to keep ahead of the Germans who were employing the newest technology to ferret out wireless transmissions.

"Found intact—disassembled—sent on."

Jerzy picked up the message during his regular rounds. His name was on the covert station's restricted 'need-to-know list,' and he was promptly notified of any change of location.

Commuting in and around Warsaw became a part-time position for the journalist. He became familiar with the routes and time tables of the rail system in the suburbs, as well as the steady routine stops of the trams that conveyed their passengers in and around Warsaw. His Aryan good looks, neat appearance, and pleasant manner held sway with the German passengers, while the Poles traveling the rails considered him a possible undercover SS agent.

Jerzy interpreted the vague text of the wireless as the important message Kaminski had been expecting from Blizna. He was on his lunch break; he had less than twenty minutes left. It was imperative that the message be delivered as soon as possible.

Back at his desk at the *Nowy Kourier*, Jerzy searched through his file of potential interviews that would get him out of the office and back on the street. He glanced at his watch; the gendarme would be changing shifts at three o'clock and the guards would be focused on the necessary documentation and assignments of the duty roster. That muddled environment always held the potential for breaking news. He informed his editor of the assignment he was taking on and headed for the stationery store.

A young man in the uniform of the Wehrmacht was at the counter trying to decide on an impressive letterhead for his personal stationery.

Jerzy approached with the official salute, *"Heil, Guten Tag,"* he offered a pleasant smile.

The soldier clumsily returned the salute; he had never before been greeted in this manner by a civilian, certainly not here in Warsaw.

Jerzy continued in German, "Personal stationery?" he glanced at the samples Potopski had displayed on the counter, "you must write a lot of letters."

He blushed and tried to make light of it, "Oh, it's just that I have just been made sergeant, and my family will be proud to make announcements of my promotion to the neighbors."

"In that case, you should have Mr. Potopski make a sort of coat-of-arms for you. Perhaps the official font of the W, with the proper insignia beneath."

He looked to Potopski, "Is that possible?"

"Not only possible, but quite easy to do."

The sergeant beamed an appreciative smile, *"Danke!"*

Potopski wrote out a receipt for the stationery, "I'll have the order back from the printer by next Friday; stop in to pick it up." He handed it to the soldier for his signature.

With a flourish, the young man signed the order, *Unteroffizier Anselm Hauer.*

As soon as the soldier left the shop, Jerzy asked to use the phone and dialed Kaminski's office. Kurt answered with the usual greeting and shop name.

"May I speak with Pan Kaminski?"

"Whom shall I say is calling?"

"This is Potopski from the stationery store and I have a large order to be filled."

"He's not here, but I will give him the message; you can be sure to hear from him soon."

Jerzy left the cryptic wireless with Potopski to deliver to Kaminski; he had invested enough time in subversive intrigue; he had to get back to his office. Fortunately, he had a human-interest story about a young German soldier who had just been promoted to sergeant in time for the next edition of the *Kourier.*

Edward Potopski repeated the message as it was told to him for the benefit of Kaminski, who was seated at his desk. He returned the receiver to its cradle on the counter. His facial expression said it all; an element of danger was implied in the message delivered by Jerzy at the stationery store.

Kaminski tightened his lips, drew a deep breath, and rose from his seat. "Finish up this order for the boot factory." He picked up his *Hamburg* from the peg on the wall as he made his way to the door.

Potopski was wrapping up a sale at the counter when Kaminski arrived with a delivery of balance sheets and notebooks. He laid his packages down and waited for the customer to leave.

"You have something for me?"

Potopski handed him the note. Kaminski was visibly shaken by the cryptic message; he stood motionless for a moment, as if deciding what course of action was needed. He lit a match and torched the note in the ashtray.

"Thank you, Edward," and then, as if an afterthought, "Write out a check for the products; I'll pick it up later."

He rushed out the door. Finally, he had the information on the Blizna story that he had been covering for months. Kumor could give him an update on the captured V-2 rocket.

"Do you have an appointment?" Kumor's secretary presented her authoritative demeanor to Kaminski's request.

"No, but this is a matter of urgency; I must see him."

"I'm sorry, but the Colonel is not to be disturbed." She went on typing the document that she was working on before he interrupted her. He chafed under the impervious attitude of this insignificant secretary. She may have considered him dismissed, but Kaminski was prepared to camp on Kumor's doorstep for the rest of the day. He settled down on one of the uncomfortable wooden chairs, opened his flask, poured a shot of vodka in the cap, reached into his briefcase for pad and pencil and began to work on an outline for his current article.

His temerity paid off when Kumor came out of his office on his way to the bathroom. Kaminski confronted him.

"We need to talk!" Kumor stopped in his tracks, gave him one of his familiar stares, a grimace pulled at the line of his lips, "First things, first. When I come back, I have five minutes to deal with you."

Kumor ushered him into his office and remained standing to emphasize the limited time he had to offer.

"What's going on with the rocket? I have a right to know. I've been in pursuit of the story since last year."

Kumor heaved a sigh, "Take a seat, Zygmunt," he walked around his desk and sat down for a face-to-face interview with the tenacious journalist. "I cannot give you any information on the V-2. You of all people, should know the degree of classified intelligence that's involved in a major new development of a war weapon."

Kaminski did not lower his glance; if Kumor was taking the time to sit down, there must be some compensatory tidbit about to be offered. He pulled out pad and paper, ready for a story to unfold.

Kumor cleared his throat and leaned forward in his seat. "This is the latest on General Anders' Polish II Corps in Monte Casino. The Nazis, entrenched in the hills directly below the abbey, are conducting repeated attacks on the Allied troops beneath them. This caused the Allied commanders to assume that the Germans had taken possession of the abbey. As a result, on 15 February, American planes bombed the facility with fourteen hundred tons of high explosives providing an advantage for German paratroopers to take possession of the abbey."

Kaminski held his pencil in mid-air, "This is the story you are handing me in lieu of the V-2, which legally belongs to me? Albert Świątek, the Swiss, gave me this much information two months ago."

Kumor stood up from his chair, "Your five minutes are up!"

Kaminski lowered his head and slowly shook it in resignation, "I apologize, Colonel, forgive my ridiculous comment. I know you have a story for me, and I'm most eager to receive it."

Kumor cocked his head to the side, dismayed by the humble apology, he sat back down. "General Anders' troops continued to advance up the mountain despite the lack of cover on the hillside. They were met with constant artillery and mortar fire from German paratroopers who had set up camp in the ruble of the abbey."

He rose from his seat again, this time with an air of finality. "Anders' Polish II Corps have taken Monte Casino after five months of pounding from the Allied forces with no gain. They accomplished this on 18 May and raised the Polish flag in what remained of the abbey. The casualties of the Allies numbered fifty-five thousand, compared to the German losses of twenty thousand soldiers, as well as a monastery dating back to the sixth century."

Kaminski let his notebook sit on his lap, opened, while he absorbed the impact of the final battle. He lifted his head and stared into Kumor's eyes; he would not settle for the Ander's story. There was a V-2 rocket he wanted to know about.

Kumor grimaced, "The Home Army in Blizna disassembled an intact V-2 and carted it into Warsaw. It arrived last night." Kumor paused and sent a guarded look at his inquisitor before he continued. "The rocket is being taken to a laboratory to be analyzed by the scientists before shipping it on to London. This is definitely not for publication."

"Understood." then a brazen request, "May I follow up on the final analysis of the rocket?"

"Absolutely not!"

The disassembled rocket and its motor were laid out on a large plank suspended by two wooden horse stands. Virski had delivered the pieces to one of the secret laboratories in Warsaw where the fragments would remain until the scientists had exhausted their analysis.

Chapter Eighteen

At 11:00 am, 6 June 1944, Home Army headquarters of General Bór received the first cryptic radio message of the day from Britain. A beachhead was established by Allied forces in Normandy. Operation Overlord had begun on Utah Beach at 6:30 am. Eighteen thousand Allied paratroopers had landed at dawn and were able to capture a bridgehead and disrupt the German lines of communication before the first landing. Bór was elated. He contacted his deputy, Deputy General Antoni Chruściel, (nom de guerre: "Monter"), Commander Warsaw District, to share the news of the long anticipated Second Front Invasion that would preclude any attempt of a Rising to expedite the withdrawal of German troops from Warsaw. The plans for the Rising had been set into motion after the *blitzkrieg* of 1939 had brought the Poles to their knees in defeat and surrender.

General Bór-Komorowski, Commander of the Home Army, had an aristocratic lineage that went back to the fifteenth century. In 1938, he was ready to retire from the military. Adolf Hitler put an end to the plan. General Bór needed to vent his aggression.

The *Nowy Kourier* news staff was scrambling. Hitler had received the news of the landings at 10:15 am. He immediately sent orders to General Rommel to fly to France and drive back the invading forces by midnight.

The British decryption on 6 June gave the assurance that D-Day plus One, June 7, would not see the full force of Germany's defense, due to Hitler's confusion as to where the invasion would take place. He had dispersed troops to Norway, where the Russians had set up a foil to safeguard the Allied landing of Normandy.

Mateusz Kizlewski, manager of the Nectar Restaurant in Center City, was the commander of the group of insurgents that served under him. Every waiter, bartender, busboy, even the janitor, had lost family and friends to the barbarous Nazi procedure of *lapanka,* the indiscriminate killing of innocent victims for the retribution of subversive activities by the Resistance movement. His staff worked together as a unit to disrupt the occupation and rid themselves of their captors. The Nectar served an excellent German cuisine to the Schindlerites, who took over their commerce, and the Gestapo, who ruled their lives. The staff kept their eyes open, and their ears pealed.

During the bustle before lunch, Kizlewski got word of the Normandy Invasion. He gathered the staff for an impromptu announcement. "Fellow partisans, the Allied Forces have invaded the beaches of Normandy," he was unable to complete his report; the applause was deafening.

Jerzy got to the Nectar for lunch, where he hoped to bump into Kaminski. He ordered a bowl of *Goulaschsuppe* and a stein of beer to occupy him while he waited. His favorite waitress, Adela, an elderly woman who reminded him of his grandmother, engaged him in mundane conversation when she brought him his soup.

"What is this? You are flirting with the woman I have been trying to woo for weeks?" Adela responded with an audible *"Tch,"* and a shake of her head. Kaminski gave her a quick hug, along with his order and took a seat.

"I was hoping that you'd stop in here for lunch, today." Jerzy said as he filled his spoon with soup. "The second front has been established," Jerzy then muttered just before he placed the spoonful of soup in his mouth.

Kaminski nodded his head in acknowledgment, "I'm just back from Kumor."

Adela brought their drinks to the table, Kaminski gave her a big smile and raised his stein for a German toast, *"Zu Wohl,"* he beamed. The waitress seemed startled by his aberrant choice, she made a grimace and walked away. Kaminski gulped a mouthful of the beer, and raised his stein again, "Just in time for my next edition."

"Zygmunt, why the toast in German?"

"If Bór has his way, as he probably will; he's been itching for an uprising for four years, he's sure to pull the trigger on the operation now. He's been chafing since the suspension of Allied drops in '43', due to Stalin's accepted recommendation that Yugoslavia receive aid because they were involved in combat with the Germans, whereas the Poles were merely involved in Resistance."

Jerzy had firsthand knowledge of what was going on, not only on the various battlefields but in Berlin as well. "The Germans are sure to retreat to the west, now that Germany itself is being threatened, and Rokossovsky is already at the Vistula. Help is available; where's the problem?"

"As I see it, there would be no problem—if we don't intervene. The Germans are losing territory and men; the German people are turning against the war. Hitler's key military figures are seeing the writing on the wall. Why can't Bór see the big picture? Why sacrifice *Warszawian* lives needlessly?"

Kaminski picked up the tab and the two journalists went their separate ways maintaining their disparate views on the subject of a rising.

Chapter Nineteen

The rain was pelting down on the apartment windows beating out an annoying staccato rhythm. This was the third day of the heavy onslaught, and Virski was showing signs of a possible breakdown; his imposed inactivity was causing a strain on the couple's relationship. Bórza was determined to come up with an idea to intervene and perhaps inject a moment or two of reduced tension; they couldn't go on like this much longer, something was sure to break.

Virski had a passion for plum pie, and Bórza was a culinary artist, baking was her specialty. She set her alarm for three o'clock in the morning to assure ample time for the project. Six hours of uninterrupted sleep were considered to be a luxury for Bórza; she averaged approximately three to four hours of sleep on any given night. Her covert operation as supervisor to the Liaison Girls left her without any semblance of normalcy in her life; stress and anxiety were taking their toll on her as well. She clung to the only thing that resembled a real life, her love for Virski gave her the emotional energy to hold on. She actually awoke a few minutes before the clock was set to ring, and while Virski tossed about in the bed, she crept into the kitchen to switch on the oven and prepare the ingredients.

Out on the street pedestrian traffic was increasingly chaotic as people bungled their way under umbrellas and splashed about in the puddles on their way to the trolley stop. Bórza's freshly baked plum pie sat on the wide kitchen windowsill cooling in defiance to the ongoing torrent.

Virski gripped the handle of his third cup of coffee; he stood in front of the window and watched his neighbors' bustle on their way to a productive day.

"Mateusz, I have to leave. Will you be alright?"

"Of course; why wouldn't I be?"

"I know you, Mateusz, you are under great stress while you wait on Kumor to call." She pulled her coat off the door peg and reached for her umbrella from the stand. "Don't worry, Kumor will get in touch with you."

He put his cup on the table and lowered his head.

Bórza placed her hand under his chin and lifted his face, "Stay with God. I love you, and I must go now."

"Go with God. You don't know how lucky you are to have something meaningful to do. Go and be safe."

The recovered V-2 rocket was still being analyzed by the group of scientists in the Office of Research, a branch of the Polish Intelligence Agency. Until the analysis was completed, Virski was to remain securely undercover. His next assignment was vitally important. He had to be ready to travel at a moment's notice.

Bórza's wit and good home cooking kept him engaged while she was at home, but her twelve-to-fourteen-hour schedules left a significant void to be filled by demons of the past along with significant angst over the future flight he must take to London. Virski, who had no trouble facing a German Luger, had never flown in a plane, nor did he ever consider the possibility that one day he might climb inside of one of the craft's tube-like structure and view the ground below.

The German V-2 rocket, a guided ballistic missile, powered by a liquid propellant rocket engine, was a vengeance weapon designed to attack Allied cities as retaliation against the Allied bombing of German cities. During the testing of the weapon in Blizna, Poland, only four out of twenty-six launches were successful, due to inflight breakup or during re-entry into the atmosphere. The analysis of the captured and reconstructed rocket at the laboratory in Warsaw was completed with an understanding of its devastating possibilities and an explanation of its failure to launch successfully.

A very large, tightly secured canvas bag was deposited at the foot of Kumor's desk, along with a sealed document addressed to Prime Minister Churchill, which was dispatched by courier and delivered directly into the hand of Kumor. Operation *Most* III [Polish for Bridge III], or if the British code name was preferred, Operation Wildhorn III, was set in motion.

The torrential rains had receded, the air remained humid, and the temperatures were rising. Virski lit a cigarette with the burning butt of the one he had just finished. He needed a shower; the typical July weather pattern was stifling, and the rising heat factor was augmented by the lofty position of the third-floor apartment. Virski had grown increasingly lethargic and despondent. Grooming and self-care were not on his agenda.

It was 2:00 pm when Bórza burst into the living room, "Virski, it's here! Kumor gave me your orders."

Chapter Twenty

Motyl, *or* Butterfly, was the code name given to the abandoned airport that was assigned by the SOE, the Special Operations Executive, Churchill's secret intelligence organization, as the loading site for the rocket that was expected in London. The airfield was not far from the village of *Wat-Ruda,* a farming district, where the Home Army unit "Urban" was under the direct command of Adam Gondek, aka Kruk.

The Nazi troops in *Wat-Ruda* were in flux. A skeleton crew would be left behind to maintain control over the villagers; the majority were already in transit to offer resistance against the Allies advancing into German held territory.

Kruk had received an encrypted code over a BBC radio broadcast informing him that a British plane would be flying in to *Motyl* to pick up passengers and a vital weapon. He immediately alerted the villagers. Able bodied men would be needed to aid in the boarding of an Allied plane at *Motyl* at a moment's notice.

An RAF Dakota KG 477 transport plane of No. 267 Squadron, stationed in Brindisi, Italy, was fitted with additional fuel tanks to endure a flight of eighteen hours. The pilot of the plane was a New Zealander, Flight Lieutenant Stanley G. Culliford.

His co-pilot, Polish Flight Lieutenant Kazimierz Szrajer, would also serve as an interpreter. Weather conditions permitting, the flight for Operation Most III [British Operation Wildhorn] was scheduled for takeoff, on 25 July 1944.

The Opal Kapitan, seized property of the Resistance, sported the swastika logo on magnetic shields that were firmly placed on the doors, the emblem was repeated on a flag that waved in the breeze from the antenna. Dysthmus donned his *Wehrmacht* uniform with a sergeant's insignia on the sleeve. Virski and the Home Army sergeant accompanying him were suited in expensive business suits, in the style befitting a proper German. Their travel to *Wat-Ruda* was without incident.

They arrived at Kruk's home on 23 July. The hermetically sealed bag was securely stowed behind a panel in the kitchen wall. Home Army soldiers and stalwart villagers kept an around the clock vigil over the premises.

At 8:00 p.m. on 25 July 1944, the weather report at Brindisi cleared the way for the Dakota takeoff. A little past 10:00 P.M. the RAF transport plane took off for Poland. Kruk was alerted by an encrypted code from the BBC, requesting that appropriate action take place. The Home Army soldiers, and the peasant partisans surrounded *Motyl* to lay in wait. They watched in numbed fear as two German *Storch* reconnaissance planes landed on the airstrip and took off shortly afterwards.

Virski's hair at the back of his neck stiffened, "What's happening here? We were assured this was a relatively safe site?"

Kruk wrung his hands, "Everything is thrown off schedule. The German troops are dispersing. This landing field has been deserted for years."

Virski wasn't satisfied, "What if another *Storch* lands while the British plane is headed this way?"

Kruk pursed his lips, a vacant look in his eyes, "We can do nothing."

Just past midnight, an approaching plane broke the silence of the night. The partisans waited until Kruk gave the signal that it was indeed the Dakota and not another German Storch; they emerged from the woods wheeling the cart carrying the V-2 components. The plane's twin searchlights glared down on the airfield. It circled and hovered above the ground for a few seconds and then rose again. The sound of the engines struggling against gravity could alert every remaining Wehrmacht soldier within miles. It circled once again before completing a safe landing. Kruk's army of peasants, some of whom were barefoot, surrounded the Dakota and rushed the four passengers off along with their luggage. One of the passengers was Zamski, the courier from London, who was sent to observe the climate and conditions of an impending insurrection and report back to the Cabinet who were out of touch with the prevailing circumstances of Warsaw.

All hands rushed to swiftly complete the boarding. The disassembled V-2 components, along with the engineer in charge of the laboratory experiments in Warsaw took precedence. Virski and the sergeant were quickly stashed on board followed by three passengers with assigned seats for Brindisi and their luggage.

The doors were securely shut, ready for takeoff. The aircraft vibrated, moved forward and stopped.

"Damn it," Culliford hissed, "the brakes locked!"

His co-pilot, *Szrajer,* stood up and pulled a set of pliers from the toolbox behind his seat. "I'll cut the cables."

The landing in Brindisi was a concern to be dealt with later. Right now, they had to get this bird in flight.

Culliford turned the ignition key, put the gear in place and was dismayed when, once again, an attempt at take-off produced the same vibrating effect with no forward movement. The wheels had become stuck in the mud produced by the recent deluge of rain. He radioed the dispatch officer to apprise him of the current conditions. It was determined that all baggage be unloaded, along with the passengers and an attempt be made to clear away the mud.

Kruk shouted out, "Farmers, raid the barns for straw; soldiers start digging trenches!"

Once the straw was obtained, the men quickly performed the task. Satisfied that this would do the job, the V-2 parts were carefully re-loaded, the passengers climbed on board and their luggage was tossed on behind them. The engines were started, Culliford engaged the gear for take-off only to be faced with the same vibrations and no movement forward. He radioed his flight commander and was ordered to unload the aircraft and burn it, the plane could not be left intact for the Nazis.

Virski strode forward, his right hand covering the butt of the gun snuggled in its holster, "I cannot allow you to do that!"

An argument ensued. Kruk raised his voice, "Let's try one more time."

Culliford snapped to attention, while his eye remained on Virski's right hand.

Kruk shouted, "We'll tear the boards off that shack over there and lay them in the trenches. That should do it!"

Fortunately, the building was old, and weather worn. The men had at it and gathered enough slats to provide a more solid structure for the wheels to roll on. For the third time the cargo and passengers were loaded on board. The engines were started, the gear engaged, and the plane took off just as the first rays of dawn were appearing in the short July night.

They landed at Brindisi without brakes. Three of the passengers left the flight. The brakes were repaired, the additional fuel tanks re-filled, and a quick safety check was performed before the plane took off for London, via Rabat and Gibraltar.

On 28 July 1944, the plane landed in London. Two British officers boarded the plane and demanded to know who on board was carrying the V-2. Their approach was intimidating. "We are here to take the weapon to Mr. Churchill!"

Virski balked, a sneer on his face. One of the officers pulled his gun from its sheath, aiming it directly at him. "Mr. Churchill has been waiting for this package for several days."

Virski pulled a knife from his pocket, his face took on a rigid, defiant look, "We have been waiting for Mr. Churchill for four years. Out of my way! This package will be delivered into the hands of Prime Minister Mikołajczyk of the Polish Government. Shoot if you will!"

INTERMEZZO

The steady stream of communications, both radio and courier, between the two governing entities proved inadequate. The climate and mood of the Government in London could not be accurately conveyed to Warsaw, and the situation and issues of the occupied capital were incomprehensible to the chain of command and staff of the Government-in-Exile. They operated in two different spheres; their individual impressions led to different perspectives resulting in a schism of policy and approaches.

In London, Premier Mikołajczyk was surfing about in the political undercurrents of the British war office and sensed a shift of policy towards the Russians. There was a conspicuous absence of commitment to the eventual return of the Polish Government to Warsaw.

Mikołajczyk was beginning to recognize the fact that Poland could indeed become the Seventeenth Soviet Republic. In that case, a Polish Administration would require a "Quisling" governing body managed by Polish communists. He was flailing about in unknown waters without a floatation device.

Commander-in-Chief, Władysław Sosnkowski, the architect, with his analytical mind, foresaw a repetition of the 1939-41 scene of Soviet tyranny over the Poles. Tactics that included mass deportation, and a false referendum that led to the subjugation of the people with an agenda to finally exterminate the will and national identity of Poland. Sosnkowski was immutable: there would be no compromise, no ceding of Polish territory.

7 June 1944: news of the Allied Invasion of Europe exploded in the media. The underground radio of Warsaw, and Kosciusko radio, out of Moscow were offering detail by detail events of the raid. The numerous underground newspapers, including *Poland's Journal,* presented huge headlines and informative text. Conspicuous by its absence was the blaring announcement over the German street speakers of Warsaw.

The emotions and mood of the people of Warsaw was divided. Those who clung to the future independence of Poland were confident that liberation was not far off with freedom right behind. The negative faction held that the German reaction to this news would be to intensify their control over the nation. The Government-in-Exile in London understood that victory over Germany would deliver Poland into the hands of the Soviets. This could not be made public. Russia was arming the communist People's Army of Poland. Stalin was in the process of organizing an underground parliament, the Polish National Council, a quasi-government to replace the exiled government in London.

Chapter Twenty-One

July 1944, Poland was a churning volcano about to erupt. Passersby along the railways were exposed to the gruesome sight of lengthy trains carrying hospital cars back to Germany. The wounded lying in the upper bunks of the cars could be seen through the windows. Germany was succumbing to the advances being made by the combined Allied Forces. The Soviet Union was invading territories held by Germans and the *Wehrmacht* toll was staggering. Moreover, Germany was unable to effectively replace these men. The average Polish citizen was able to read the handwriting on the wall.

14 July, 1944: General Tadeusz Bór-Komorowski reported to Sosnkowski, the Commander-in-Chief in London, the need to stage an insurrection.

Bór was haunted by the propaganda, released world-wide, regarding Poland's defensive attitude toward the Nazi occupation. The global media failed to grasp the intensely debilitating effect of underground disruption on the German regime.

Meanwhile, the Kosciusko radio and Soviet propaganda were falsely accusing the Poles of being silent allies of Germany.

General Sosnkowski, Bór's superior, was against a general insurrection. However, the Government-in-Exile in London, under Prime Minister Mikołajczyk, adopted a totally different stance. On 26 July, a wire was sent from London to the Government Plenipotentiary in Warsaw, Jan Stanisław Jankowski, endowing him with permission to proclaim an insurrection at whatever time he judged appropriate. This information was not relayed to Sosnowski.

The Poles in Warsaw knew that the battle would not bypass the city, they had been hearing the ammunition blasts from further up the Vistula coming from Rokossovsky's Soviet troops. The population's lust for vengeance, accumulated under years of tragedy and domination by the occupying German forces, was a tinder box waiting for the fuse to be lit. In this atmosphere the danger existed that perhaps that fuse would be ignited by less disciplined elements and trigger an unplanned rising.

General Konstantin Rokossovsky, one of the most brilliant officers in Russian history was ordered to fight off the retreating Germans in Poland along the banks of the Vistula. He was at an exceeding disadvantage. He was forced to move with caution; his front-line troops were exhausted after the fighting they had encountered at Byelorussia. His second line positions needed consolidation. The infantry reserves and heavy artillery were still moving up and not readily available. Stalin had placed him in a severely weakened position.

The effects of the Russian troops along the Vistula did have a persuasive effect on the German garrison. Threatened from both the south and the east, they prepared to withdraw. Civilians in the administration were ordered to evacuate. This condition was expected by Rokossovsky. The German command decided to throw in reserves to strengthen the defense lines to the east of the city in anticipation of the reaction from Polish citizenry. There was, however, a noted conundrum: if the German garrison pulled out too soon, Warsaw would be encouraged to rise. If the reserves were sent in too late, under heavy Soviet assault, they would not be able to move their heavy equipment in to offer some resistance. Meanwhile, the streets and roads leading to the railcars were filled with vacating German civilians.

Chapter Twenty-Two

During the month of July, the Germans experienced crushing defeat, not only by Soviet advancement, but by unsustainable German loses throughout their battlegrounds. Out of six armies, three were completely annihilated, two were pushed aside, and only the Second Army survived. They had no adequate reserves in their immediate rear on the Western bank of the Vistula.

The weather had not yet turned crisp but a cool breeze from the north made this sunny Saturday a day to brighten anyone's attitude. Albert Świątek approached the Napoleon Café with a quick step, a serene smile on his face, and the *Nowy Kourier* tucked under his arm. He took his usual seat and waved a good morning to Jushka, the waitress who was approaching his table with a glass of prune juice in one hand and a hot cup of coffee in the other.

"Good morning, Jushka; how goes it by you?"

"I'm awake and alive," she grunted, "what more could I ask for?"

Świątek leaned back in his seat, a fond smile parted his lips. "So true, my dear," he offered in the way of consolation. "By the way I noticed several trucks along Malikowski Street on my way. Do you know what's going on?"

"They're dropping posters to be hung on the walls of the city."

Świątek shrugged his shoulders in a manner that conveyed, "an accepted routine". He drank his juice, positioned his newspaper on the table and sipped his coffee while he waited for his *pierogi* and eggs. When Jushka brought him his platter, he glanced at his watch; eight-thirty-seven. He scanned the room, then looked out of the window. Where were Kaminski and Jerzy?

The ceiling fans were spinning overhead to stir away the stale, stifling air in the basement refuge of the Department of Intelligence. Kumor had been most benevolent this morning; he allowed Kaminski to sit in on his morning briefing in the conference room.

The large table hosted five people; Kumor sat at the head, to his left, Elka, his secretary, to take notes on the proceedings; to his right, Virski with Bórza seated next to him, and Kaminski seated next to the secretary on the other side. He was also engaged in note taking.

Kumor took a long drag on his cigarette, "What have you got, Zygmunt, that you're so anxious to discuss during this vital meeting?"

Kaminski straightened his posture his voice carried a note of assertiveness. He knew he had a scoop of outrageous proportions.

"Twenty July, at Wolf's Lair, in Prussia, Hitler's top men bungled an assassination attempt on der *Führer*." He uttered it like a headline.

"Shit!" Kumor crushed his cigarette butt in the ashtray. "What is this, the fifth attempt on that bastard's life? Don't those sons-of-bitches know how to murder someone? They sure as hell know how to exterminate Poles and Jews. What happened?"

"It was the second effort at Wolf's Lair. The first one occurred fifteen July, in the conference room with the timer running in a bomb set in a briefcase that was positioned by Hitler's chair. He was unexpectedly called out of the room minutes before the bomb was set to go off."

"Where did you get this information?"

"Jerzy got it off the wireless at *Nowy Kourier.*"

"And the second screwup?"

"Even more bizarre. The briefcase was once more positioned, all systems precisely set, next to Hitler's chair in the conference room. Hitler stood up to make an announcement, after which the official puppets rose to salute him, and Colonel Heinz Brandt, seated next to him accidentally nudged the briefcase with his foot and pushed it against the table leg. Brandt lost his foot and his life. Hitler's trousers were singed, and he suffered a perforated eardrum."

Virski banged his fist on the table, *"Psia Krew!"* he cursed. "Satan protects him from harm. No ordinary human could lead such a charmed life! He's the devil's disciple."

Bórza lifted her thick eyebrows and tipped her cap back, "Could Fischer have been in on this? He just got back to Warsaw on Thursday, the Twenty-seventh."

"Never!" Virski blurted, "Governor Ludwig Fischer is one of der *Führer's* most devoted puppets."

Kumor took the reins back in hand. "The Gestapo must have gotten wind of a potential rising. Fischer has returned to post orders for the citizenry. He's demanding that a hundred thousand *Warszawian* men be mobilized at the parks and markets to receive orders on procedures to safeguard the city."

"Bór knows about this," Virski quickly followed up on this breaking news, "He is going to post a proclamation on the door of Fischer's Headquarters declaring the Home Army's intention to fight for the homeland and throw off the German yoke."

"The idiot!" Kumor unleashed his contempt. "The Nazis are facing defeat on all of their battlegrounds. The upper echelon under Hitler's command are plotting to assassinate him, the Allies are advancing on all fronts, and Bór wants to annihilate *Warszawians?* Is he becoming senile?"

Virski's reaction was vehement, "Bór knows how we have suffered under the Nazi rule. All of us *Warszawians* are hungry for freedom and revenge. With Rokossovsky on the Vistula and Allied aid, we can make it. Just today, on my way here I saw Germans retreating to the rail station with barely more than the clothes on their back. They know that they're doomed."

Kaminski intoned a rational touch, "The Russians are our greater enemy. Don't count on anything happening on the Vistula that will benefit us. And don't count so much on the Allies, as they are cow-towing to Stalin whose troops have borne the brunt of this war. An insurrection at this time will result in a fruitless mission and we will be massacred."

Early Saturday morning, Jerzy made his way to Bór's current hideout outside of Żoliborz, where radio operations were going on twenty-four/seven. Bór had been holding daily conferences with several key people and a few messengers.

Bórza was able to attend every morning meeting; her position as supervisor of telephone operators kept her occupied during the swing shift, 3:00 pm to midnight, but her mornings were then free. The messengers in attendance were her Liaison Girls. There was a "letter box" a few streets away. The same situation was accommodated for at the other secret locations of Mokotów and Centre City. Telegrams and reports from other units were collected every hour. Between the transmitted radio messages and the letter box messages, Bór was kept apprised of movements being made by the Germans and the Russians.

Jerzy was looking for copy for the Journal, the radio set-up was fertile ground. Sergeant Janek Slota, formerly Corporal Slota, the only survivor of the sixteen members of the Home Army who were captured by the Russians in Volhynia in November of 1943, was re-engaged as a radio operator. He was putting in eighteen hour shifts seven days a week. Jerzy walked in just as Slota was jotting down the latest message. He stood over his shoulder and waited for Slota to decode the cryptic message.

"29 July 44, German defense lines broken by Soviet forces now occupying Otwock, Falenica, and Józefów."

These were villages at the outskirts of Warsaw. Further reports from the letter box described Soviet patrols had crossed the Vistula to the south of Warsaw and were approaching Mszczonów, 30 miles south of Warsaw.

Jerzy jotted down the information and glanced at his watch, 6:42 a.m. Kaminski was headed to a meeting with Kumor; he'd have to wait until the meeting was over. He headed out the door; artillery and ammunition would be needed—there would be a rising.

Chapter
Twenty-Three

J erzy eventually caught up with Kaminski and Virski at the café, where they were indulging in hot coffee and *pączki.*

"I've been sitting in the park, feeding the birds. I have a radio report I think you will find most interesting." He handed them his scribbled note of the events taking place in Otwock, Falenica, and Józefów.

Kumor was on his way to another meeting being held by the Deputy General Monter, Chief Warsaw Delegate Jan Jankowski, and the Council of National Unity; Virski took it on his own to investigate the ready supply of arms and ammunition hidden in the forest.

The morning was warm and humid as he made his way to Sochaczew. The sound of artillery grew louder as he drove on. He noticed a tank column ahead, but he wasn't close enough to discern whether they were German Panzers or Soviet tanks. He would need serious help from his Guardian Angel if they were Panzers. As he moved along he was relieved to discover they were Russians. He pulled up alongside, got out of the car and saluted the group of men who were preparing to climb into their vehicles.

"Dobroye utro!" The men returned the salute and smiled warmly at the friendly Russian greeting. He addressed the sergeant in his almost perfect Russian.

"Have you had much trouble with the Germans?"

"It goes easy, the bastards are retreating; we should be in Warsaw in the next few days."

The drive to the Furtak farm was made all the more pleasant under the optimistic view that now embraced him. *"The Russians are our greater enemy!"* he scoffed, remembering the comment made by Kaminski at yesterday's meeting.

Furtak was out in the field with his family. They were harvesting the ripe barley. Virski called out to them, but that weak throaty mumble of his could not be heard; he had to come in closer to be noticed over the machinery. It was Olga, Furtak's oldest daughter who sighted him, "Papa, Virski is here!"

Furtak jumped off the truck, "Something bad must be happening to drag you up here."

"I must see Dysthmus!"

"And what's the emergency?"

"We begin the Rising."

Furtak escorted him up the hill to the little barn that was the Gudzynski home. Pola answered the knock, and Virski was surprised to see how very pregnant she was.

Furtak was apologetic in his approach, "Good Morning, Child, this is Virski, here on an emergency mission. Where's Dysthmus?"

"He left with Kurt, an hour ago."

Virski got to the point, without acknowledging the lovely Pola, "Where did they go?"

Pola looked to Furtak, as if to question this man's need to know.

"It's alright, Pola, Virski is from Intelligence." He assured her.

"They went to the forest to load ammunition on the truck. Marek says there's to be a rising and the Home Army needs the weapons."

Over the intervening years of the war, ammunition and weapons were successfully stored away at Home Army Headquarters deep in the forest. They had amassed machine guns, rifles, and pistols. Much of the stored ammunition was acquired from Allied air-drops and confiscated weaponry obtained during underground skirmishes with the Germans. The underground maintained factories that produced hand grenades and Molotov cocktails. They even possessed a PIAT anti-tank rocket, courtesy of the German Army.

The total cache yielded enough ammunition to keep an insurrection going for several weeks. Now that the Allies had finally opened up a second front, it would surely maintain the Home Army until the inevitable intervention of Russian support arrived to reclaim Polish territory.

Dysthmus knew every backroad that transited Warsaw to the forest. This information was all the more important now that the Germans were filling the usual routes with escaping German civilians and retreating troops, due to the advancing Soviet tanks.

Immediately after the Allied invasion of Normandy, soldiers stationed at the hidden bunkers in the forest compound began the cleaning and preparation of the arsenal of equipment. The provisions were bundled and ready for transport.

Dysthmus drove the truck provided for him from the Schultz Sewing Machine Company, and Kurt drove the provisions truck requisitioned from the Nectar Restaurant. Dysthmus' battered truck would never hold out. Both trucks were loaded and headed for the secret depots for distribution.

Chapter Twenty-Four

Father Lipinski pulled the green chasuble over his head and hung it on the peg. Mass on the 29th of July celebrated the family of Martha, Mary, and Lazarus, Jesus' friends. Jesus arrived too late to save his friend Lazarus from dying and Martha and Mary were resentful. Jesus wept for his friend and then resurrected him; Lazarus emerged from the cave wrapped in burial cloth and the odor of death. Poland reeked from the smell of death. So many people slaughtered under the Nazi regime, so many thousands of Jews murdered in the hellish Nazi concentration camps sprinkled about Poland. When would justice come along to intervene in this holocaust? Would Poland rise again? Would the smell of death ever be blown away?

The unrest in the congregation at this morning's mass was so palpable, it was almost a visible entity; *Warszawians* were prickling under the pressure of an imminent rising about to occur any day.

There was a light tap on the screened door of the vestry and the sound brought Father Lipinski back to the present moment. "Come in."

"Ah, Heinrich, is it settled yet?"

"Let me join you for coffee. I need to update you."

Pani Trypka served the coffee and *babka* in the kitchen; the dining room was too formal, whereas the kitchen offered a more secluded atmosphere including the added comfort of a window which overlooked the garden. A huge linden tree offered shade to the table and the two chairs.

"Lord, God, bless this day and this food. Give us the strength to endure the coming events, according to your divine will."

"Amen."

"Heinrich, all of *Warszawa* knows the Rising has begun. Artillery fire has been keeping us awake."

"That's not the Rising, Father, that's the Soviets outside of Praga. There was talk of Bór initiating an uprising set for yesterday, but that fell through. He's still trying to get everyone on the same page for a commitment."

"With the Russians intervening, is it Bór's intent to join forces with the Soviets?"

Heinrich's lips stretched into a grimace, he looked out the window and then back at the priest, "There is a faction that does not believe Stalin has any intent to rescue Poland from the Nazis, while Bór believes the Home Army can successfully begin a rebellion before the Russians fight their way into Warsaw; the combined effort will see the defeat of the German oppression."

"So, there will be a rising?"

"Any day, now."

"What can I do to help?"

"Those catacombs beneath us can serve as a hospital facility. I have opened my home as a storehouse for ammunition and I have a stockpile of canned and packaged food for Home Army soldiers. All of *Warszawa* is preparing for the outbreak, whenever it comes."

Father Lipinski tempeled his fingers and bowed his head; Gruber followed the cue.

"Lord, creator of the universe, take this little corner of earth and protect it from the evil we have suffered under for years. If there is to be conflict, lead us to freedom from the barbaric foe."

"Amen."

'Heinrich, if the basement is to be used as a hospital, I shall have to petition the congregation for bedding."

"You'd better set out on it now, there's not much time!"

29 July 1944: General Tadeusz Bór-Komorowski, known simply as "Bór," was Commander of the Home Army. He had requested a meeting with the Council of National Unity, the underground parliament. He already had the endorsement of the Government-in-Exile in London to proceed with an insurrection at the timing of his discretion. He had need of further conviction from the Warsaw governing body.

The Government Plenipotentiary, Jan Stanisław Jankowski, aka "Prezes," arranged for the meeting to take place. Kaminski was there to cover the meeting. The Home Army's officials, Kumor from Intelligence, General Bór from Military, along with Deputy General Antoni Chruściel, aka Monter, and Bór's two deputies, Niedźwiadek (Bear Cub) and Grzegorz were in attendance. Zamski, the courier, who just flew into Poland on the Dakota that transported the V-2 rocket to London, sat in as mediator between the Council of National Unity and Mikołajczyk's Cabinet. The meeting was called to order and Bór was introduced as the speaker.

There was a round of applause for the esteemed general as he stood before the podium. He thanked the audience and assured them that, "Poland is not yet lost!" the traditional battle cry that had been uttered over the centuries of repression that Poland suffered from one nation or another. He then posed this question.

"Is it absolutely necessary that Warsaw be liberated before the Russians enter to capture the city?"

There was a short pause while the assembled members conferred amongst themselves. Jankowski then took the vote which turned out to be a unanimous, "Yay".

Now Bór needed some definite idea as to how the parliamentary members would proceed after the battle to regain control over the city.

"How much time should elapse between our gaining control of the city and the entry of Soviet troops?"

Jankowski convened a brief meeting to establish a general consensus.

It was agreed that twelve hours should be sufficient time for the parliament to get together and establish their corners before hosting the entering Soviet Army.

Zamski appeared increasingly uncomfortable as the proceedings went on. He had been in the midst of the nocuous division that had split the London Cabinet. He had not yet been apprised that an insurrection was agreed upon. He raised his hand.

Jankowski acknowledged his request for the floor. Zamski, disarmingly young and handsome, made his way to the table. His baritone voice and dignified demeanor caught the audience's attention. "Gentlemen and Ladies, I was not aware that we had come so close to a rising. I must inform you, there will be no Polish Paratroops to engage in the battle. They are fighting in Italy."

Bór was stunned, he had counted on the troops. His voice did not flinch, "Will the Allies support us with continued resources?"

"That I cannot answer to, General. I can only speak of what I have knowledge. The Allies are fighting not only on the fronts of Europe, but also in the Pacific. They are totally embroiled in these strategic commands."

The assembly had become as divided as the London Cabinet. A consensus could not be reached. Jankowski closed the meeting with the issue of a rising unresolved. He set the date for a subsequent meeting, July 31 at 6:00 pm. The information presented by Zamski would have to be authenticated before a vote could be taken.

Kaminski caught up with Kumor as he was getting into his car, "Kumor, come have lunch with me at the café."

"I don't indulge myself in sitting at public tables about town. I live a cloistered life."

Kaminski wasn't about to let him get away without a comment on how the meeting went. "What do you think the consensus will be at the next meeting?"

"I see no rational reason for a subsequent meeting. Zamski couldn't have made the prevailing situation more clear. An insurrection is out of the question."

"Can I count on your vote of Nay?"

Kumor scoffed in annoyance. He pushed Kaminski away from the car, opened the door, and took his seat. He gave the insistent man a piercing look as he slammed the door, and drove away.

Chapter Twenty-Five

Meanwhile, in the Eastern battle zone, Stalin, to mollify the Allies, reported that his 2nd Tank Army had suffered a crushing defeat. He stated that the Russians retreated 120 miles, when in fact the Germans had destroyed 100 tanks in heavy fighting and the Soviets retreated 12 miles, but soon advanced again. Under that ruse, Stalin's troops could remained idle while the Germans shredded the Warsaw Rising a few miles away.

30 July, Sunday: Premier Mikołajczyk [Mik] arrived in Moscow for a meeting of resolution with Stalin. The post-war status of Poland and the expected Soviet aide for the Rising in Warsaw were at the top of his agenda. A jeep and a military sergeant awaited his arrival. There were no members of the press champing for a story with note pads and pencils in hand. The sergeant offered a salute, and the Prime Minister of Poland was whisked away to his place of lodging. He had his secretary phone the British Ambassador, Clerk Kerr, for a briefing. He was advised to curb his Government's stance on anti-Soviet elements and accept the Curzon Line of the territorial dispute. It was also important that the Exile Government disavow the condemnation of the Katyń massacre.

The following day he was ushered into the office of the Minister of Foreign Affairs, Vyacheslav Molotov, who greeted him with a question, "Why have you come here?"

Mik offered an insolent stare.

"Premier Stalin's time is consumed around the clock; you would do better to speak to a representative of the Lublin Committee."

The Lublin Committee was a newly established umbrella organization with ambiguous tenets and a hidden agenda to come forward as a Soviet "Quisling" government to administer communist policies to Stalin's future plans of a 17th Soviet State— Poland, after the war. The premier was offended by the rebuff.

"*Dziękuję, Nie!*" Mikołajczyk had a strong peasant stubborn streak, but a genuine concern for his country's future independence. Compromise was bending the man.

Mik was left to cool his heels for three days before he would meet with Stalin. He was becoming more rigid in his stance; his temper might jeopardize his long anticipated meeting with Stalin. However, just before he was to meet with the Soviet leader, he received news of the Rising. Now, the ball was in Stalin's court. Russia's aide was sorely needed in Warsaw.

At the same time as the Polish Government Premier awaited Stalin in Moscow, the Polish Commander-in-Chief, Sosnkowski, was reviewing the troops of the Polish II Corps under General Anders in Brindisi, Italy. Before he had left London, Sosnkowski had dinner with the Premier Mikołajczyk. Sosnkowski had no intention of indulging in polite conversation with the Premier. In his usual forthright manner, he had voiced his strong opinion on Mikołajczyk's proposed upcoming meeting with Stalin in Moscow.

"You leave with no clear proposals? Have you been given guarantees from the Western Allies that they will support you? Stalin holds a sword over their heads, I suspect they will compromise."

Sosnkowski lit a cigarette from the butt of the one he was about to discard and logically summed up the issue. It was vitally important that a clear understanding of the situation be recognized by both parties, sitting that it would be, "politically unjustified and militarily nothing more than an act of despair."

In Brindisi, he had not been apprised of Mikołajczyk's diktat to Bór to organize an insurgence at the latter's discretion, but something stirred his sixth sense. He had his secretary send a wire to the commander of the Home Army in Warsaw, dated 28 July 1944, with the dire warning, "…an armed rising would be devoid of political sense, capable of causing needless victims."

The message was interrupted enroute and did not arrive in Warsaw until 3 August 1944.

Chapter Twenty-Six

July 31, Monday, a sunny day with a cool breeze, a good beginning to the week. Deputy General Monter, sat at his table, preoccupied with events at hand and not attending to the plate of *bigos* in front of him. He stared out the window, *"God is in His heaven, and all is right with the world." Empty words!* He could not come to a resolution. His deepest desire was to crush the barbaric Nazis who had murdered and maimed so many who were dear to him, but the realist in him acknowledged the possibility that with an insurrection, *Warszawians* might experience the very same barbarism inflicted by a rising that might be successfully employed but violently crushed by the Germans. He blessed himself and uttered a contrite prayer to St. Michael, the Archangel, who drove the devil into hell. He took a deep breath and remained silent for a moment. A smile etched its way across his mouth. This was a good day for a bike ride.

Monter pedaled his bike toward the eastern suburbs, where all the action was taking place, He needed to see for himself just what were the real life conditions of the skirmish going on between the Germans and the Russians.

He rode along the streets of housed German installations that were obviously abandoned. Virski had mentioned that he had seen German civilians, "…*with only the clothes on their back racing to the rail cars.*" He sighted Soviet tanks on the immediate perimeter of the road to Praga. St. Michael had answered his prayer. He was confident. An insurrection was in order.

The meeting venue was moved to Mokotów Street, where exploding shells over the Vistula would be less of a distraction. Albert Świątek brushed his napkin over his lips, carefully folded it and replaced it on the table. A light snack of ham and cheese with a green salad would sustain him until later that evening. Jacob, his servant came to clear away the table.

"No bridge tonight, Pan?" He offered in a teasing manner.

"Hopefully, Jacob, there will be a bridge erected this evening. Do we have enough seats set up for the meeting?"

"I think so. Take a look, Pan."

The living and dining rooms had been set for an assembly. Every chair and bench on the premises was marshaled to use.

Bór and his deputies were the first to arrive, followed immediately by the Chief Deputy, Jan Jankowski and Deputy General Monter. The members of the Council of National Unity continued to arrive on their scheduled intervals, two at a time, ten minutes apart. Kaminski took a seat in his preferred spot, the middle of the audience where he could span the members to pick out any nuances of reactions.

It was 6:08 pm and Kumor had not yet arrived. Jankowski stood to begin procedures. "Good evening, Colonel Kumor is obviously late. But we must proceed with the meeting, General Bór, if you please?"

"Thank you, Prezes, Gentlemen and Ladies, I have validated reports of the Soviets moving tanks and using heavy artillery advancing into Praga. Deputy General Monter has firsthand knowledge of declining German forces."

He took his seat and Jankowski called Monter to the floor.

"Please, Ladies and Gentlemen, I was unable to arrive at a decision this morning, so I rode my bike into the eastern suburbs to verify the conditions myself. All of the German held installations have been vacated, all German civilians are gone. I spoke with Virski from Intelligence, who drove into Sochaczew and spoke to an officer of the Soviet tank unit near Praga and was told that they expected to be in Warsaw within a week. The time is ripe!"

From his seat at the table, Jankowski raised his right hand, a defiant smile on his lips, "Let's Go!"

The last to leave was a well-dressed gentleman, Secretary of Treasury, Ignatz Walczak. He had been lingering in the background.

"Albert," he handed over a small package, "This is a monetary gift from the Allies, with the oncoming conflict I have fears that it might come into unfriendly hands. I beg you to keep this in safeguard..." Świątek interrupted before he was given the option to refuse, which he knew to be forthcoming.

"Not another word, my friend," he placed his finger to his lips. He went to the doorway and called out for Jacob.

"We will have this vaulted while you are here to witness."

"Ah, Jacob, we are to have a deposit from the Government Plenipotentiary concealed within our home. Where would you suggest that we put it?"

They were standing in the living room. Jacob's eyes lifted up to the left, while he gave the matter some thought, then he scanned the area. He walked over to the large, round tea table that took center stage, pulled it to the side, and reached into his pocket for his Swiss knife. He got down on his knees and plied up a wooden tile from the parquet flooring.

"Give me some time to grind out some of the cement and we will have a nice little deposit box."

"V" Hour was set for 5:00 PM, Tuesday, 1 August 1944.

Chapter Twenty-Seven

Janina stood looking out of the window that overlooked Zielona Street, coffee pot in hand, engrossed in the scene below. Michal and Leona glanced at one another; they were waiting for a second cup to finish breakfast. Michal cast a puzzled look Leona's way, she responded with a shrug, "Janina, what are you looking at?"

The maid gave a start and the coffee pot twitched in her hand, "Oh Pani, something very wrong is going on. The street is bustling with people and bike riders. One boy was driving so recklessly that he knocked old Piotrek over."

They both rushed to the window, the street below was a scene of frenzied activity. Leona touched Michal's arm, "Could this be an uprising?"

Michal jerked his head in her direction, "It couldn't be; I would have heard of it." He turned his attention to Janina who still held on tightly to the pot. "Never mind the coffee for me, Janina, I've got to get to the office. I must untangle this mystery." He kissed Leona's cheek.

"Michal, please be careful, I don't like the look of things out there!"

He grabbed his hat from the peg in the foyer and shot into the hallway. Before he got to the outside door, a young man flung it open, he was dressed in a tan shirt, the Polish Eagle Badge was wound around his left arm.

"*Dzień dobry, Pan Bednarek,* I'm Janek Szepua, a student of Professor Bednarek. I want to say goodbye to her, I'm off to join the Home Army."

"Has the Rising begun?"

"Yes Sir, we are preparing to destroy the Nazis at 5:00 pm!"

Michal retained his civility, "Please, do go ahead. Pani will be most anxious to see you."

Michal jostled his way to Napoleon Square. A crowded tram went by, and he noticed a cluster of young boys standing up front, in the *Nur Fur Deutsche* section, which under ordinary circumstances would have brought instant reprisal. Women, in groups of two and three were hauling heavy bundles; arms and ammunition? No doubt about it, this had to be an insurrection, but when he looked up to the corner, he saw the usual patrolling gendarme at his post, seemingly unaware of anything extraordinary. He decided not to open his office, instead he made his way to Warecki Street and the café; he had to find Kaminski.

Approximately 48,000 Home Army fighters were mustered in Warsaw and its suburbs. Another 4,000 Resistance fighters, both men and women from all walks of life, workers from factories, restaurants, railroads, shops, and offices and from different political units; Communists, Socialists, and Right Wing NSZ sections.

Home Army fighters wore a mixture of old Polish Army uniforms, captured German camouflaged smocks, and even Polish Postal uniforms. The Polish Eagle Badge was worn to identify soldiers from insurgents due to the articles of war.

The early curfew hampered the spread of Bór's orders, leading to confusion the next day. The population was restless, almost at first light *Warszawians* reacted to the sounds of fighting in the east with patriotic fervor. A deep state of excitement prevailed among the Home Army fighters and many civilians. Optimism and aggression floated among the crowds. Among the younger, minimally trained, fighters of the Home Army there was a rising swell of unwarranted bravery.

As soon as the door clicked shut behind Michal's dash for his hunt for Kaminski, Leona made a scrambled exit from the kitchen, causing Janina to drop the cup she was setting on the drain. A knock on the door derailed her rush to the bedroom.

"Janek Szepula!" One glance at the thrown together uniform, brandished with the Polish Eagle Badge that he wore wrapped around his arm, and she was overcome with unleashed sobbing.

"Pani," he wrapped his arms around her shoulders and allowed her tears to splatter on his used and tattered army shirt. "It's alright, Professor, I'm on my way to help save Poland. You've always made us proud to be Poles and to love our country."

He eased her away and looked into her face. She swallowed hard, grabbed a breath, and managed a smile. "God bless you Janek!"

She grabbed his face and kissed his lips.

She would forego the shower. There was no decision making process involved in the selection of her apparel. She quickly pulled on the sleeveless blouse that she wore the day before, pulled a skirt from a hanger in the closet. She rushed a brush through her hair and slipped her bare feet into her sandals.

Janina heard the bedroom door close and made her way to the hall. "Pani, where are you going?" Her tone was a pitch higher and genuine concern wrapped itself in her phrase.

"Janina, you're not to worry! I'm on my way to the church, to pray for us."

"You could pray here with me. It's not safe out there!"

"How can you say that when you saw all of those women milling about, unharmed?"

"Who's to say that they won't come to harm?"

"Did you see the German soldiers on the street? Did they take any notice?"

There was no response, "I'm on my way to the church. Prepare a nice lunch for Irena and me. And don't wake her. Let her enjoy these last few peaceful moments."

"And just how am I to enjoy any peaceful moments when you and *Tatush*—the whole of Poland is under attack?" Fear and anxiety appeared in her voice; tears filled her eyes; her arms folded tightly across her chest as she stood before them in her nightgown.

"Jezu Kochanie!" Janina blurted.

"Irena," Leona took a deep breath, shook her head and reached out to hold her daughter in an embrace, "I must leave. I'll try to be home to have dinner with you."

As soon as the door shut behind her mother, Irena made a dash for the phone, "I must call Bórza!"

Janina dropped onto a stool and let loose, with tears and sobs she stammered her way through a litany of prayers.

"Hello, this is Wanda Hebdowska, I am having difficulty with this application for employment, I need your help."

"I'm really quite busy…very well, I'll meet you in my office, but get here quickly."

Chapter Twenty-Eight

The steps to the church presented a steady flow of traffic. There was only one mass on Tuesday, and that ended forty minutes ago. Once inside, Leona had to confront the fear that overwhelmed her when she realized that she was witnessing a scene she could never have imagined. Father Lipinski was in the middle of it all. Heinrich Gruber and Jerzy were speaking German to deliver instructions to the members of Heinrich's organization of *Volksdeutsche* sympathizers. Father, who had a good understanding of the language, was handing out weapons that were recently delivered by Jerzy from the arsenal set up at Heinrich's home in Czerniaków.

Out in the narthex, the flow of traffic continued. People entering the church bounded down the stairs to the basement. Those who were exiting the building climbed the steps carrying revolvers and grenades.

Curiosity overcame fear, and Leona directed her feet to the stairwell. In the huge hallway, Virski was giving a quick course on how to fill the chamber of a revolver with bullets and how to aim for the best results; how to pull the pin from a grenade and count before tossing it on a specific target. Those who had completed the course were waiting in line for the distribution of weapons.

Some dallied about trying to familiarize themselves with the weapons, while others rushed out, eager to employ them. She wandered over to the northwest corner, where she previously held her covert history class. The floor was covered with bedding. Here and there, a proper cot stood ready to accommodate a victim but spread about were blankets and pillows to offer some comfort against the hard, cold floor.

Leona ran back upstairs and wiggled through the crowd to approach Heinrich. She touched his arm, "Heinrich, what can I do to help?"

He handed off a revolver to the next in line, "Leona, behind me is a crate of Flipinkis; would you mind handing them out?"

By the time Michal approached the café, he no longer needed Kaminski's validation. The insurrection was primed and ready.

An ominous feeling greeted him at the door of the café. It was not yet 9:00 and the counter and tables were empty. Instead of the usual bustling ambiance of early morning fast-breakers and scurrying waitresses, only a few elderly *Volksdeutschers* sat scattered about the room. Michal scanned the occupants and recognized one of his clients. With a smile spreading on his lips, he offered a greeting, "*Dzień dobry,* Albert."

"Ahh, Pan Bednarek, *dzień dobry.* Won't you join me for breakfast?"

"I would like some coffee, so, yes, but I am too unsettled to eat."

"That's because you will be involved in the day's events, while I have only a bridge game to look forward to. And if my usual partners don't show up, I shall have to challenge Jacob to a game of Gin."

The old man's stoic nature and complacency had a soothing effect on Michal. The waitress delivered his coffee, and he appreciated the comforting aroma of hot caffeine.

"Had you arrived ten minutes earlier, you would have been able to bid Pan Adamski farewell."

Michal stiffened, "Aaron!" the name was barely audible.

"He rushed in for some breakfast buns to take on a trip. It seems there was little planning time invested in the trip. I looked out the window and saw his wife and little girl waiting for him, there was only one valise on the ground next to them." He watched Michal's reaction to his story. "He whispered to me that they were going to catch the next train to Danzig, with hopes of boarding a ship to England."

"If only there is a train to Danzig." His voice was soft, intoned as a prayer.

Michal sipped at the brew, which by now had cooled. "I must find Kaminski," he muttered.

"The upper echelon of the military are meeting as we speak at Home Army Headquarters; no doubt, you will find Kaminski there, gathering news items."

Chapter Twenty-Nine

Bednarek's step was ever so much brisker than his usual stride. There was a soft rain falling and he reacted to the weather as a paradox. Was this an omen? It certainly wasn't a condition for cooling things off. The very air he breathed seemed to be charged with the prescience of oncoming thunder and lightning. Or was it a message for hope and renewal?

Michal pushed and wove his way through the congested traffic. *Where were the gendarmes?* He noticed a pattern of idle men spaced, perhaps ten feet apart in the midst of bustling boys and women at the entrance to Bór's Headquarters. He made his way to the stair well. At the bottom, he was greeted by three Home Army soldiers who would not let him pass.

"You have no business here. Go back upstairs."

"I do have business here. I'm a magistrate of the secret court." He pulled out his defunct business card which labeled him an attorney at law.

"That card means nothing. Turn around and go back upstairs."

Michal had nowhere to be and no task to perform. He stood rooted to the ground in open defiance.

The Honorable Judge Peter Butkowski needed no identification. The sentries stood in salute to him when he appeared at the bottom of the stairs.

"Bednarek, why are you standing there?"

"I'm not allowed admittance."

"Gentlemen," he lowered his chin and looked up at them over his spectacles, "this is the honorable defense council for the Court of Warsaw. He will join me at the meeting."

"Michal, we will get a valid ID card for you, and you will not suffer these indignities again. You will need easy access to the daily meetings we will be holding. Bór-Komorowski has mandated a set of rules regarding the disposition of prisoners and property. We shall begin recording events as they occur, in order to expedite these events after the Rising."

The meeting had begun. Michal scanned the room until he came upon the figure of Kaminski settled in his usual spot, right in the middle of the gathered commanders of insurgents. Kumor, Bór, Monter, Grzegorz, and *Niedźwiadek* (Bear Cub) held forte at the main table. Kaminski was not the only one taking notes. Pad and pencil were in the hands of everyone in the audience. Kumor was the first to speak.

"I apologize for not attending yesterday's meeting. I went to Praga to confirm the report of Soviet tanks on the Vistula and got stuck behind a roadblock." He turned his hand to signal Bór, who offered a polite nod as he made his way to the lectern.

"I have tried to send a message to London regarding H hour and the initiation of the Rising. However, it seems it did not go through."

Kumor interjected, "First of all, that message was sent *en claire* which is inexcusable. We have been having a problem getting messages as well as sending them. This matter will be corrected."

Bór made the announcement, "Home Army Insurgency Headquarters will be moved to the Kammler Factory. I will be joined by my Chief of Staff, Grzegorz, Prezes Jankowski, and Chairman Puzak of the CNU."

He made his initial address and then went on to follow the agenda. Michal was fascinated by the unpacking of an instant bureaucracy as members were chosen from the ranks to head programs for the transportation of troops and the necessary requirements: food, ammunition, utilities, medical care.

Administrative command posts were set up in the territories of Mokotów, Żoliborz, Riverside, and the Central Borough, each with a commander and block captains. Within these units, a detachment was allocated to raid the supply depots and stores held by the Germans for emergency provisions. The stash was to be brought back to the unit until Dysthmus or Kurt could arrive to pick up and deliver the provisions so that no area would be left undersupplied.

Every home was prepared for fire-fighting with sandbags, pickaxes and buckets. Center City residents were an auxiliary arm of the insurgency. Pre-selected homes were handed requisition orders for the billeting of Home Army soldiers, and once the Rising went into effect, they would also be housing civilians who were unable to get safely past the fire zone.

The Secretary to Prezes Jankowski, sat squirming in his seat. Finally, he raised his hand to approach the floor. "I am unable to quell my anxiety of the chosen H hour. At seventeen hundred, people will be returning from work and will be caught up in the barrage. Couldn't we push H hour up a bit until people are safe in their homes?"

Bór's facial expression never displayed congeniality; this remark evoked a visage that sent a shiver up Michal's spine.

"Our intent, Sir, is to produce a surprise attack on the Germans. They would never expect an organized revolt against them at the busiest hour of the day. That is what strategy is all about."

Bór's then raised his steeled eyes to address the room at large. "Tomorrow, at seventeen hundred hours precisely, we will start operations in Warsaw."

Chapter Thirty

It was after 2:00 P.M. when Bór had crossed his last 't' and dotted his last 'i' to head for Rising Headquarters at the Kammler Factory located near the shattered Jewish Ghetto.

Michal waited by the door until Kaminski had finished his customary kibitzing.

"Michal"… he made an abrupt stop at the confrontation, a chagrined expression led into his apology. "I know I left you in the dark, I bumped into Leona, and she really let me have it; so, take it easy on me."

Michal shook his head, a smile whisked away his anger, "Zygmunt, I really do not care to hear your feeble excuse; I just need to be brought up on current events."

"Come with me to the Nectar for what is sure to be our very last meal there. My treat."

At 3:00 p.m. only a few diners were left at the Nectar. A couple of SS men sat at the bar, three scattered tables held the remains of coffee and dessert that some lingering German civilians enjoyed while they indulged in banal conversations.

Kizlewski, the manager, ushered the two new arrivals to a table in a secure corner of the room.

"There's nothing hot available on the menu. I can make you a sandwich or slice some *babka* for you. No wine available either, some coffee left over."

He sat down next to Bednarek, obviously to direct his remarks to Kaminski seated on the other side of the table. "My entire staff is on force for this afternoon. We have all the materials ready to build a barricade on the street."

"You're ready to do battle?"

"My hidden storage room has been harboring the munitions we've been gathering for years. We're set to go!"

"God be with you."

"Now, what will it be, sandwich or *babka?*"

"Both!" they exclaimed as a duet.

Kaminski added, "Who knows when our next meal may be?"

Bednarek used the wait time to unload his news. He prepared to absorb the information Kaminski would offer during the meal.

"Chief Justice Butkowski informed me there would be daily meetings to prepare depositions for war hearings after the Rising."

"Yes, Kumor had the Information Bureau print up fliers for newsboys to deliver tomorrow. The rules of engagement - only four, but very powerful - are very specific in detail," he reached into his pocket and pulled out his notepad.

"One, the dead, both German and Polish, are to be given temporary burial, and all personal documents preserved. Two, all self-appointed courts are banned. Three, all enemies of the Polish nation, Germans, or *Volksdeutsche* are to be protected pending trial. And four, all property belonging to German citizens, or the German state, is to be guarded and inventoried."

Michal scoffed, "You can't be serious; in the midst of a raging battle? What? Are we going to have spiritual angels directing the scenes as a staged play?"

"Personally, I'm proud of our Insurgent Administration, we've never been any good at propaganda. And Kumor must have ordered the printing with his tongue in his cheek; he's far too realistic and pragmatic to indulge in such fantasies."

"Well, I'm sure the Secret Court will do what it can to expedite these measures."

Doretka, the waitress brought their order to the table. "*Na zdrowie,*" she muttered, and left their table with a sharp salute.

Michal picked up the check and they made their way to the register.

"It's on the house," Kizlewski saluted, "*Jeszcze Polska nie zginela!*"

Michal returned the salute, recognizing Kizlewski's reference to the Polish National Anthem, "Poland Is Not Lost!"

Kaminski muttered under his breath, "Not yet."

Out on the street they shared a *déjà vu* moment of another time when their parting occurred on this very spot, Christmas of 1943. Kaminski was off to Blizna to cover the V-2 story and Michal was left in charge of *Poland's Journal*. The situation was different then, they were off on a reckless adventure; now there were grave doubts that they would ever see one another again.

Kaminski held onto Michal's hand, "Will you come with me to the Savings Bank? I have to be in on the immediate plans for the city."

"I'll meet you there. I'm off to the Stationary Store. Butkowski has called for a pre-Rising meeting."

Chapter Thirty-One

The activity along Buxom Street was incredible. People were actually bumping into one another as they scrambled across the street loaded with parcels and bundles. The Stationary Store had never seen such a bustle. Irena weaved her way through the crowd and entered the shop; she threw a nod Potopski's way and made her way to the basement hideout. The area was occupied with several small groups that were meeting to discuss plans for their particular unit and how they would participate during the inevitable rebellion that was about to take place. She scanned the area; almost at once she spotted Bórza's corps huddled near one of the bracing pillars and the judiciary faction at the opposite corner. Luckily, her father was entirely involved in the procedures and gave her no notice.

"You're late!" Bórza delivered the reprimand in her gruff, military style.

Irena grimaced, took a seat and accepted the admonishment. Bórza continued with her instructions.

"The Telephone Exchange will doubtless be held intact by the Nazis. Therefore, all communication rests with us and the radio. Administrative command posts are set up at stations in Central Borough, Żoliborz, Mokotów, and Riverside, with each site having a commander and block captains. You will be working in league with these block captains who will pass their unit's messages on to you. Develop a close relationship to maintain consistency. Praga is under siege by the Soviets. Hopefully, they will succeed and bring their artillery to Centre City before long. I have written down the individual locations and routines for each of you to follow."

She dealt out 3X5 cards to every one of the Liaison women who were there. Their very presence was a declaration of commitment to the cause.

"Do whatever is necessary to get your house in order and deploy to your stations by 4:00 pm. I understand that H Hour is scheduled for seventeen hundred. God Bless you; stay in contact with me. I must leave now to take care of my own personal duties."

Irena checked her assignment card, "Church Basement, under Liaison Captain, Gwiazda."

She was not as fortunate at eluding her father as she exited the premises.

"Irena!"

Bednarek must have been distracted; she might very well have been the distraction. She had been trying to slip away as she tried to hide herself in the midst of Liaison Girls. She stopped and separated herself from the group and turned to face her father's inquisition. He had been so involved in his covert actions he never gave a thought to the possibility that his daughter might be likewise engaged.

A concerned, as well as a puzzled expression addressed itself to the situation. "What are you doing with Bórza? Why aren't you at home with Janina?"

She placed her hands on his shoulders and kissed his cheek. "*Tatush*, I am a Liaison Girl; I have been for over a year," she smiled broadly, "I am trusted with Rush Service."

Michal went limp. He had been in dangerous situations, life threatening conditions, but he held on tight, working his way through. But his stress provoking moments were centered around Leona and her involvement in the Resistance, now he learned that his only daughter had been conducting covert duties on her own.

"Don't worry about me *Tatush*, I carry my *Częstochowa* rosary with me everywhere; Mary won't let any harm come my way. And I'm stationed at the church where Mama is!"

What could he say? She was an independent adult with parents involved in trying to obtain a free and independent Poland.

"*Idz z Bogiem!*"

Kaminski traveled the route on foot. Driving about town in an automobile during a Rising would be suicidal. He was just about to turn onto Marszałkowska Street when a passing truck stopped a few feet in front of him. 'Schultz Sewing Machine' served as its label.

"Hey, old man, where you off to?" Dysthmus' rakish voice called to him.

Kaminski sniffed a smile and walked over to the cab. When he was close enough to answer quietly, "To the Savings Bank."

"Hop in, that's where we're headed."

Kurt moved over to make room for the new passenger. *"Dzień dobry."*

"Who's minding the store?" Kaminski feigned an authoritative voice.

"No one is shopping today."

"What are you delivering? Ammunition?"

"Some, but also food and medical supplies that Dysthmus was able to finagle from a German stooge he's been bribing."

"How do you manage that?"

Dysthmus chuckled, "I've been doing it for years. It's a setup that Kizlewski used to fill his wartime closet at the Nectar, and I just fell into it."

Chapter Thirty-Two

Bednarek looked at his watch, 4:02, did he have time? It was only two blocks to the church, a seven to ten minute walk from the Savings Bank. Now that he knew where his wife and daughter would be…he'd have to chance it, he may never see them again.

The transiting milieu that confronted him at the church was overwhelming. It was similar to Easter Sunday services, but with a totally different aspect. This scene was not spiritual, it was militant.

Bednarek noticed the mostly elder parishioners seated in the nave, reciting the Rosary as he followed the din from the basement. No one noticed his presence. He stood at the foot of the stairs trying to make some semblance of the flurry of activity. Virski almost stumbled over him, obviously he was in a hurry.

"Oh, Bednarek, your family is here."

"I know, I'm here to visit with them before I run onto the Savings Bank. Where are you rushing to?"

"I have to report to Kumor before I begin my rounds to collect and distribute information. *Pozostan z Bogiem!*"

"*Idz z Bogiem.*"

Bednarek shifted his eyes through the crowd, he caught site of Gruber's big head and pushed his way through the horde.

"Heinrich, have you seen Leona or Irena?"

"Leona is with Father, organizing the hospital beds in the northwest corner." He lifted his head and scanned the area looking for something. "The last time I saw Irena she was over in that corner," he pointed his finger to the left, "talking to the Block Captain. I don't see her now; I don't know where she is."

Bednarek touched his arm, the gesture implying an array of emotions; friendship, concern, gratitude, and possibly, 'Good bye.'

"Thank you."

Gruber gave him a warm smile and a nod of his head. His sentiments were returned.

He elbowed his way through the crowd…the northwest corner, where Leona held her covert history class. For a brief moment, a shiver of nostalgia ran through him; he sniggered, *I thought I had reason for concern, then.*

Father Lipinski was the tallest person in the room, he was struggling to set up an old army cot, using words from scripture to alleviate his stress and get him through the exercise.

"Here, Father, let me help."

"Michal, thank you, I think this is from the war of 1920."

After a bit of tussling, the cot made its home firmly on the floor.

"There really are not enough of these," he gestured ahead, "Leona and Irena are putting makeshift beds together with blankets and sheets donated by the parishioners, there aren't enough pillows either." He gestured a blessing on him, "Go, make the best of this time with your family."

Leona put the finishing touches on a mat bed, straightened up and saw Michal coming toward her, "Irena, *Tatush* is here."

There was no greeting, no words—an embrace said it all.

Irena waited while her parents clung to one another; when they appeared ready to return to reality, she joined in the hug.

"Good you are here with Mama, here in the church, the good Lord will take care of you."

Irena took his hand in both of hers and squeezed gently.

"Where are you off to?"

"To administrative headquarters, Judge Butkowski is holding court there."

"Are they holding trials during the Rising?"

"No, Irena, they are keeping a running documentary of war crimes that will occur during the Rising." He noticed a folded cot on the floor.

"Here, let me help you with this, you'll never manage it on your own."

After the intractable cot was stretched to its fully functional condition, Leona glanced at her watch. "Michal, its 4:43, you'll never make it!"

"Jezu kochanie," he looked at his watch, "I have to!"

Cheek kisses were their parting gesture along with the traditional, 'Be with God' affirmation.

Chapter Thirty-Three

By the time Bór and his staff were entrenched in the Kammler Factory, *SA-Gruppenführer* Ludwig Fischer was alerted to the situation by an unprovoked skirmish on the outskirts of Wola. Bór's concern of a pre-empted strike by youthful zealots had become an actuality.

At 4:30 PM, Fischer put the entire garrison on alert and notified his superiors. Loud speakers along the streets of Center City were blasting warnings against "Bandits" actively involved in armed protest, this would not be tolerated. There would be severe reprisals.

A thundering noise alerted the residents of the homes that extended from Pious Street to Marszałkowska Street. In the kitchens of the first floor, where the evening meal was being prepared, the pots hanging on the wall were rattling. A detachment of Home Army militia was moving into position with all of the artillery they could carry over the roofs and lofts.

Virski reported to Bór that the German's strongholds surrounded the Telephone Exchange on Pious Street, with positions beyond the Square of the Redeemer. Until an underground passage could be constructed, rooftops were the safest way to initiate a Rising.

There was no 'flow' of traffic, the tramcars deposited their passengers onto streets that were currently military thoroughfares, the congestion was palpable. Bednarek could not forge a clear path, he had to push and prod his way along, anxiously marking time on his watch. At 4:58 pm, he was approaching Raven Street; before he made it to the corner the scene was bombarded by Home Army militia from every window and door in the vicinity.

He ran for cover into the nearest house. Exiting militia pushed past him, gunfire was incessant, a passing formation of German soldiers fell, unwitting targets for the newly unleashed offensive attack by Polish soldiers.

The foyer of the invaded apartment became a crossroad for a flux of citizens rushing in to seek shelter and insurgent troops, who had climbed down from the roof tops to unleash their fire of ammunition. After a few minutes, things settled down and the shelter seekers were left to seek some semblance of reality out of what had just occurred. The anxious breathing among them sounded like a low hum. Reactions were varied; some cried, others prayed, while others cursed the situation. A steady mantra was, "How will I get Home?" "What will my family think happened to me?" Here and there a positive statement, "When the firing stops we can make a run for it to get home."

An attractive woman in her fifties was the obvious resident of the apartment; she was baffled! She stood in the midst of the invaders wringing her hands. Bednarek stood near her, she fixed her attention on him.

"What shall I do?, she queried, "My husband, my son, and my daughter have all joined with the Home Army," she wailed, "but why? And why are you all here? I can't take care of you!"

He gently reached for her hands to stop their agonizing twirl. "Pani, we are all in the same boat, but with different problems. We must settle down, so that we can be sensible about our situation and decide on what we must do next."

August 1, 5:30 pm: Himmler received news of the Rising. He immediately sent a wire to Commandant Sachenhauser with orders to kill General Rowecki, aka General Arrow, the former commander of the Home Army who was held prisoner since 4 July 1943. He followed up with another wire to Adolf Hitler. In it he addressed his long seething passion against the Poles.

Hitler's response was delivered as orders to have every inhabitant killed, no prisoners to be taken, and every house to be blown up and burned.

Himmler's first impulse was to destroy the city by air bombardment but the fact that German troops occupied the area put a damper on that.

Himmler's mission was about to be fulfilled, there would be total destruction of Warsaw and Poland would cease to exist.

Chapter Thirty-Four

The transient residents of the apartment on Raven Street were at loose ends. As in any typical group of people, the immediate grasp of the situation was met with an array of emotional responses. Most of the women were hysterical; they knew their families were also in jeopardy; they knew their family members were angsting over questions that could not be answered as to the whereabouts of their missing relatives. The few elderly gentlemen who were not engaged in the insurgency, were guilt ridden and raring to become involved in the skirmish. The few who stood with Michal, were trying to bring some order to the situation. Food and water were a priority. The one definite bit of knowledge that they shared was the name of the woman whose apartment they had raided, Wanda Trawińska.

The Trawińska cupboard held a goodly supply of staples that would accommodate a family of four. There was barley for coffee and cereal, sugar, and flour. The icebox still held a large block of ice to maintain the freshness of four eggs, a half-pound of lard, and a few slices of bacon. Pockets were being emptied of snacks and bits of uneaten lunch morsels. All told, there were nine people in the apartment. If they were very careful they would have a bite to eat for dinner and something to munch on for breakfast.

The only item that did not appear on the table was cigarettes. Smokers would not relinquish the coveted tobacco.

Resounding artillery was taxing not only the hearing but the emotions of the residents who had to shout to be heard above the din. During the sparse meal, the noise level was sharply increased as a German panzer tank tore around the corner of Raven Street. Home Army defense retaliated with gunfire and Flipinkis. The result of the excessive amount of ammunition the insurgents spent on the fracas was the capture of the first German tank.

At 8:00 p.m. Michal climbed the three flights of stairs to get to the roof and assess the damage. To his incredulous astonishment, the red and white flag of Poland was flying over the Prudential Building, the tallest building in Warsaw. Another laid claim over the Main Post Office on Warecki Street, formerly a German barracks with stores of hand grenades, rifles, liquor, cigarettes, and other treats. A third flying flag announced that the Town Hall was now under Polish domain.

It was exactly 4:00 pm when Schultz Sewing Machine truck pulled into Bright Street. Sentries carrying live ammunition patrolled the area around the Post Office Savings Bank. Dysthmus pulled the truck onto the pavement to unload the supplies he had gleaned. It would be the last delivery the truck would make. The Schultz Sewing Machine's vehicle was retiring, cars and trucks were easy targets for grenades and machine guns. Supplies would be delivered on foot.

Kaminski entered the front door. The sentry recognized him and pointed to the right where a large marble hall offered office accommodations on both sides. He followed the sound of voices that led him to an office three doors down. The meeting was in progress, the administrative staff included Deputy General Monter as commander of the troops in Warsaw and the mayor of the City of Warsaw, Sowa, an old and experienced city official.

Monter stood before a map of the city, "Sowa and I have allocated eight units throughout the city comprising six hundred soldiers." These were brightly marked in red. "The units have been issued Thompson machine guns, grenades, Flipinkis, and cans of petrol. The flexibility of these units to integrate and separate will pose a real strategy problem for the Germans who will find it difficult to pin a specific unit to ambush. We have tried to distribute equal amounts of the munitions, hoping that the supplies will last until the Russian forces arrive, but in guerrilla warfare in 'an everyman for himself' ground combat, much ammunition is wasted…we can only pray."

At precisely 5:00 p.m. all of Warsaw resounded with the blare of exploding artillery; Monter lowered his head. Sowa offered a prayer.

Wednesday morning, Michal stood up from his berth on the floor of the apartment and leaned into a long stretch. The rain continued to pour, intermittent gunfire, broke through the gray atmosphere. German or Polish, it didn't matter; it was evidence of the continuing skirmish. The incessant barrage of artillery drowned out the droning sounds of snoring and weeping that went on in the Trawińska apartment. No one was sleeping. The final phrases of the day were addressed to the expectation that the Soviets were on their way to aid in the destruction of the iniquitous German forces.

In the middle of the night the bombardment had diminished somewhat, and Michal could no longer tolerate the incessant caterwauling within the apartment. He went into the street where heavy rain was lashing down to quell the fires of the combat zone. He smiled; *Did Father Lipinski order this deluge?*

There was no escape. In the cellars beneath him pick-axes were pounding through the walls, passing from one cellar to another over courtyards following a path from Raven Street to Buxom Street. Here and there, in the doorways of the houses people were whispering, the glow of a cigarette gave him a bizarre sense of normalcy.

He looked at his watch, the absence of sunlight made time indeterminable, it was 8:00 a.m. He realized that a few of his invading neighbors were gone. Had they left to find their way home? Surely, Pani Trawińska would be relieved. A sardonic smile swept across his face; he would be one more missing occupant.

In his usual summer business attire, he was definitely not prepared to wander through war-torn streets. His stomach growled, the few mouthfuls of the thrown together repast of last evening, had not left a lasting impression. He assuaged himself that this was a condition he would have to get used to.

The heavy rain covered him as he stumbled over broken glass and ruble on his way to Administrative Headquarters, *Did Kaminski make it through yesterday?*

The devastation he witnessed en route was horrific. Collapsing houses strew ashes, smoke and flames into the air, bodies exploding midair landed to rest in the prevailing debris of earlier victims of the unfortunate people caught in a confrontation between aggressors and liberators as they tried to make their way home. *Are these the lucky ones?*

Chapter Thirty-Five

Father Lipinski had left the doors on both sides of the basement unlocked. The steady flow of traffic overnight was unremitting. The hastily thrown together hospital was sorely lacking in medical supplies. There was no X-ray equipment. Fortunately there was enough morphine to keep the seriously wounded sedated. Two doctors had made it to the church to administer to the injured. Doctor Razinski, a man in his sixties, initially took charge of allocating the patients priority according to the extent of their injury, but the hands-on application of dressing wounds and performing immediate surgery, made this necessary task impossible. He called to Leona, who was helping a patient to drink.

"Pani, I need you to take on a vital duty. There may not be the possibility of someone else with a medical background able to join us. In the meantime, I must rely on your judgement to sort out the wounded according to how badly they have been injured." He handed her a prescription pad and a red pen. "According to your determination, designate a large one, for extremely wounded and attach it to their collar. For injuries that seem able to delay, write a three, and for those in between label a two." He returned to the patient he was administering to without another word, or a positive response from a woman he barely knew.

Leona had now became the triage nurse. The responsibility relieved her of the initial squeamishness that had overcome her when she witnessed fire-pocked faces and open festering wounds from hand grenades and bullets inflicted upon them. This was no time for sensitive, empathetic feelings. This was life or death.

The stealth walking pace and the spiritual presence of his Guardian Angel got Michal past German pillboxes and sporadic gun fire from both sides as the rain pelted down on him. He tucked his head between his shoulders as a reaction to the pouring rain; this may have been a blessing as he was unable to see the brutally burnt bodies and the severed limbs of civilians blown from their houses.

Once he arrived at Bright Street he was safe; Home Army sentries had headquarters secured. He strode through the entrance and the waft of coffee put his stomach in control. Nothing was more important at that moment than a cup of coffee and a morsel of food. He followed his nose and the din of conversation to the cafeteria in the basement, where an array of unshaven, loosely attired men were breaking their fast. Conversation was at a minimum, each man appeared to be reflecting on his own issues of this surreal adventure.

When he finally did locate Kaminski, he surprised himself by the outburst of laughter that issued forth from his mouth, drawing unwanted attention to his presence. Zygmunt was in his shirt sleeves, without a tie, his hair was rumpled, and a five o'clock shadow filled his cheeks and chin. *Where was the carnation?*

A look of annoyance flooded Kaminski's face, "What the hell are you laughing about? Are you shell-shocked?"

Without waiting for a retort, he called out to the men in the room for articles of clothing to allow Michal to shed his suit which was drenched from the rain.

Over coffee and stale dark bread, they exchanged their latest experiences. Michal filled in the whereabouts of Leona and Irena, and Zygmunt relayed the pertinent information of the organization of troops within the city as laid out by Monter at the meeting the night before.

"Has Britain replied to our situation?"

"Well, you know that the original messages sent by Bór were undelivered. Also, with so many wires traversing the globe, messages are lost or delayed. However, my greatest fear is that our message of a Rising will be looked upon as a fable; the way the allies disregarded the various alarming messages we sent regarding the conditions within the Jewish Ghetto. If you remember, they assumed our alarm to be a fabrication to get their attention."

The administrative staff left the cafeteria to resume a meeting upstairs. Michal and Kaminski followed. Virski was standing in the hallway, he had just arrived with news from Intelligence. Unlike Michal, his uniform was dry, indicating there was some sort of vehicle involved in his transportation.

Virski '*Ahem*'ed his way to the lectern, announced in his raspy voice, "We now are able to determine the German strongholds within the city; Gestapo Headquarters on Szucha Street, the Sejm Parliament Building, the Bank of National Economy, and of course, the seat of the General Government, Buell Palace. These strongholds are fortified by Panzer units and pillboxes." He allowed a lengthy pause for the audience to absorb these facts before his exiting speech. "Please, that was the bad news …Wola was captured in a team effort of both the Home Army and the Socialist Party Militia, in less than three hours."

Exhilaration subdued the stress and the overflow of adrenaline that had demoralized and weakened their resolve. They now had reason to allow their expectations to command a positive attitude.

Monter grinned and nodded his head, "Thank you, Officer, we'll concentrate on the good news." He called for a bottle of vodka to celebrate and repose on the good news, *"Na zdrowie!"*

Sowa wanted to know, "When can we expect the Soviets to intervene?"

"We are unable to maintain radio contact with Moscow, or with the Socialist Kosciusko Station, we are relying on news from London as to their position on the Vistula and their inevitable entry into Warsaw. The Germans have Praga under their control. Our immediate concern is that Russian bombing of strategic German objectives over the area have ceased as of Tuesday evening. Also, artillery fire coming from the Russian side of the Vistula has been silenced."

Kaminski pulled Virski on the side, "Listen, Virski, you remember the trouble we had trying to get global coverage on the Warsaw Ghetto? Could we be going through the same denial from the Allies regarding the Rising?"

"Kumor is on that same vein. He is in touch with an Englishman, who escaped from a German prisoner of war camp; he has been kept undercover by the Resistance group long enough to speak tolerable Polish. Lieutenant Ward has witnessed the atrocities of the Nazis against our citizens and is eager to testify to London what he has seen and what is happening now. Once the British have certified his credentials, you can expect the Allies to take on a positive point of view of the Rising and our need for aid. Our hope is that Churchill will then intervene and nudge Stalin to rush into Warsaw with his troops from the Vistula and influence him to maintain communications with us."

Chapter Thirty-Six

At 5:45 p.m. the BBC Polish radio announced the news of the Warsaw Rising with as much detail as it could provide. International radio stations picked up the breaking news item and the world was apprised of the latest offensive against the Nazis in this checkerboard conflict. Moscow radio and the communist controlled Kosciusko station remained silent.

Now that radio transmissions appeared open, Bór sent a wire to London requesting ammunition and anti-tank weapons. He stipulated the areas which provided easy access for pick-up, Napoleon Square and the Jewish Cemetery. He suggested the Polish Parachute Brigade be dropped in Wola.

The heavy downpour had been slashing at the windows since 8:00 p.m. The gunfire began at 5:00 p.m. with the rumble of tanks and the deafening roar of 'Billowing Cows', the German *Nebel Werfer* artillery that produced a series of six blasts that sounded like the mooing of cows prior to blasting off.

Janina sat in the dining room chair, her only solace was the Rosary she was thumbing through her fingers and the bottle of vodka that sat on the table. She was not good at being alone. Except for evenings, when the Bednareks went out for a visit or an event, she could not remember a time when she was left alone. She felt abandoned and overwhelmed by a foreboding sense of imminent death.

Five chimes from the clock on the mantle announced daybreak, there would be no sunrise. She rose from the chair and went to light the lamp and when the room was flooded with light, she was comfortably surprised, at least the power station was still functioning. Reassured by this minor blessing, she turned the dial on the radio, nothing but static resounded from the available stations. She eased herself back into the chair and rested her hand on her lips. Her senses were dulled, there was not a thought in her head. The horrendous bombardments had gradually decreased during the night, but the downpour of rain seemed to be nature's own retribution against the deadly pursuits of men.

She began a new recital of the Rosary and felt the love of the Holy Spirit bestowing itself on the only family she knew, the Bednareks. Last year, at this very table, after the Katyń massacre had been revealed and the family was about to attend the German mandated propaganda film on the subject, Janina had declined an offer to accompany them.

"I have seen enough of restrictions and retributions. The bodies of innocent citizens shot in the streets for acts of violence they never committed are enough for me. I don't need to see Ruskie massacres."

When the family acquiesced, she summed it all up, "Besides, I'm nobody! I would never be brave enough to do anything to help in resisting, I just want the occupation to end."

She was at the 'Glory be…' of the fifth decade when a resounding clamor of voices came up from the street, followed by loud thuds of thrown objects. She folded the Rosary in the palm of her hand and took to the window. There, in the pouring rain the neighbors were screaming and flinging furniture into the road to provide a barricade to hamper German traffic. Tables, divans, mattresses, anything movable within their homes that was available. Several men were using pickaxes to tear up the paving and hurling the blocks of the cement onto the pile.

She blinked several times, *Is that old Piotrek out there, swinging an axe?*

She ran to the hall closet and pulled on her galoshes, she yanked her raincoat off the hook and slipped it on, she tugged at Irena's brimmed hat from the shelf and popped it on her head. She then looked around for something she could carry with her. The small, upholstered chair that sat by the closet as a convenience for shoe removal was of a weight that she could handle. She ran to the kitchen for a carving knife which she slipped into the pocket of her raincoat and then struggled to get the chair out of the doorway and down the hall to the front door.

Out on the street, she became part of the milieu. Men, women and children were vandalizing the street scene. Ladders were employed to tear down the German named street signs. Posters extolling portraits of Hitler, Frank, and Fischer were being hung on the barricades inviting the Germans to take a shot at them as they flayed the rioting citizens with bullets. Janina delightedly draped a portrait of Frank across a mound of furniture just as a whirling bullet passed through her ribs.

Chapter Thirty-Seven

The rectory dining room was finally receiving the functional utility it was designed for. Father Lipinski avoided the room by indulging his preference to the cozy, tree shaded kitchen where he could stretch his long legs under the table and enjoy a close up view of the garden. Now the rectory was housing eleven people who were forced to seek shelter during the surprise onslaught of the five p.m. Rising. Father also played host to the messaging unit of the Liaison Group whose mission it was to collect information of interest in the vicinity and deliver the messages to Bórza at the base of operations.

By mid-morning on Thursday, six of the victims of the surge had left the rectory to try to make it to their homes through the exchange of fire, the others took advantage of the chapel, where they could vent their misgivings and seek the solace of God in His heaven

Irena was awaiting orders from her lead messenger, Captain Gwiazda. She helped herself to a cup of barley coffee that was brewed and left standing in a pot over a candle warmer. She was a novice at fetching food for herself; this was always provided for her by Janina, the maid, and barley was not her idea of coffee, but…she held the cup in her hands and found some comfort in its warmth. Would she ever be able to tolerate the tumult exploding around her?

"Oh, please, I hope you don't mind if I join you," a tall young man stood in the doorway and practically shouted to be heard, "I could use a break, I've just made some food deliveries to houses down the street that are also housing perfect strangers with no reserved rations."

It was the Block Captain, Edziu, a tall young man with a rakish demeanor and a head of bushy, brown hair.

"Not at all, actually I appreciate the company, it will turn my head to other thoughts." Irena shouted back.

Edziu slid a large cup from the china closet and poured the warm barley to the brim. He took a seat across from her. "We haven't had time to get acquainted, and since we'll be working together, this is an opportunity to learn about the person that I'm teamed up with."

He took a seat across from her.

"How is it that you're not fighting with the Home Army?"

"Oh, I'm a different type of insurgent. I'm a machinist and I work in the insurgent factory on Marszałkowska Street. And what about you?"

"I've been a Liaison Girl for over a year. I'm pretty good at it," she bragged.

He made a quick glance at her left hand, unmarried, not betrothed.

"So, what was life like for you before the Rising, besides being a prize Liaison Girl?"

His smile was warm and softened what could have been construed as a jibe.

"I was the pampered child of a successful lawyer turned resistor and a brilliant professor who taught her students in underground classes."

"Pampered, eh, and is there a handsome young man in the picture?"

Irena didn't answer immediately, she lowered her head, a soft, tender smile appeared at the thought of Jerzy. Without looking up, "Yes." Was her only reply.

Edziu had a far-off look in his eyes.

"Ah, love… there's nothing better; I'm still madly in love with my wife Barbara. We are blest with a five year old son, Michal."

"That's my father's name!"

The former headquarters of Home Army had become the nerve center for local messaging. Bórza requisitioned Bór's cot. His trunk that sat at the foot of his berth, now held her personal items. She and Sergeant Slota had arranged a schedule that would cover the six hours sleep pattern of their eighteen hour days; the radio would maintain constant coverage by an alert agent operating the transmitter.

Insurgents controlled the powerhouse. Former employees of the German General Government, they risked their lives 24/7. Under constant gunfire many lives were lost as these brave technicians strove to keep the cables repaired. The entire operation was controlled by Bór and Monter.

The tactics of guerilla warfare had secured isolated German districts in Center City and Olde Town, together with two districts on the banks of the Vistula, and the towns of Czerniaków, Powiśle, and Wola. It was necessary to interconnect these units into a network for communication purposes.

The gathering and dissemination of pertinent information was processed according to military operations. Each Block Captain was required to gather military and supply information from his neighborhood and report to the Liaison Girl in charge of his district. Each Liaison Girl was responsible for the information to be delivered to the drop boxes allocated to her within the two nearby districts assigned to her by Bórza. The outlying districts of the Vistula, Czerniaków, Powiśle, and Wola, were covered by radios operated by individuals who mostly lived next to the transmitter where they could respond to the tapping codes emanating from other sources.

Jerzy Gruber maintained the transmitter in the basement of his Uncle Heinrich's home in Czerniaków.

Messages were to be transmitted as soon as possible to the headquarters of Bór and Monter.

Chapter Thirty-Eight

There was plenty of time for Premier Mikołajczyk to revise any sensitive areas on his agenda that might be displeasing to the Soviet leader. Perhaps the interim between the start of the Rising and his eventual meeting with Stalin was a God send. He was practicing obsequiousness. His nerves were taut, he had eaten little and slept less. The weight of his country rested heavily on his shoulders; he must not be swayed by the opinions of his divided cabinet. Under his authority the Rising had begun in Warsaw while the Commander-in-Chief, Sosnkowski was reviewing the Polish troops in Brindisi; he would bear the consequences. It was imperative that he obtain military aid from Russia. For now, the issue of Poland remaining independent after the war was secondary on his agenda.

During breakfast in his room on 3 August, Mik was advised that he would meet with Stalin at ten a.m. He rounded out his breakfast with several shots of vodka.

Mik entered Stalin's presence with an entirely changed demeanor, not groveling, that would only incite Stalin, but with an air of confidence and rationality. He was the leader of a country, and he would represent his country in an exemplary manner.

Stalin rose from his desk and offered his hand, "Good morning, Premier Mikołajczyk."

"Good morning, Marshal Stalin. Thank you for taking this time to see me."

Mikołajczyk took the seat that Stalin motioned to him from the other side of his desk.

"Be precise, I haven't much time."

"I have a request for military assistance for the insurgents fighting in Warsaw."

"My troops are already involved in battle with the Germans on the Vistula."

"Chairman, the Rising was prompted by that very issue. General Bór-Komorowski undertook this revolt as a measure of weakening the German forces until your forces could arrive. They have enough armor and ammunition for only a short period of time."

"If that is the case, why was I not informed before he set out on this rampage? If we were to be partners in the endeavor, should not the partner have been able to agree or deny the conditions?"

There was a long pause while Mik absorbed the impact of this valid statement.

"Will you at least supply these people with weapons?"

"You will have to speak to the Lublin Committee on this point. After all, your units have had no experience in fighting the Germans; they have been skulking in the woods receiving aid from Britain and America. They are not proven fighters. If the Lublin Committee acknowledges the need for assistance, I will order it."

The Lublin Committee was a newly established umbrella organization with ambiguous tenets and a hidden agenda to eventually become the Soviet "Quisling" government that would replace the current independent Polish administration in London. Their intent was to rule Poland with communist policies at the end of the war. Stalin's plan was to make Poland the 17th Soviet State in its territorial expansion.

It was time for Mik to turn his hat once again. The Allies were waiting for a positive response from Stalin before they would consider aid for an insurgence. The war had spread into a global conflict, and they had to keep their priorities straight. Time was of an essence; Mik took an unreliable positive approach and informed Britain that Stalin had agreed to give orders to provide aid to the Warsaw conflict.

Chapter Thirty-Nine

Janusz Szepua wielded the heavy machine gun over the uneven ground of the Presbyterian Cemetery. He would get a good shot at the enemy. Why did his commander trust him with such an ungainly piece of equipment? Why not grenades or a rifle? Not that he knew how to handle a rifle, but at least it was lighter and had a good sight on it. His unit was right on the target within a few hundred yards range. He blessed himself and took aim…his aim was too high, two more shots were fired over the target, then, to his amazement, a shot dead on. German troops commenced to forge into the cemetery firing at the insurgents in an effort to clear them out and regain their position. Janusz took aim at a group of Germans and watched in surprise as a string of the men fell where they stood.

Nearby residents ran to throw petrol soaked flaming rags and homemade petrol bottles onto the German troops. In the midst of the fray, a captured armored car waving the red and white flag drove into the street and set off a clamor of applause from both civilians and insurgent fighters. The haul for the day included a grenade thrower, three heavy machine guns, and three lorries filled with ammunition against Tiger Tanks.

Heavy smoke billowed over the city; the Germans were shelling homes with aircraft above and 'billowing cows' on the ground. Bodies flew through the air from the exploding homes sending fragments of body parts spewing forth through the smoke and haze; thousands of civilians were shot as they tried to rush into the streets from their burning homes.

Father Lipinski had his breviary open before him as he knelt before the icon of Saint Michal thrusting a spear into the side of Satan. While he acknowledged that God was in His heaven, he knew all was not right in the world. The barbarism he had witnessed was consistent with the inhuman conditions the Nazi were conducting in the concentration camps. How could such satanic evil proceed from an ethnic group endowed with intelligence and the practice of Christian religions? Women were being raped; citizens were bound and tethered to the front of tanks as they maneuvered their way into the line of fire creating a moral reluctance on the part of the insurgents to fire on innocent civilians. These monstrous acts could only be performed by men who had lost their souls.

There had been a major haul the first day of the Rising. A German warehouse in Stawki stored SS uniforms as well as food, munition and cigarettes. This huge cache laid Bór's mind at ease. He had registered grave concern over the excessive use of ammunition by insurgents firing from all sides at one specific target in the absence of a central command. If booty obtained from the Germans could be depended on, it would surely offset the waste.

SS uniforms were cut from the finest cloth and neatly tailored. Virski got his hands on a set that fit him as though it was tailor-made for him. He adjusted his red and white armband around his left arm to distinguish which side he was fighting under; he checked his reflection in the mirror and appreciated the possibilities that this cover-up look might afford him in his in his future endeavors.

Messages had to be collected and delivered to Bór as soon as they were received. Virski had obtained access to the captured armored car, which he used sparingly; vehicles were open targets to fire on from both sides. He continued his errands on foot, between barricades and the underground passages that were gradually being extended day by day. Among the messages collected from Captain Gwiazda's boxes were the number of wounded that were being treated in the church basement along with a plea for an X-ray machine, and the latest Home Army capture of a nearby German unit, complete with stock and ammunition.

The messages collected throughout the eight districts presented a checkerboard pattern of loss and gain. At least the insurgents seemed to be holding their own.

Chapter Forty

At the Klammer factory, Bór received a radio message from Britain regarding future aid, "The English are making all significant assistance for you dependent on the results of the talks in Moscow." From Praga in the west, he could hear the barrage of fire between the Russians and Germans. His strategic mind led him to speculation. At the onslaught of the Rising on Tuesday, the sound of artillery coming from over the Vistula had ceased. Was the weather responsible for the silence? Well, now that it had resumed, it was quite possible that aid was forthcoming in time to alleviate the loss of his men and the limited supply of ammunition. He took a deep breath and allowed a slight smile to etch its way across the lips that had become accustomed to a rigid grimness.

The anticipated cooperation of the Russians was short lived. On Thursday August 3, Bór awoke to a deafening silence from across the Vistula. It was a silence to be endured throughout the Rising. He could only pray that Mikołajczyk would be able to convince Stalin to join the Home Army in its fight for Warsaw. His supplies were limited. At the onset of the Rising, he could count on ten days food for his forces that had been stored away during the Resistance. There was enough weaponry to last eight to ten days.

He had hoped the insurrection would hold for three or four days until the Russians would enter the fray.

On the plus side, the fighters had collected food and ammunition supplies during their raid on German stockpiles, and fifty German tanks had been destroyed with the cooperation of citizens who armed themselves with petrol soaked bottles to heave under the oncoming tanks.

Logistically, the insurgents had carved some strategic territory to their benefit. Although the Germans had recaptured the bridges across the Vistula, the Home Army was in command of the roads leading to the bridges. While Wola blocked the German's to the west, Old Town and Mokotów cut their routes to the north, south, and west. The Post Office across from the railway station controlled the rails from the east and west. By destroying a considerable length of rail, no trains could get through with German reinforcements and supplies.

The conflict had reached a tug-of-war stage; neither side having a clear advantage.

At two a.m. on Friday, August 4, Bór awoke to the sound of aircraft. It wasn't the all too familiar throb of the German Stuka engine, yet there had not been the usual radio message from London announcing a planned RAF flight. The long held, standard procedure of a delivery broadcast was cryptically transmitted in the form of a familiar song, one current tune was played if a drop was cleared and ready to fly over a prearranged site. A different tune would indicate if the flight was cancelled. Since there was no such message, Bór suspected the planes were being flown by Polish pilots out of Italy who weren't concerned with Soviet cooperation. The yield was twelve cartons of ammunition.

Churchill sent a wire to Stalin on 4 August 1944, informing him that an airdrop of 60 tons of ammunition and equipment was bound for the Southeast portion of Warsaw to aid the insurrection.

Stalin responded with a wire on 5 August, denouncing the capability of the Home Army. He informed Churchill that they had few detachments, were without aircraft and tanks, and would not be able to hold their own.

The reply was ambiguous—it did not deny any help, neither did it affirm the need for aid that Russia might respond to.

Twelve special waterproofed metal containers weighing 330 pounds each were dropped on Krasiński Square and Wola during the night of 4/5 August.

Sunday morning mass saw actual participants in the pews. A few of the ambulatory patients from the clinic in the basement were there to observe the sacred rite with a renewed appreciation of life. An eighty year old invalid woman, Lucisia, sat limply grieving in her wheelchair. Her son was able to wheel her into the subterranean passageway before their home was blown up by German fire. He, his wife, three children and their cat were still in the building. Lucisia was now a physical resident of the rectory, oblivious to the care and shelter being given her and the horrors going on around her.

A few of the mobile patients made it to the rail for communion; for the rest, Father walked the holy chalice to the pews to deliver the body and blood, soul and divinity of Christ.

When mass ended, Father descended to the basement clinic. He asked one of the sturdiest of the patients to serve as altar boy and hold the silver tray under the chins of patients who were physically able to receive the Host.

Blood and the smell of death filled the environment. The doctor's gowns were covered with blood. Doctors Razinski and Kozak worked in shifts that allowed them to take turns for a four hour nap out of every twenty-four hours. The women of the parish worked around the clock to maintain a clean environment.

"I need an X-ray machine," Doctor Razinski shouted when he noticed Kurt and his team delivering supplies.

"It's number one on our priority list. We'll find one."

Leona had been to confession on Friday. She was in a frightful state. One of the wounded, whom she had labeled as a two for the triage, had slipped into a comma. His wound, which was not obvious, was a bullet that had lodged at the center of his spine where it had shattered his liver. He fell into a comma and was dead within the hour.

Chapter Forty-One

Saturday, the fifth of August, *SS-Ogrufführer* Erich von dem Bach, whose expertise was in quelling rebellions, arrived with his staff in Warsaw to take command and squash the uprising. The first thing he did was to check the current information of the ongoing anti-insurgent operations. Laid before him was the documentation of mass murders of civilians, and heavy bombardments.

On Sunday, a new diktat was instituted. Only men were to be shot; civilians were to be incarcerated in a newly set up transit camp; executions were under the province of a specialized task force. The immediate thrust was to concentrate on the insurgent forces.

The Luftwaffe began targeting the rebel-held districts.

On the Polish side, there was still no contact with the Soviets; still no word from Premier Mikołajczyk.

The Commander-in-Chief, Sosnkowski, returned to London 8 August. To his amazement, he discovered that his colleagues in the Government-in-Exile had ignored his advice regarding the Rising, and that his telegrams to Bór were delayed or hampered with.

Once more he sent a wire to Bór, he was sure that this one would travel the wires to its destination. He had met with considerable resistance in his talks with British Air Marshal Wilson and Secretary for Air, Sinclair, but Churchill had agreed to resume relief flights over Warsaw. However, at this point, Sosnkowski's position was greatly damaged in London.

There was a gnawing concern over the apartment and Janina's welfare that was causing Michal Bednarek a good deal of angst. Also, he hadn't showered or shaved since the Rising began. Was it worth the risk of dodging bullets and shellfire from tanks? He clutched at the crucifix attached to the rosary that he kept in his right hand pocket. A handsome beard had ripened on his face after nearly two weeks of neglect. Except for Monter, the disciplined military officer, all of the men that he was now bunking with had taken on a seedy, unkempt appearance. Monter, on the other hand, did have an aide-de-camp, Władziu, who performed valet services for his distinguished General.

Michal made use of the underground passage that was already half-way to its completion mark, destined to end at Jerusalem Street. Local residents had already moved in with what little baggage they could muster. It was the light from their candles that allowed him to take advantage of this protective roadway. The heat was stifling, the air was thin, and the smell was noxious, but his survival instincts did not prejudice the circumstances.

Active pounding and digging resumed to extend the passage and Michal had to climb out to street level; he rushed behind available barricades until, at last, he was on Zielona Street in sight of the apartment building.

The destruction of the street held little impact on him, it looked no different from every other street in Warsaw. He climbed down the steps that were still intact to the manager's apartment and prayed that he was still alive. He knocked on the door and put his ear to it for any sound of life. He heard a scuffling sound and then a click on the knob. The door opened and he was face to face with a significantly altered Antush who stood there gazing at him. The man was distraught. Michal threw his arms around him, and the two men cried in each other's arms.

"How is Pani and Irena?" he uttered between shuddered breaths.

"As far as I know, Antush, they are alive and volunteering their aid in the insurgency in the church."

"Pan, there is no Janina," he lowered his head while blessing himself, "she lost her life on the second day of the Rising, when the neighbors turned the street into a roadblock to halt the Germans."

Michal allowed the news to impact him, as he caught an image of the maid who cared for his family as though she was their mother. Janina, who shared his early morning jokes as they drank coffee. Janina the gourmet cook and obsessive housekeeper, who had been a part of their household since Michal had married Leona. Janina had come along as a part of the dowry.

"Where is her body?"

"Only the good Lord knows, Pan. The street was plowed over by tanks. Whatever body parts remained to be seen were put on a pile and set fire to."

Chapter Forty-Two

During his interactions with the British high command, General Sosnkowski provided Air Marshal Wilson with a list of drop off sites in Warsaw where access to the insurgents would be most effective.

Churchill kept his word. The Warsaw Airlift was in full swing. Transport planes flew the eight-hundred-fourteen miles from bases in Apulia and Brindisi, Italy over the Adriatic and Croatia at sunset to reach the Danube in Hungary in darkness, then climbed northeast over the Carpathians in Soviet held territories in Poland to approach Warsaw.

Stalin did not yield to Churchill's request for permission to allow the planes to refuel on the route back. A Soviet landing strip was within a hundred miles of Warsaw, another air strip was a mere fifty miles distance.

The planes were forced to fly over Eastern Germany and East Austria. Barring any hazards, the planes would arrive back in Italy by mid-morning the following day.

The second airlift was expected. The BBC broadcast that evening, signed off with the agreed upon popular tune; the appointed personnel were at their posts in the vicinity of Kercelego Square. Searchlights beaming south of the city lit the skies signaling the oncoming air traffic. Fifteen women from the Sapper Unit marched onto the square in single file, each one carrying an unlit lantern. They took their assigned positions in the street, and at the sound of the approaching aircraft, ~~they~~ lit their lanterns and laid down on the ground in the formation of a cross.

The planes circled about for a while before descending lower. The red-white-and blue roundels, the insignia of the British Air Force could be seen from the ground. Home Army shock platoons surrounded the area to fight off any aggressors and to collect the precious supplies. The Germans increased their heavy machine gun fire as a plane flew over the square and six, slowly opening parachutes floated to the ground. People left their hiding places, the cellars, and the barricades to rush into the streets shouting, cheering, and waving. Seven more planes discharged their cargo under heavy anti-aircraft firing. One plane was hit, one of its engines was on fire, within moments it spread through the wing, the plane was being consumed. It was descending rapidly at any moment it would crash. At that very second the hatch opened, and six containers headed for the ground near Napoleon Square, The plane managed to fly on, away from the gaping throng to cross the Vistula where a great spurt of flames and smoke filled the sky.

The shock troops scrambled over rooftops and barricades under heavy machine gun fire and managed to glean eighty percent of the much needed supplies.

The early possession of Wola was definitely a morale booster for the insurgents, and a liability for the Germans. It was a strategic roadblock that had to be opened for Panzer tanks and Wehrmacht troops to maneuver through in open warfare; also, the block disrupted their east to west communication system. The surrounding area included the obliterated Jewish Ghetto, the Jewish and Christian Cemeteries, and the suburb of Pawiak, home of Pawiak Prison, a solidly held German fortress. The Kammler factory, Bór's Headquarters, was a mere five-hundred yards away.

On the sixth of August, the Luftwaffe flew its planes over Wola dropping incendiary bombs. Wehrmacht forces moved in while the flames were still raging, forcing Home Army soldiers from behind their barricades to surrender. Twenty Panzer tanks continued to shuttle in and out of the streets clearing anything in their path until Wola was once more in the hands of the Germans, opening a direct route for troops to reach the Western Gate of their bridgehead on the Vistula.

Chapter Forty-Three

"Jesus Christ!" Kumor slammed his fists on the desk, "We've lost Wola! What the hell is Rokossovsky up to? He's never run from a fight. He's here on the Vistula, the Nazis have a bridgehead on the Kierbedź Bridge, and we lost Wola! Is the son-of-a-bitch dead?"

He slumped down in his chair, his staff stood at servile attention, scarcely blinking an eye while they waited for his ire to cool. He grabbed a cigarette, lit it, took a long pull.

After two more puffs, he said, "I need a clean Wehrmacht non-com uniform, I need a sergeant's insignia, I need a soldier to fit into it, I need a letter drafted and signed by von der Bach. I need them now! Get Virski in here."

The Royal Castle in Old Town had housed Polish Royalty since the 16th century. The Castle and the Arch-Cathedral of St. John the Baptist were the most outstanding features in the neighborhood of narrow streets that housed the tall, thin buildings constructed in the architectural style of the early Renaissance.

Air raids by the *Luftwaffe* had done serious damage to the Arch-Cathedral as well as several other ancient buildings, but as of 6 August there was no ongoing street battle raging. The German divisions had been stripped to provide reserve units for the battle in Warsaw. Old Town would become Bór's new headquarters.

In sight of the diminished German militia, the residents of Old Town wantonly plundered the stocks of the shops and German supply depots. They lugged the contraband material on their backs in whatever sack, bag, or basket they could lay their hands on. The basements of the homes of Old Town were filled with the reserves of what they could not cram into their homes.

During the pre-dawn hours of 7 August, Bór and company divided into three groups and proceeded to vacate the Kammler factory. They set out on foot to Old Town. Last minute communications managed to secure an old school building on Borakowa Street, formerly the site of a German held hospital.

The trek through the ruins of the ghetto proved to be death-defying as the company was forced to dodge machine gun fire from the German fortified Pawiak Prison. Several bodies fell along the way. Dawn was breaking as the troops and staff managed to reach Krasiński Park.

Virski gave one quick rap on the door, without waiting for a response, he opened it and peeked in to gage what sort of humor Kumor was wearing.

"Elka said you wanted to see me."

He looked up and seemed at odds; should he be irritated by the intrusion, or should he just get on with it?

"Sit! You have your SS officer's uniform; we shall put it to good use. I need you to take that armored car, along with a soldier in a German sergeant's uniform and perform an investigative mission to find out what that son-of-a-bitch Rokossovsky is up to. Is he with us or not. Bach has brought men with him who are undoubtedly unknown to the districts along the Vistula so there should be no problem infiltrating the Praga district."

"You want me to take on the role of a Nazi SS man and check on the German position on the Vistula."

"Correct."

Virski took a deep breath while he shook his head. "That won't work. I can't act and my German is not that good. SS men are well educated; I'd be shot on the spot."

Kumor sat back in his chair, his chin down, his eyes raised to the right. He nodded his head, offering no response.

Virski took advantage of Kumor's apparent attempt to analyze the situation.

"I think you should get Kaminski to play the officer. He's a *Volksdeutscher*, and he's educated and if anyone can play a role well, it's him. I'll go along as his lackey."

Kumor actually chuckled. "Get him on board and tell him not to overdo the play acting."

Although Old Town had not entered the battle of the insurgence, it was not spared the shelling of air raids which caused the entire population to seek shelter in the deep caverns beneath its medieval structures.

Residents of Center City sought refuge from the endless skirmish and migrated there seeking a safer environment. By the time Bór had settled into his new headquarters on Borakowa Street the population of Old Town had doubled, causing chaos. The co-mingling of the two populations produced a skirmish of another sort.

The first officer to report to Bór was Karol Ziemski Wachnowski, accompanied by Dysthmus. They were sent by Monter to study the situation and sort it out. Wachnowski was dismayed by the bizarre behavior of the inhabitants who were unruly and literally fighting amongst themselves.

He reported to Bór. "I have requested a unit of senior combatants from Deputy General Monter to impose restrictions on the population. Once I have maintained some discipline among them I will assign responsibilities and tasks to organize them into functional units. Meanwhile, Dysthmus will take stock of the supplies and products this population has confiscated from the stores and warehouses."

Half a smirk spread Bór's lips as he nodded in agreement with the outlined strategies, "You have my full cooperation, proceed with your plan."

"I'll begin by dividing this sector into four districts with commanders assigned to each one. Certainly, the eastern flank of the Vistula deserves some consideration, and the roof of the Treasury Printing Building offers a good observation point of not only all of Old Town, but a good spread of the activity going on in Warsaw."

The inhabitants of Old Town, residents as well as the refugees, had wantonly raided the stores and warehouses; they carried away the booty in sacks on their backs endeavoring to stock their larders. The vaults of Old Town were filled with left-over contraband.

Dysthmus realized that he was no match for the hostile citizens and requested three strong, armed men from Bór's unit to help manage the people and lug the merchandise.

By the second week of the rebellion the administration in Warsaw, under Monter, had organized procedures for the distribution of food supplies. Volunteers were recruited to operate a food chain. A central storage deposit was allocated to each of the eight districts within the city with a Home Army officer in command. Neighborhood volunteers were weighted down with sacks of food to carve their way through the underground passages and sewers during the night. The products, including medicine and ammunition, were rationed off in order to be equally distributed. Citizens organized communal kitchens to share meals. Dysthmus modified this procedure to accommodate the citizens of Old Town.

All of this was accomplished in two days. The bounty of the stored supplies kept the population going for six weeks into the uprising.

Bór hosted a dinner of chicken, barley bread and canned vegetables. "I apologize for the fare but as you know, our food supplies are staples, the chicken is out of our compound. I will try to get the farmers to smuggle some vegetables and fruit into the city and Old Town; they have no staples." He gave a little chuckle, "Perhaps we could barter." He raised his tumbler of vodka, "In the meantime, *Na zdrowie!*"

When dinner ended, Dysthmus approached Bór, "Sir, I see that you have three German lorries in tow. Might I requisition one of them?"

Bór paused, as if to weigh the matter before he responded, "That may prove a dangerous risk. *Warszawians* have developed a real skill in tossing petrol bottles under German vehicles."

"I have to take that risk, Sir, I have my eye on that X-ray machine that the Germans left behind, it is sorely needed in the basement hospital of the church."

Bór nodded his head, a little half-grin spread his lips. "I understand, yes, take it, and God be with you."

Chapter Forty-Four

Throughout the long history of the Polish Intelligence Agency, forgery remained a hallmark within the process. Within twenty-four hours a letter was drafted regarding the need for an on-sight report of the situation between the offense of the Russian troops and the defensive measures taken by the German troops, along with the official signature of *SS-Ogruführer* Eric von der Bach.

Within the context of the letter was the introduction to SS-*Oberleutnant* Wolf. Fastidious identification cards were created for *Oberleutnant* Marcus Wolf and *Unterfeldwebel* Elias Koch. Proper insignias were carefully sown in the appropriate position on the uniforms, and Kaminski donned a pair of spectacles and a neat little mustache that he obtained from an actor friend of his, complete with the necessary glue.

The irony of the loss of Wola was that the road leading to Praga was being maintained by the *Wehrmacht*. The German armored car traveled safely along Marszałkowska Road to Praga, it took less than forty minutes.

Unterfeldwebel Virski escorted his officer to the door where he stood his post to wait for Kaminski to complete his mission.

"Heil Hitler," Kaminski gave a sharp salute and a loud click of his heels to the sergeant sitting at the desk. He handed the sergeant his letter of commission, "I am here to speak with your commander."

The letter carried its weight. The sergeant re-appeared, "*Oberstrumführer* Memming will see you, follow me."

Commandant Memming stood up from his seat to offer the proper salute, "Heil Hitler!" A tall wiry type with a firmly set jaw gauged his visitor.

"Heil Hitler," Kaminski lowered his hand and took the seat proffered to him. "I had a professor Memming in Poznań; any relation?"

"Not that I'm aware of. I see that you are here to observe the conditions we are engaged in at present. Except for one brief encounter on 3 August, the Soviets have not fired a shot."

"What, in your opinion, is the reason of their withdrawal from battle?"

"Warsaw," he jutted his chin forward in a gesture of satisfaction. "Russia has future plans for Poland that will never be accomplished. Germany will eventually ride herd over both countries."

"What do you expect the outcome will be?" Kaminski was comfortable in his role of interviewer.

"Once we have determined that there will be no further intervention from the Russians during the Warsaw conflict, we will pull our units from the skirmish along the Vistula to do battle in Warsaw, until it ceases to exist. If and when the Russians are back in the fray, those troops, and all the men fighting the insurgents will be available to flatten the Russians and regain the territory."

By August 10, Bór was able to complete his aggravating jigsaw puzzle. Between the daily messages and Kumor's recent account of the Russian vs. German situation, he had a momentary feeling of abandonment; however, the possibility that the talks between Mikołajczyk and Stalin might still prove fruitful allowed him to push on with positive energy.

The latest edition of *Poland's Journal* was on its way for distribution with the devastating news of the capture of Wola by the Germans. Kaminski tucked a few copies under his arm and left his underground office to gather news for his next edition. While he was on his usual underground trek to the Post Office Savings Bank, the *Luftwaffe* made a direct hit on Raven Street, engulfing most of the homes in flames.

By the time he reached his destination, Monter and his staff had been apprised of the situation. His printing press was set up in the basement of one of those homes; did he still have a press to operate?

He sent a wire to Jerzy in Czerniaków, "I need you. Get a couple of *Volksdeutschers* from Heinrich's band of conspirators to operate the radio transmissions. News is very important to all *Warszawians*. I can't delay an issue."

He spent the night at Monter's quarters and had breakfast with the staff the following morning. He and mayor Sowa had been longtime friends and Sowa was genuinely concerned for him.

"Whether or not your press is destroyed, you will need to establish new accommodations."

Kaminski nodded, a forlorn expression reflecting his immediate concern.

Sowa turned to Monter, "The Bulgarian Embassy on Ujazdów Avenue is a relatively safe place; is it not?"

"Surely. I'll wire Commander Bereszyński to prepare a space for you."

Michal was seated next to him, "Zygmunt, I'll go back with you today. You're going to need help getting organized. I'll miss my meeting, but I'll catch up on things when I get back."

Dysthmus had the lorry loaded with one state of the art X-ray machine and a cache of food and medicine to be distributed in Warsaw. He still had his Wehrmacht sergeant's uniform from the time he played chauffeur to courier Zamski's role of a German general in 1943, just after the news of Katyń had shocked the world. He had no difficulty traveling the newly German captured road through Wola.

He commandeered two stalwart Home Army soldiers to help unload the X-ray machine and transport it against the ongoing flux of traffic that transited the basement of the church. From the time they opened the door, *'oohs and ahhs'* were sent up by everyone they encountered. Dr. Razinski stood frozen to the spot, unable to wrap his brain around the situation. As Dysthmus approached him, he blinked his eyes and shook his head; he threw his arms around Dysthmus and unloaded two weeks of stress on his benefactor's shoulder.

Leona watched the scene unfold and got such an exhilarating emotional flare from this, the first positive experience since this whole ugly mess began. The load she bore as triage nurse had overwhelmed her; also, the process of labeling the incoming victims was a twenty-four hour situation. She trained three of the volunteer women with the minimal knowledge that she had gleaned, and remembering how devastated she was when she mislabeled the soldier with the shattered liver.

She apprised them, "You have no medical training, you are not a doctor or God, you cannot know for sure if your rating is correct, but your service is very important for the doctors to treat the most serious wounds promptly. So, do the best you can, and God be with you."

After Dysthmus left, she got back to her post and immersed herself in the job at hand. It was almost four p.m. and in another few minutes Emilia would be coming on to relieve her. She leaned down to examine her next patient and shrieked his name, "Janusz, Janusz Szepua!"

Dr. Kovak rushed to her side, "Pani, get a hold of yourself!"

Janusz was suffering third degree burns inflicted on him by a German flamethrower. Kovak pulled her away and Dr. Razinski rushed over to inject a dose of morphine into the arm of a victim who would die peacefully.

The Germans had cut off the water supply and water had become as necessary to them as air was to breathe. The residents were already engaged in digging underground roadways, shallow gravesites, and latrines. More than a hundred captured German prisoners were being housed in the basements along Buxom Street. Monter had assigned Home Army officers to guard them in squads of twenty. The task of digging wells, out in the open was sacrificing the lives of *Warszawians*. Sowa, the Mayor of the City of Warsaw, was concerned over the loss of its citizens and he appealed to Monter to have the prisoners of war swing the axes, supervised by their armed squad leaders.

Kaminski and Bednarek had traveled the available length of the underground passage until they were detoured by the diggers who were working to complete the road. Up on street level they were confronted by more digging.

The POWs were digging wells for water. Ever the charismatic newsman, Kaminski smiled, *"Verzeihen Sie mir"* or *"Pardon me, please."*

All digging stopped. The soldiers, most of them young, all of them frightened, cried out, *"Bitte!"*

They gathered around him, finally someone who speaks German and appears friendly. Their main concern was would they be shot, What would happen to them?

"You will not be shot. If that was the plan, you would not be here. You will be held prisoner until the Russians take over Warsaw, and then you will be captured militia until the war ends."

They clamored around him to shake his hand, pat his back, or just to touch him.

"Poor Bastards," Kaminski mumbled to Michal, "They're just as likely to be killed by their own Luftwaffe mistaking them for Poles doing the digging."

Chapter Forty-Five

Deputy General Monter was faced with a dilemma. Except for a few mishaps, caused by gunfire, his organized plan of the distribution of food supplies was running smoothly but if he wanted to avoid a scurvy outbreak, he'd have to get fruit and vegetables included in his distribution plan.

The meeting was in progress, the possibility of obtaining a printing press was discussed, and Monter brought a new objective to the table.

"I have grave concerns over the food distribution; we must find a way to include fresh vegetables and fruit in the process. The Peasant Battalion can be depended on, but we need someone in charge who is capable. I cannot spread Dysthmus or Kurt that thin; they are too important, and I cannot think of a soul to take on this mission."

Colonel Wachnowski, officer in command of supplies, slapped his hand on the table. "I have your man!" Everyone's eyes were on him.

"Professor Putczyński."

The recognition of the name ran across the faces of the members. Putczyński, a professor of philosophy courageously maintained Flying University clandestine classes during the Resistance but was unable to submit to fighting for the Home Army. In his late forties, hale and hearty, a bachelor, Wałek Putczyński was also a conscientious objector. He had shown pluck in running errands for Monter under fire, but he refused to harm another human being. Professor Putczyński was considered by many in the vein of a pariah.

Jerzy Gruber rowed his way through the Vistula from Czerniaków to Warsaw during the middle of the night. He stealthily slipped through the barricades until he arrived at the Bulgarian Embassy on Ujazdów Avenue, where he faced the most serious obstacle—the sentries. He certainly could not use his NSDAP card. And the sentries knew nothing of a Zygmunt Kaminski who supposedly had moved into occupy office space the day before. Jerzy was ejected and left to sit out on the pavement, leaning against the wall.

An officer behind the barricade that flanked the building recognized him but was involved with matters of life or death. When he glanced in that direction sometime later and noticed Jerzy still sitting there, he left his post.

"Gruber are you holding the wall up?"

"Kaminski has moved in here. His printing press was blown up on Raven street. They won't let me in." He was too exhausted to be confrontational.

Sergeant Staszek walked over to the sentries, "This man is the printer of the newspaper, *Poland's Journal*, if you value your daily news bulletin you'll let him in."

Wojtek opened the door and laid a broom to the steps. It was not yet five o'clock in the morning, the sun had yet to waken, there would be no customers for at least another hour, but this was the time of day that he most cherished. The moisture of humidity and dew permeated as the ripening smell of fruit and grain wafted on the air. He filled his lungs with the aroma and went inside to say his rosary, have a hearty breakfast of bacon, eggs, and pierogi with a large cup of barley coffee. While he ate, he looked up at the fan that was still stirring the air to maintain some coolness in the store; the power had not been lost even though Warsaw was raging in battle. He blessed himself, comforted by the availability of electricity and the recent removal of Wehrmacht guards from the village. They were called in as reserves to fight in Warsaw; a skeleton crew had been left behind.

He was busy stocking shelves when the bell over the door rang to announce a customer. He stepped down the ladder and turned to offer a smile and a greeting to a man he had never seen before.

"Dzień dobry," a pleasant baritone voice uttered by a handsome, well-built man with a thick head of hair and spectacles addressed the storekeeper. He was accompanied by a young man who could be no more than fourteen years old, dressed in a tattered old Home Army shirt with the red and white badge on his left arm.

"Dzień dobry." Wojtek's expression asked the question.

"Deputy General Monter sent me," he handed Wojtek an envelope. "I'm Professor." There was no reason, at this time, to assign an alias, Professor would be his insurgence name.

The note was cryptic, in lower case print, "need fruit and vegetables" underneath the password to be used, "For Monter from Censorship," followed with a scrawled sketch of a mountain, Monter's logo.

Wojtek turned his attention to the young man, "Is this your son?"

"No, this is my second in command, Antoni."

"What do you need from me?"

"A meeting with Furtak, commander of the Peasant Battalion."

"How did you manage to get here from Warsaw?"

"A member of the Judiciary Committee who traveled the back roads during the Resistance drew a map for me."

"Ahh," a smile lit his face, "Bednarek."

"I will take you there myself, only wait while I get my wife to mind the store."

A sentry ushered Jerzy to the office of Commander Bereszyński.

"Pan Kaminski is waiting for you." He motioned to one of the soldiers in the room. "Take Pan Gruber to the new office downstairs."

Jerzy's eyes wandered around the architectural grandness of the building, the iconic frescoes, and the profuseness of gilding along the walls. *It surely out does Raven Street.*

"Jerzy!" A smile burst on Kaminski's face, he rushed forward, threw his arms around him and pecked at his cheeks with a kiss. Jerzy was overwhelmed.

He gently separated himself from the embrace. "Good to see you too, Zygmunt."

"You already have a printing press?"

"Yes, I'll bet that Sowa knew that when he suggested this place. While my main requirement has been provided, the stock of paper is lost to me. I don't know how long it will take to get enough of a supply to keep us rolling."

Michal joined in on the scene, "Jerzy, good to see you. But I must be going, I've missed my meeting yesterday." Kaminski grabbed his hand.

"Thanks, friend," Gruber replied, "you went out of your way for me. I've lost my verified documentations of war crimes committed but I'll make it up to you in a few days."

Michal smiled and nodded his head, "There is no need for gratitude, Jerzy, you would do the same for me. I will try to stop by the church on my way back. Is there any message I can deliver to Irena?"

"I can't believe she hasn't been in my thoughts, but don't tell her that. Tell her, now that I'm back in Warsaw, I'll try to make it to mass one day…and please, give her my love."

A pattern had developed under Monter's strategy of battle. All of the won barricades in Warsaw were fortified by a front line, which made travel by foot a bit safer.

Michal followed the same route back, zig-zagging between barricades until he was at the basement door of the church. His sense of smell must have developed amnesia, for the odor of decaying flesh and death had not presented itself to him. He cast a quick eye to scan the premises to find Leona.

Dr. Kovak noticed him and walked over to him, "Pan Bednarek, Leona is in the rectory, I don't have time to speak with you, but please, seek Father Lipinski before you see her and have him tell you." He turned to go.

"Doctor, what is the problem?"

Kovak continued to walk away, shaking his head; patients were dying, there was no time for conciliatory chats.

The insurgents barricade enveloped the church and rectory, Michal ran the distance, his heart beating rapidly; the last thing he needed was a mystery involving his wife. There was no need to knock, he pushed his way in. Pani Trypka, the rectory housemaid came out of the living room carrying a tray meant for the kitchen.

"Pani, I must see Father!"

"Oh, Pan Bednarek," a mixture of care and concern edged her greeting, "he's not here, he is saying mass in the court behind Warecki Street."

She laid the tray on the hall table and blessed herself. "Please, Pan, you must not be upset. Pani has had a terrible experience and has not been in the hospital. She is now cleaning the church; she spends most of her time there and is not eating much. Be gentle with her and do not question her, she can't bear to talk of it."

"Talk of what?" his voice had an edge to it and Pani Trypka seemed to be intimidated.

"Her student, Janusz Szepua was brought in, badly burned by a flame thrower."

The ire was gone, Michal lowered his head and let the tears flow. "Thank you, Pani. I'll go back to the church. God Bless you."

Leona was on a kneeler in front of an icon of Mary. She was silently staring at the image. Michal let a cough signal her of his presence. She turned around and ran into his arms.

"Michal, God kept you, you're alive!" She wept as he cradled her.

He whispered softly in her ear, "Shush, shush."

They took a seat in a pew and Michal told her the latest news, keeping everything on a positive note.

"Kaminski has a new printing press and a new office in the Bulgarian Embassy and Jerzy has come to join him; he sends his love to you and Irena. I have been to the apartment and the building still stands."

There was no mention of Janina.

She took his hand and rose from her seat, "Come, we must take this news to Irena."

Wojtek's horse began to lift his head sniffing the air and neighing as they approached the Borowski farm; he had been foaled there and his mother was still pulling the wagon for harvest. The family was out in the field, but a lovely young woman sat at the kitchen table shelling peas, next to her was a wicker woven basket with a new born child.

"*Dzień dobry,* Pola," God's blessings on you and the child."

"And for you as well. They are out in the fields picking the barley and rye, Wojtek."

"As I figured. How are you feeling?" There was genuine concern in his tone, Pola had experienced a difficult time in labor, but Bianca and the good Lord brought her through safely.

"I'm still weak but when I look on little Ludwiga I feel as strong as an ox."

Wojtek remembered his manners. "Pola," he said as he turned to look at the other visitors, "this is Professor and Antoni, they are here to gather produce to take to Warsaw."

Professor nodded, "It's a pleasure, Pani." Antoni smiled and a tint of red glazed his face.

"This is Pani Gudzynska, Dysthmus' wife. Your commander."

"Your husband must be very proud of you and your beautiful baby."

"Oh, no! Please, Dysthmus knows nothing of the baby, and he mustn't hear of her."

Her tone was so dramatic that Professor let it drop and Wojtek moved the show along. "Come, we must find Furtak. Stay well, *Laletchka*,"

Out on the road, Professor needed clarification, "Why was Pani so vehement about Dysthmus not knowing about the baby; isn't it his?"

"Pola is living in agony that Dysthmus might be wounded or killed. He is a bold man who does not fear death. Should he rush home to see his new baby, Pola fears he might get killed. Do not tell him of this, you either Antoni."

They came upon Helcha, Furtak's young daughter, on her way to the well to fetch water for her jug.

"Wojtek, what are you doing here?"

"Looking for your father."

She heard Wojtek, but her eyes were on Professor. With her empty hand, she brushed her hair behind her ear and smiled radiantly.

"Tata is in the pear orchard," her eyes never moved toward Wojtek, who pulled on the reins to get his horse to turn to the right.

"Will you be staying for lunch?" This time she looked directly at Wojtek her tone held a sort of pleading quality.

"Gee-uh!" Wojtek pulled on the reins and the horse trotted off.

Furtak heard the rattle of the wagon and stepped off the ladder, the weather had been good, pears were in abundance, he wiped the sweat from his brow with his bandana and looked in the direction of the sound to see who was approaching.

"Wojtek, what are you doing here?"

"I've brought you a new member, Professor, from Warsaw who wants produce for the city."

The meeting was held there in the midst of the trees, the clouds in the sky, and the scent of ripening fruit in the air.

"I have been granted the privilege of commanding the shipment of fresh produce from the farms to Dysthmus for distribution among the military and citizens. Monter requests that we maintain secrecy and has issued a password to be used by trusted men." He handed Furtak the cryptic note from Monter.

"For Monter from Censorship," Furtak read the note aloud.

"I will call a meeting. There are four commanders from here to Warsaw, each one about ten kilometers distance apart. They will receive the code word and the one nearest to Warsaw will be the final liaison for Dysthmus. We will begin immediately."

"Wojtek, stop by the shed and pick some burlap bags to gather produce for your first shipment, here take this basket of pears."

"Whoa, Furtak, these men are walking the distance."

Professor interrupted, "We shall take as much as we can handle; we can't begin soon enough."

Chapter Forty-Six

Dysthmus came through again. Kaminski had his shelves stacked with a hefty supply of paper and *Poland's Journal* was on a roll. It was five in the morning, the usual lull in gunfire made conversation possible. Zygmunt and Jerzy were having their breakfast of bread and coffee laced with vodka.

"I've got my lead article together for the press today," he handed the script to Jerzy. "This will be of special interest to Michal."

Jerzy read the article, grimaced and laid it aside his cup; he would arrange the text for the press after breakfast.

Wola was not surrendered. There was no one left to surrender. The village was bulldozed by heavy artillery on the ground and incendiary shells from above. The SS and the Gendarmes used machine guns, grenades, and flamethrowers on victims who survived the onslaught. No one survived. Once that situation was resolved, the units spread their tentacles further. They attacked the hospital in Old Town and killed the wounded, the doctors, and the nurses. No one survived.

The Professor was now a member of Dysthmus' crew. He and Antoni had delivered nearly eighty pounds of produce collected from Furtak's farm. Their Guardian Angels watched over them as they lugged the weight on their backs over the back roads and barricades to Warsaw.

Dysthmus bombarded him with questions, the first, "Did you see my wife, Pola?"

Professor prickled and shot a glance at Antoni to firm up the lie. "Yes, she's lovely and safe." Another glance at Antoni.

"Is she in pain?"

"No, she appeared quite healthy."

When Dysthmus concluded the interrogation, Professor reported on the provisions that Furtak had laid out, "Our contact will be Kuba, just a mile and a half out of Warsaw."

It was another two hours until sunrise when Dysthmus and his crew of five set out on the path to Kuba's farm. Each man was expected to carry 50 to 60 pounds of produce on his back in burlap bags. Antoni would manage what was comfortable for him. The trek to the farm took the best part of an hour; barricade hopping took up most of the time.

Kuba was not yet out of his bed when Dysthmus pounded on the door. "Kuba, this morning you wake the cock. Open up!" He gave another bang.

The disgruntled farmer opened the door dressed only in his underpants. He said nothing, he stood there waiting for an announcement of why he was being so rudely disturbed.

"Have you got supplies ready for us? We have to get back on the road."

"Yes, the crates are piled inside the barn door. You'll have to fill the bags. Go, I'll be there in a few minutes."

Dysthmus introduced the Professor and Antoni, the new members who would be visiting on a regular basis.

Kuba gave a sharp slap to Dysthmus' back. "Congratulations, *Tatush*, that's some beautiful little girl God blessed you with."

Professor stopped packing, and looked over at Dysthmus, who seemed to be reeling under the remark thrown at him. "What are you talking? Pola has not yet delivered!"

"She has, over a week ago. A healthy girl, Ludwiga, for her *Babcia.*"

Dysthmus stood still, reflecting on the news, then he looked at the Professor. "You told me she looked well but you never said a word about my baby!"

Professor stumbled and stuttered, trying to get a coherent phrase together.

"I...I...they, Furtak and your wife were emphatic that you not be told. Your wife is afraid you will rush to see her and get wounded or killed in the doing."

Dysthmus didn't bother with a response, instead, he gave directions.

"Divide my load among you. I'll see you back at the distribution center," he threw a glance at Professor, "you're in command."

Tuesday, August 15, 1944, Soldier's Day, a national holiday commemorating Poland's victory over Russia in 1920 presented an ironic twist of events; Warsaw was once more engaged in battle, this time with Germany while Russian troops sat idly on the sidelines within shooting distance.

A dour atmosphere hung over the Home Army Command in Old Town; two weeks to the day of the Rising. Bór knew at the onset that he had, at best, a ten days supply of food and ammunition. He had counted entirely on Soviet intervention.

Mikołajczyk arrived in London on Sunday, the 13th of August, without a pledge or a proposal. He had engaged in a series of talks with Stalin, Molotov, and the communist Polish National Committee, the PNC, to no avail. Stalin's contempt was obvious; in his heart, the Poles were no better than the Germans. In his mind, the many invasions of Germany into Russia over the millennia were occasioned by the lack of resistance on the part of the Poles. They failed to defeat the plundering hordes; Poland could not be an independent state. The Soviet Union must claim that territory for the future security of Russia.

Dysthmus was faced with a long and arduous trek, albeit the journey would take him through cultivated lands dotted by farmhouses and barns and the quiet, sandy roads lined with poplar trees, compared to the odious trudge through the sewers fouled by years of accumulated detritus, and the recent addition of dead bodies and feces. The comparison did not impinge on his senses; there was no thinking or feeling involved in his mission, only an overwhelming drive to arrive at the Furtak farm.

Pola was asleep in her bed, the linden cradle that had bedded down four little Furtaks was within her reach; Ludwiga rustled about in her comfortable crib. A soft rap on the door and a gentle voice, "Pola." issued forth in her dream, she smiled and squirmed, "Pola." this time the voice accompanied a touch. She was stirred in her dreamlike trance and fully engaged in the embrace which allowed her to vent all of the emotions and passions she had held in check all these weeks.

Dysthmus was home.

The finely tailored SS uniform was tucked away. Poles held such an abhorrence for the Nazi elite union that the very sight of one elicited the killing instinct within them. Mateusz Nowacki, aka Virski, was dressed once more in his aged Polish Army uniform, disheveled as it was. His rucksack was filled with fresh produce, which included four perfectly formed plums. These would be a treat for Bórza. They would express the conditions of his heart that he could never relate in words or gestures. Virski was the victim of a system that made no allowances for emotions, heartfelt expressions were detrimental to the professional who was trained to kill or be killed.

He set out before daylight, he would hazard the streets and hope that he could evade any gunfire. It would not do to travel the sewers and arrive with a coating of sludge and the noxious odor of filth and death.

Virski's Guardian Angel served him well, he was blessed with safe passage to Bórza's door. Sergeant Slota was on duty.

"Virski, friend, you are well."

"And you as well."

"Bórza sleeps on the cot in the hall."

"I'll find her."

"No need! Mateusz, you know I never really sleep." Bórza stepped into the room, seized him in her arms and peppered his cheeks with kisses. Virski seemed to tolerate the onslaught with dignity. She grabbed his hand and pulled him to the cot in the hall.

Bórza inspected and smelled every item presented to her; Virski held on to the plums for the last delight. "Close your eyes, smell, but don't look." Bórza was up for the game, a big smile on her face.

"Plums," she shouted and opened her eyes to appreciate the sight. "Oh, Mateusz, how very sweet you are. The many plum pies I made for you when we shared our lives together."

Mateusz indulged himself in the oncoming embrace; he no longer required an armored heart, here was a vital woman who had saved his life and added meaning to it. Here was a woman who desired him as much as he desired her.

Slota kept the earphones on and busied himself with note taking.

They smoothed their clothing, shared a kiss and sat on the cot, holding hands and enjoying the peace beyond all understanding.

"Mateusz, I have some vodka." She popped off the cot and went to get the bottle and glasses; Mateusz sat there grinning.

"The Telephone Building has been taken," he said after he drained his glass. Reality took hold once more.

"Rusza from Minerki told me about it."

"Yes, those mine-laying women were heroes along with Albert Kryzostanski who burrowed his way underground for two weeks to initiate the onslaught."

"My God, what kind of man is he? He's over sixty years old."

"He's a lion! Once he tunneled through a hundred yards or more, land mines were laid by the engineers to widen the passage so troops could slip through. Then, Rusza's Minerki women laid bombs for the German troops who would be trying to escape. The Germans were chased up to the tower, floor after floor. They tried to escape through a fireproof cable tube back to the basement where the mines were set. So, mines and flamethrowers won the victory for the Home Army."

"How did Albert make out?"

"Oh, an exploding bomb gave him a minor wound, but he's alive and well."

"He should receive the Virtuti Militari for his service and bravery."

"Bór has already presented him with his reward; he has been given a revolver with ten cartridges."

Chapter Forty-Seven

The Allied Air Lift had ceased operations, the last mission was on 14 August. A shield of anti-aircraft shelling by the Germans over Warsaw made the flights virtually impossible, it had become far too costly in men, planes and supplies. Bór's only hope for survival depended on the continued supplies of food and ammunition. The German blockade was steadily growing in strength. To the north of Warsaw, lying on the western bank of the Vistula, lay the Forest of Kampino, a strip of land thirty miles long by ten miles wide. Bór sent a wire off to London requesting the drops be continued on sites within the forest. He further declared that henceforth Kampino would be assigned the central depository for supplies and arms.

Vapors of past meals of cabbage and beet soup hovered in the air while *kielbasa* and eggs added yet another layer to linger in the mist during Sunday breakfast at the Furtak table. Ludwiga lay gurgling in her little woven basket on a chair that sat between Pola and Dysthmus. Furtak and Bianca shared the happy meal with them.

Furtak passed the bread plate and queried Dysthmus, "When will you be going back to Warsaw?"

"I must leave tonight!"

"I'll be going with you. Bór has ordered all peasant units to leave at once to be available on the outskirts to cover the units within the city."

Bianca dropped her fork, "You can't leave! Haven't I given enough with two sons, their lives at risk. And there's all of the harvest ahead of us."

Furtak lowered his head to avoid eye-contact, "The Germans are showing their force, the Russians are refusing to help; there may be no need for a harvest. Poland may cease to exist."

He looked up, a tenderness softened his face, "I must go."

The rucksack lay on the cot where Virski had left it, he needed to travel light by treading along a safer but more noxious route. He would have to negotiate through one of the narrowest tunnels to get back to the office of the Intelligence Bureau.

The passageway was three feet high and two feet wide. He hunched over and maintained his balance by clinging to the walls. The tunnel was pitch dark, the foul air took its tally on his lungs and brought tears to his eyes. Mud was up to his knees and every step was forcefully pushed against the weight of the sludge. He mulishly struggled along until he came across an obstacle that was immovable, a dead body. There was nothing for him to do but to backtrack and brave the gunfire along the streets. The lack of air was intolerable, Virski's heart was weak, his lungs depleted of life giving air rendered him incapable of proceeding. He would go no further.

Bórza sat on her stool, her earphones in place, she polished the plum and bit into the thin skin to savor the sweet taste; in her mind's eye she saw a plum pie cooling on the window sill for Virski's supper.

By 19 August, the migrating city refugees had increased the population of Old Town by twenty-thousand people. All of the spaces in the subterranean passages and the cellars of the old wooden buildings were filled with the mixed population. Bór's anxiety had been increasing. His daily incoming messages alerted him of the possibility that the Germans were about to attack Old Town.

The Wehrmacht strategic plans were under the command of an SS general, *SS-Ogruführer* Rohr. The concentrated area was a semicircle stretching from the citadel in the north of Old Town. At his disposal was an infantry of ten battalions, a platoon of mine throwers, an armored train, two gunboats, and fire from Praga across the Vistula. Overhead, he had the support of Stukas flying in formation an hour apart. The area under attack was a mere half mile square.

In the first hour, the artillery fire, the shelling from the gunboats, and the bombing from the Stukas set the old oak buildings ablaze, spewing flames and smoke into the air and collapsing the structures on their foundations. The Town Hall, Bank of Poland, the Old Arsenal, Treasury Printing Building, Royal Palace, and St. John of God Hospital were no longer in the hands of the Home Army. By the third day of the attack three-hundred homes out of a total of eleven-hundred had been burned, four-hundred were demolished.

Soldiers' faces were blackened with smoke, their expressions bore the trauma of a living experience in hell. They were physically and emotionally exhausted. The line of defense somehow managed to struggle on for one entire week.

By Friday, the 25th of August, Bór prepared to evacuate headquarters. The steady bombardments and mass attacks had reduced the Home Army legion at his disposal from eight-thousand to fifteen-hundred men.

Six-hundred-fifty feet from the German held positions an unused sewer continued on its route directly under Bór's headquarters. At 1:00 a.m. 26 August the executive staff, Bór, Jankowski, Puzak, and Grzegorz walked the short distance to a manhole cover on the corner of Krakowskie Przedmieście. One by one they entered the sewer and were guided through noxious sludge that reached their thighs. They were guided through this detritus refuse by the *Kanalarki* sewer girls who not only guided people through the muck but administered aid to those who did not have the stamina to complete the journey. Two hours later they were hauled out of the sewer by manhole guards in Center City.

Bór was deeply affected by the loss; he had revered the ancient homes and palace since childhood, "Six-hundred years of history lay in those ruins."

The remaining troops had to be extracted from the ruins. Bór staged a furry of counter-attacks from the units on the periphery of Old Town to engage the Germans while the main attachments escaped the territory. The final stage of the exodus was to remove the rear guard from the periphery. These two stages were accomplished over three consecutive nights from 31 August to 2 September.

The tragedy that befell the civilian population was devastating. The victims who survived the smoke and flames of the collapsing buildings over their cave like existence in the subterranean passages numbered thirty-five-hundred mobile, able civilians and several hundred wounded who were left to be captured by the Germans.

The SS arrived to evaluate the population. The old and the wounded were shot, The others were queued up for disposal to the concentration camps of Mauthausen and Sachsenhausen.

Alexander Werth, a Western war correspondent, interviewed Rokossovsky on 29 August. The General stated that the Germans had driven his troops back some sixty miles, once they had reached the outskirts of Praga on 1 August. Werth asked if he was still retreating, and was told that they were advancing, slowly.

The general was evasive, offering that the capture of Warsaw and Praga would prove most difficult for the Russians.

In response to the unreasonable denial of the Soviets to allow Allied airlift planes to refuel at the Russian held landing strip, just a few miles outside of Warsaw, the general defended their position by stating it was a military stronghold and therefore not available to British and American planes.

The interview ended with the general carping about the interference of the Home Army. Poland's territory was in the capable military command of the Soviets. He then went on to analogize the insurrection to a circus clown that pops up at the wrong moment. Rokossovsky summed up the situation with his own forecast; the rising would result in a tragic loss of hundreds of thousands of lives.

Chapter Forty-Eight

Bór and his staff moved into the Post Office Savings Bank with Monter and his crew. The building itself was a fortress. Constructed of concrete, its domed roof stood in defiance to the enemy's air attacks. Upon their arrival, Monter sent two members of his military unit to fetch water from the wells being dug. The recent newcomers were caked in slime, they dripped the foul sewer water onto the floor where they stood. Jankowski and Puzak, both in their sixties were in wretched condition. Bór did the best he could to clean up, and with a change of clothes went to lie down in a corner on the third floor. His plan was to set up headquarters in the basement.

At the CNU meeting, the next day, Jankowski appeared weakened and thinner, a quiet mannered gentleman, he smiled at Bednarek inviting conversation.

"Thank God you were able to endure the horrors of the sewer."

"Michal, I will never do that again; death is a much better alternative."

Kaminski asked the ever present question that hovered in the air.

"The Germans are increasing their force with fierce aggressive tactics and ammunition. Is there still a possibility of Soviet intervention to rout the Nazis from Warsaw?"

"They are monstrous felons!"

These meetings occurred every two to three days on Przeskok Street, a few hundred yards from the Post Office Savings Bank. Representatives of the eight districts of the city reported on the conditions within their precincts, the supplies and ammunition needed, and the ongoing mortality rate. The information gleaned at these meetings held great importance for both Kaminski's newspaper and Bednarek for the documentation of atrocities. Jerzy accompanied Kaminski at this meeting; he planned a stopover at the church afterward.

An air attack that occurred over Marszałkowska Street during the meeting increased the noise level to the degree that reports had to be written on the board; this only served to escalate Monter's angst. His immediate concern was about the supply line delivery to civilians; it took precedence over the ongoing battle at the front lines.

During the Resistance over one-hundred bakeries, legitimate and black market underground ovens kept the citizens in bread. The Germans had destroyed the bakeries. The current stock of bread would be depleted by 2 September. The lack of water created a catastrophe beyond the needs of the people, there was no water to put out fires. The lack of milk was devastating to the children. Mothers of newborns were traumatized by the interminable battles and were unable to produce milk for their suckling babes. Dysentery was spreading throughout the city.

When the uproar of the bombardment decreased, Chairman Puzak of the CNU rose from his seat and in his unruffled, self-possessed manner terminated the meeting.

"Friends, we cannot count on the next minute for our lives, but we can maintain a stiff upper lip and courage in our hearts. We must not let the enemy attack our reserve, for if we lose that we are nothing."

Jerzy made his way through the hazardous streets to the church barricade and managed to wiggle his way through the two-way traffic of the hallway into the hospital. He peered through the frantic medical scene of cots and medical staff in search of a tall, big-headed man, his Uncle Heinrich. He had to caste his eyes lower to discover his uncle on his knees, helping an elderly woman take a few sips of water, he placed the cup on the floor and gently laid her head back on her pillow.

He looked up and saw his nephew watching him from the other side of the cot. "Jerzy!" He grabbed a hold on his arm, "Come, we'll go upstairs where we can talk."

They sat on a bench in the narthex, Jerzy queried, "How are things going in Czerniaków?"

"My crew is holding everything in order; so far, there have been no casualties. Emile and Moritz are manning the radio transmissions and they've assigned Fritz the position of distributor; he's working with Dysthmus and Kurt.

"And what about you?"

A light chuckle, "I feel like a diplomat, working in the Bulgarian Embassy. The building is quite beautiful. I'm on my way back after Monter's meeting but I wanted to stop by and see you and Irena."

"Irena surprises me. Coming from her *szlachta* background, she has shown a bravery and resilience I would have never suspected possible."

"It doesn't surprise me, Uncle. Under all of that soft feminine fluff lies a mother tiger."

"I don't know if she's in the Rectory or out on her calls, but go, find your girl and may God be with you."

The setting was eerie, the open fireplace, the two fireside chairs, the round tea table complete with the ceramic tea set, the varied religious icons looking down from the walls, and the Victorian loveseat which was occupied by Irena and Jerzy was incongruous with the blasting gunfire that resounded in the streets.

There was no conversation. The couple were communicating by exploring each other's body.

"No, no, Jerzy, no," Irena pushed him away, "This is a holy house, the home of the priest and God. No!"

Jerzy paused, swallowed hard and began to pull at his shirt while he grudgingly popped the buttons back in place; Irena straightened her hair and smoothed her skirt.

They sat up straight on the loveseat and held hands while they tried to convince themselves that they could be content with just being in the presence of one another without indulging their passion.

And then, "Irena, this cannot go on. We don't know how much time we have; we have no time together, and if I'm to get through this horror, I must have some peace of mind. We'll have Father marry us."

The women volunteers of the hospital enjoyed a glimpse of the vestige of past wedding celebrations. They remembered the long weeks of preparation and the long days of celebration, when spirits were high, and hands were busy. Here and there among the bombed out courtyards a patch of flowers remained waiting to be picked, but no one was thinking of flower bouquets while ammunition was firing away from both sides. Several women dug them up and placed them, soil and all into whatever type of container they could find, as there was no water to keep them fresh.

Pani Trypka dug into the drawers and cabinets for the hand embroidered altar cloths and Leona led a crew of volunteers to scrub down the sanctuary before placing the containers of wilted flowers upon the altar. The vows were to be exchanged immediately after Sunday Mass.

The women volunteers had gleaned articles of clothing from whatever corners they were able to stash their treasures and brought them to the rectory. The artillery fire around them did not discourage them from frivolous charades of modeling the items in mock vanity. The battle was forgotten as laughter eased away weeks of stress and put them in a party mood. Leona and Irena chose a fetching outfit from the available pile. A long sleeve satin blouse, the color of cream with a keyhole neckline and a pleated white cotton skirt served to showcase her tanned complexion, her lush brown hair, and her turquoise eyes.

Father Lipinski had served the last communicant at the rail and then proceeded to carry the chalice up the aisle so that those members of the congregation who were incapacitated would be blessed with the divinity of Christ. Stukas flying overhead began blasting the nearby area by dropping incendiary bombs. The very pews were vibrating under the bombardment. Father maintained his usual measured stride, unperturbed by the disruption, he moved along from pew to pew and serenely delivered the sacred host to the waiting celebrants.

Jerzy had borrowed a fresh shirt from Monter. Clean shaven, with an anxious glow on his handsome face, he shifted about in the pew up front; occasionally he traced a finger around the shirt collar and stretched his neck in nervous anticipation.

Mendelssohn's Wedding March set the stage as Michal held tightly to his daughter's hand that she had thrust under his arm, and they walked the one, two, pause, way to the altar where he would surrender her to the man who would cherish and protect her.

Father talked them through the responses after which he wrapped the wedding cloth around their joined hands over the nuptial tray on the altar. The *"I Dos"* were muttered under the reverberating bombardment, and then the kiss. Blatantly unconcerned with their audience, they lingered in this moment that was so intense it provided a virtual reality of its own.

The honeymoon would be celebrated at the Bulgarian Embassy in one of the elaborately decorated bedrooms. Pan Jerzy Gruber and Pani Irena, nee Bednarek, Gruber were now one.

Chapter Forty-Nine

For thirty-five days, the technicians and linesmen of the Power Station fought and died to fortify the facility so that Warsaw would continue to have the necessary electricity to survive the brutal ongoing battle. On the 4th of September, the Nazis repeated a *blitzkrieg* operation on Riverside; the entire area was demolished.

The relationship between Irena and the block captain Edziu in all respects had become compatible. They covered for one another, supported each other, and gained strength from one another. While the battle endured in Riverside, Edziu was presented with a new directive. Warsaw must have power.

Warsaw would be unable to maintain the necessary communications that stoked the 24/7 strategy of warfare. Further requests for aid from London would be terminated. Medical personnel would be unable to care for the wounded. Germany would not have to fire another bullet. The insurgent factories would have to pick up the slack. Edziu was needed at the factory to produce power by using accumulators to charge automobile batteries for life sustaining electricity.

Irena was on her own.

By 6 September, Bór and company had settled into the damp basement of the Post Office Savings Bank, and his staff was involved with the issues of the day. The typewriter was clacking away, several soldiers were reviewing and organizing recent messages, while an off-duty soldier provided background music on a mandolin and sang, off-tune, a song about rebellion. Bór gave a final check of the situation before he left the building for a meeting on Przeskok Street.

German Stukas filled the sky overhead and began strafing the area with bombs. A 600-mm shell exploded on the Post Office Savings Bank, chunks of cement were sent flying into the air and then thudded to the ground. The entire area was covered in a heavy smog of dust with fragments of cement. The mighty dome of the building was also projected skyward and landed upside down to crown the rubble.

The destructive shell shattered Bór's office area killing the staff members he had left behind. Chief of Staff Grzegorz was hit by a falling beam, his jaw was fractured, and the accompanying debris pock-marked the flesh on his face.

Bór would later appointed General Leopold Okulicki, (nom de guerre: "Niedźwiadek" or "Bear Cub") as his new Chief of Staff.

German planes were littering the air with leaflets, not bombs, and Bór was involved with his third move since the Rising had begun six weeks ago. He and his retinue would take up residence in the newly acquired Telephone Building on Pious Street, which was within 300 yards of a German post, a relatively safe move, as the Germans would not risk shelling an area so close to their own position. Przeskok Street, a few hundred yards away from the Post Office Savings Bank was also devastated.

The Government Plenipotentiary along with the CNU moved to Central Borough South on Basket Street, while Monter and company settled in the originally held insurgent's barricade, the Palladium Cinema on Golden Street.

The leaflets were a solicitous invitation from the Germans offering: combat status to uniformed military, safe conduct for civilians wishing to leave the city, and a cease fire. Bór sent out orders to ignore these messages. However, There were those who saw this as an opportunity to escape a nightmare; what could be worse than the constant hell they had endured for five weeks. Home Army soldiers were on hand to maintain order. There was quite a scuffle when insurgent sentries discovered that several elderly citizens were discovered to be young healthy youths masquerading to escape a battle worn city.

Kaminski was on the scene for a story. He had interviewed several people when the ruckus broke out over the youths. He reached out for the arm of one of the masqueraders and pulled him aside.

"What made you take a chance like this? What's your name?"

"Wałek!" he screamed, and then vented his anger. "What a stupid question! Are you alive? Does this look to you as a reality? And these people, acting as though they are patriots! They're goddamn fools! There's death and stench everywhere; I've lost my hearing over the constant bombing and destruction. We are starving, there's no water. I have lost my parents and two brothers, and now I have conscription to look forward to. Well, fuck them; I'll kill myself and save a Nazi bullet."

Military planners in Berlin were appalled with the lengthy involvement of the Warsaw insurgency. Over one month of armed conflict with inadequately trained troops branding homemade weapons against the *Wehrmacht* and the *Luftwaffe* was a baffling proposition. Actually, the Nazis were fighting two wars; the war of attrition was every bit as challenging. The mortality rate among the German military ranks was unsustainable. The Nazis were filling their ranks by enlisting or conscripting other ethnic groups. The Allies were stripping away at the German's confiscated territories, Turkey had turned neutral and would not supply the chrome to build the armored Panzer tanks. Not only were the inadequate Poles making a mockery of the military force of the Third Reich, but the troops, artillery, and Stukas were needed elsewhere.

The turnout of evacuees was not what the Germans had hoped for, the authorities opted to raise the stakes. An envoy, under a white flag of truce, made the 300 yard trek with a message for Bór, signed by *SS-Uberführer* Rohr, Commander of the German Sector, suggesting that representatives from the Polish Red Cross be invited to work out an agreement for the protective coverage of citizens wishing to leave the city. Bór was apprehensive about the investment of representatives in a vis-a-vis meeting with the German authorities.

The perplexing issue was presented at the September 8th meeting of the CNU. Bór handed the message to the Prezes without comment. Jankowski read the short context, bit his upper lip and did not raise his eyes. He seemed to be trying to absorb the significance of the opportunity. He handed the note back to Bór, "I think you should read this to the group."

Puzak spoke up first, "This is a total departure from the usual savagery we have become accustomed to. It is evident that they are trying to wrap up this venture as soon as possible to alleviate the increasing cost of men and ammunition. I feel certain that they have our capitulation in mind."

There was a lengthy pause and a good deal of murmuring among the members, then Jankowski spoke up. "I agree with what you say Kazimierz, but I think we should see this through; we'll play dumb and see the monkey for free."

Countess Zofia Tarnowska and Manya Wachowiak wore their Red Cross Badges and presented their credentials to the German *SS-Uberführer* Rohr, who presided over a very short meeting leaving the representatives with yet another message to deliver to Bór.

It was precisely what Bór had expected. Rohr requested that he send his official representatives to discuss certain proposals. Reluctantly, Bór called on one of his staff officers, Lieut. Colonel "Zyndram".

Zyndram, in his early thirties made a snappy looking military officer, plus he had impeccable manners, a pleasant sounding voice, and perfect articulation.

Zyndram was escorted to Rohr's quarters where two interpreters would ensure that each word was understood. The General's interpreter precisely articulated every word that the loquacious Rohr had to offer. He droned on about the obvious foolhardiness of continued fighting.

He concluded, "We have taken Wola, Old Town, and Powiśle and we are advancing on Żoliborz. We are concentrating our efforts on the remaining bridges of the Vistula. It's only a matter of time."

Zyndram maintained a courteous military attitude while the General touched on the continuing specter that hung in the air, the dubious intentions of the Soviet Union and their reluctance to offer aid to the insurgents.

"They are sitting back, with their hands folded, waiting for the ultimate collapse of Warsaw before they continue with their endeavor to grasp up Poland and install their own puppet government of Communism."

With a punctuated blow, he continued, "Poland will never become an independent state. Russia has plans of making Poland its Seventeenth State, which is foolhardy on their part." A disingenuous smile stretched his lips, "Germany will conquer Poland and exploit its plans for *Lebensraum.*"

The final segment of his oratory was a strategic harangue of a humanitarian nature.

"Your General Bór has witnessed the devastation of the land and the people of Wola, Old Town, and Powiśle. Is he prepared to allow the very same desolation to occur to the people of Warsaw? We have the weaponry and the forces to level the city of Warsaw and all of its historic sites."

He lifted an envelope from his desk and handed it to Zyndram, "Since your commander was not present to hear my intentions, deliver this to him, these are the conditions that I offer."

Chapter Fifty

Sunday, September 10th: Warsaw was awakened by Soviet fighter planes circling the city two at a time. Stuka planes remained grounded. Once more Bór was confronted with a fork in the road.

Rohr's letter contained the conditions of surrender: The Home Army would receive combatant rights in captivity; the civilian population would be evacuated with adequate assistance, assured of safety. Rohr expected a response to his conditions that same evening, the 10th of September.

Bór decided to stall for time; he was faced with two unreliable foes. Before he chose the lesser of two evils, he would respond to Rohr's letter in a timely fashion with his opinion of the conditions of surrender.

Since Rohr was merely a sector commander, there was no way to ascertain that these conditions were valid. Bór required that the conditions be confirmed by at least the commander of the 2nd Army. Also, the conditions as stated should be broadcast to the world at large over the German station, Deutschland-sender. Bór concluded this missive with the provision that unless these requirements would be met, he could not consider signing any document.

Rohr's ego was assaulted. He was furious to be so demeaned by an insignificant Pole. He replied that this was a final offer, and it was Bór's choice to accept or reject the conditions as stated.

Bór spent a sleepless night angsting over his actions. Would the Russians once more fail to follow through? Had he closed the bridge to further negotiations with the Germans?

As the sun rose over Warsaw, the Soviet barrage continued over the Vistula, the sounds appeared to be approaching Praga. German Stukas and Junkers disappeared from the sky.

Over the last two days, only Russian fighters had taken to the air. Father Lipinski hadn't said a courtyard mass in days due to the constant Nazi bombardment. During his last mass in a courtyard off Basket Street, he had barely escaped with his life, which was not the case for the communicants who risked their lives for the Body and Blood, Soul and Divinity of Christ. He would not have that on his conscience again. With Stukas grounded, it seemed relatively safe to enter the courtyards again. The devout would risk their lives by climbing out of their underground chambers to participate in the holy ritual from which they derived emotional comfort.

On Tuesday, at 11:00 a.m. mass was being said in the courtyard off Pious Street; the sky was free of enemy aircraft. Communion was served, Father was giving the last blessing when a sniper took aim at the tall figure of a priest. The bullet made its home in his left thigh.

Kaminski was en route to the Bulgarian Embassy from a press conference on Pious Street when he came upon the scene of women with stretchers and witnesses wringing their hands.

"Father!" he pushed through the throng.

Lipinski was wincing and trying to appear undaunted, the medical assistant remarked, "It's okay. The wound is superficial, it is no place near the bone."

"Zygmunt, don't tell me you were at mass!"

"Not this time, but I will be there for Sunday mass. I see this as a miracle; it's only because your long legs make an easy target for a sniper that you were wounded," he chuckled, "I'm sure the good Lord has a suit of armor covering you."

With that benign smile of his, Father raised his right hand and bestowed a blessing on him. Zygmunt crossed himself.

Chapter
Fifty-One

A letter was drafted by Bór and sent off to Rokossovsky by the only route possible, through London. He made a sincere effort to make him aware of the fact that the Home Army was anxious to join up with the Soviet forces in offensive action against the Germans. He informed the General that the Poles still held forces in Mokotów to the south and Żoliborz in the north, as well as Center City. As for the supplies that the Soviet fighter planes had bestowed on the city the night before, "…drop what you can on Marszałkowska Street and Napoleon Square."

At 9:00 a.m. on 12 September, Soviet bombers flew over Praga; the air battles continued all day. That same day, Bór received a wire from London apprising him of consequential information on current events. Churchill and Roosevelt had pressured Stalin to open the Soviet airstrips and allow access to Allied planes. Once this issue was resolved, the Allied Airlift would continue.

An operation of 100 bombers would begin in a few days, the musical announcement chosen as the cue would be, "One More Mazurka Today" which would be played the end of the BBC broadcast to Poland.

While Soviet bombers held command over the skies, the Germans retaliated with increased offensive artillery on the ground. Panzer tanks and infantry attacks plunged into the Polish held territories near the Vistula.

Perhaps it was a baptism for fire that sent the rain pouring down on Warsaw on the night of August 1, the first day of the Rising. Perhaps there was some significance in the fact that for the next five weeks there was no rain. The Vistula shrank to an all-time low. Stretches of sand were exposed, the highest point of flowing tides was at most hip length; one could walk on water.

Although there had been no forthcoming reply from Rokossovsky to Bór's invitation to join forces, Marszałkowska Street and Napoleon Square had become a bread basket. On the nights of 13 and 14 September, Soviet planes dropped supplies over the city without parachutes; the packages split open when they hit the ground. Wheat, oats, barley, and kasha, mingled with the detritus of deteriorating body parts and the rubble of shattered buildings. In the midst of the 'bellowing cows' and ongoing artillery men, women, and children - civilian and militia alike - were scrambling along the streets to gather whatever their bags and pockets could hold. The saving grace was that the skies were free of Stukas.

Over the next two weeks, small Russian bi-planes, PO-2s delivered a total of 156 50mm mortars, 505 anti-tank rifles, 1,478 sub-machine guns, 520 rifles, 669 carbines, 780 hand-grenades 37,216 mortar shells, 131 tons of food, 515 kilograms of medicine.

In his mild manner, Jankowski did his best to exert himself and bring to order the meeting of the CNU. The last few days had seen the cessation of German bombing, the resumption of Russian fighting over the Vistula, and provisions being dropped on the city by Russian fighter planes. The members, reeling under emotional spasms of renewed energy, were not inclined to be compliant.

Monter rose from his seat and hammered the table with the gavel, "Order, Order!" he barked in his loud and powerful voice.

The din was reduced to a murmur, "The Prezes is here to address you."

Jankowski nodded to Monter and offered a grateful smile. "We have been revitalized by recent positive events brought about by the Russians, but that does not in any way offset our dwindling resources. Our capital is gone. Treasury Secretary Walczak has been wounded and may even be dead. The hospital that he was being tended to on Bright Street was captured by the Germans. His deputy was killed in the Savings Bank bombing. The few known buildings that vaulted our savings have been demolished. As far as we know, there are no reserves."

Kaminski shook his head and grinned, "I know the place where a stash of American dollars was hidden."

A general gasp was emitted by the audience. "Where?" Monter and Jankowski asked in tandem.

"Not very far from here; I was there when Walczak requested the space."

Bednarek and Kaminski set out for Mokotów Street. During the last few weeks, Mayor Sowa had put together another digging force. Civilians and POWs dug four foot trenches behind the front lines of the Home Army. Sowa's concern for the many people who had to travel the sewers evoked this possible solution. Although there was heavy fire along the route, Bednarek and Kaminski managed to make it to Mokotów Street to accomplish the mission Jankowski had set upon them.

Conveniently situated between a German held district on the left and the frontline barricade of insurgents on the right, sat the home of Albert Świątek. Kaminski's knock on the door was answered by Jacob, who passed a quick glance over Kaminski,.

"Pan Bednarek, you are alive and well, come in." He pulled the door ajar and stepped back to let the visitors enter.

"Come this way." He led them to the living room where an active game of Bridge was going on. Świątek rose from his seat to shake hands.

"You're playing Bridge?" Kaminski staggered, "How do you manage to play cards with the battle going on?"

"There's not much noise. The Nazis don't want to have their safe position defiled and the insurgents are happy to comply."

Bednarek chuckled, "Kaminski is keen on Bridge; aren't you, Zygmunt?"

"If I wasn't engaged in an important mission, I'd sit down right now!"

"Please, Zygmunt, join us anytime; we will gladly take a few *zloty* from you."

"I'll keep that in mind, but we are really here for the deposit that Pan Walczak left with you. Is it still here?"

"Of course." He called to Jacob.

"Jacob, do you feel like digging? These gentlemen are here to pick up their deposit."

Raging fires over Praga could be seen in Warsaw; the Citadel was blown apart by Soviet bombs. Along the southern banks of the diminished Vistula, the Germans were retreating to the north; on their way, they blew up the eastern ends of both the Poniatowski and railway bridges.

By nightfall of Wednesday, 13 September, the Soviets had captured Gocławek and were plying their way into Praga. By midday of the 14th, Rokossovsky had taken Praga.

While the Russian invasion was gaining territory in Praga, the Germans were pushing to gain territory in Czerniaków. By 15 September, only a shrunken river separated Soviet positions from Polish units in Czerniaków.

Kumor's daily information on German positions within the battle zones netted enough valid information for Deputy General Monter to be able to outline a strategic battle plan that would incorporate the forces of both the Russians and the insurgents to encompass the German held sectors. The Russians had maintained their hold on the territories they captured in early August, Falenica and Otwock in the south. Together with Jabłonna in the north, they would be able to weaken, if not capture the German positions. Monter did not receive a response.

In the beginning of September, General Zygmunt Berling, Commander of the communist Polish Army, was involved in conscripting young male peasants in Kraków to undertake a battle in Czerniaków. The river was low and there was every chance that his newly organized troops would be able to make the crossing with relatively few lives lost. Berling was under the direct command of Rokossovsky, and one of Stalin's groveling puppets.

Under the cover of night on 14 September, Berling's five-hundred raw recruits forged the shallow Vistula. They were ordered to keep their weapons over their head during the entire process of treading over slippery strips of sand and wading through waist-high water. Farmers all their lives, they were familiar with ploughs, scythes and hoes; weapons of war were an anomaly in their leathered hands. During Berling's short term of mobilization, there was little chance of gleaning efficiency in weaponry or battle tactics. They were lambs being led to slaughter.

As soon as the peasants reached shore they were fired upon, there was no contest. A few of them reacted by retracing their steps across the river.

Chapter Fifty-Two

Dysthmus held a seat at the table for the CNU meeting of 15 September. He had an exact tally of the food supplies that were available for the 260,000 people still alive and hungry in Warsaw.

Jankowski called the meeting to order, "My friends, we are in devastating straits. The accumulators are in no way capable of providing us with the power needed, especially in the makeshift hospitals. Wells are running dry, at present there are only 92 that are still functioning; people are risking their lives standing in line to get a cup of water. There's a report of a scarlet fever outbreak, and dysentery is now a part of our daily lives. It's been five days since the British advised us of an airlift of considerable proportions on the way. We have been listening intently for "One More Mazurka Today," as yet we are unable to dance to that tune. Have we been abandoned? Dysthmus, what is the condition of food reserves?"

Dysthmus held a small card in front of him, but he made his announcement without referring to his notes. "We have available, a hundred tons of barley and fifty tons of wheat. As of tomorrow, there is no lard or oil for cooking; we have enough sugar for four days. Most of us are living on boiled wheat and barley coffee."

It had become a ritualistic observance. Every morning, at 9:00 a.m. the administrators had their ears pinned to the BBC broadcast to Poland. Once the announcements were delivered, the program would end with a final tune. Lately, the final tune had been "Military March," the cryptic cue that pronounced the airlift was cancelled.

"Weather not permitting," was the usual response to Bór's queries. Sunday morning, after mass, on the seventeenth, "One More Mazurka Today" beamed forth from the BBC. Bór received additional information on the wireless. The airlift was due over Warsaw between 11:00 a.m. and noon the following day.

The sun was approaching the overhead position in a bright cloudless sky when Allied planes were spotted at a very high altitude. At first there were two or three at a time; soon the sky was filled with planes and white specks were spotted falling from them. The streets in Warsaw were filled with people braving the skirmish to witness the much needed supplies.

Here and there, shouts rang out, "They are paratroopers," and "Our commandoes are coming to fight the Nazis." As the chutes descended, the colors of them, black, green, yellow, and white, distinguished them as supply pods.

The Germans had managed to gain advantage over the chessboard of battle. There were only small segments of the city being held by the Poles. It was only a matter of time until checkmate. Most of the 1,800 containers of food and medicine dropped by the Allies fell into the hands the Germans.

The house on Mokotów Street was absorbed into the German district on the left. There was no longer a Polish frontline on the right. Albert Świątek, as a Swiss citizen, had lived a privileged life, indulging in the finer things that wealth could buy in the way of creature comfort. He had chosen to remain in Warsaw after the *blitzkrieg* of "39". In his late seventies, he was not about to pull up stakes. After all, he was a Swiss citizen which labeled him invulnerable.

The Commander of the German sector was well aware of his status and developed a monetary relationship with the old man. He was also available to take part in the bridge games whenever he could make the time.

All of Warsaw eagerly awaited the sound of Soviet fighter planes. As of 20 September, the last reserves of wheat and barley had been exhausted. Broken containers of food dropped without parachutes were looked upon as manna from heaven. However, the skies remained clear, there were no Soviet fighters, and no German Stukas. The events on the ground offered a different set of circumstances, the Germans had intensified their artillery attacks; Panzer tanks, machine guns, grenades, billowing cows, were ripping apart the barricades and frontlines of the Poles in Center City. In the shadow of the bombardment, another war was ravaging the insurgents, the war of hunger. Men had not eaten in days, they were dehydrated, exhausted and demoralized. The very same situation plagued the civilian population. They had become immune to the ceaseless cries of their neighbors who were buried in the basements of destroyed homes. Compassion took energy, the specter of death had defeated them, the cries were ignored, no one had the energy or empathy to come to their aid.

Kaminski become a daily communicant. He had been a lifelong agnostic, although he appreciated the resilience and fortitude religion seemed to offer the people whose faith was strong. His conversion was not the reaction to the fear of death and the immortal soul gaining its way into heaven. It was the transformation of an egoist into a compassionate individual who had learned to honor life and to abhor the ever present evil in the world that sought to destroy it. As everything surrounding him was being decimated, he became philosophical. He yearned for the attributes of peace, truth and beauty, all of the amenities that he had taken for granted before the war. His observations of the patterns of nature and its life-giving energy that remained unaltered in the presence of the wanton destruction that he witnessed daily persuaded him to acknowledge the presence of a life-giving force that was independent of the crude statistics of science. There had to be an undeniable force in charge. The realization humbled him. He no longer went to press with the news, the people were all too aware of the daily situation; they didn't need to read about it. Instead, he kept a journal.

20 September, the hoped for medical supplies have not materialized. The Germans are benefitting from the Allied drop of yesterday. The entire hospital staff is suffering from diarrhea, as am I. There is not enough light for the surgeons to treat their patients, candles and carbide lamps are insufficient. Operations are being conducted without anesthesia, and whatever paper products are available are being used to absorb blood as there is no longer any cloth to be had.

The Bureau of Justice held their meetings in the building on 9 Pious Street, the former Telephone Building, where Bór had set up his quarters. Judge Peter Butkowski was walking with the aid of a cane. He had earlier tripped over debris in the street as he rushed for cover and fractured his ankle. Although he had received immediate first aid, needed further assistance. A woman sapper, knowledgeable in herbal medicine, had prepared a salve for him from a plant known as *ziwokoscz* and a pain reliever of salicylic acid. He winced with pain at every step.

Judge Anton Matewski, had been in ill health and suffered a fatal heart attack during the first week of the insurrection. The Bureau was reduced to a trio; Judge Butkowski, Albert Pierski, former District Attorney, and Attorney for the Defense, Michal Bednarek.

The Powiśle attack by the Germans was under review for the documentation of war crimes committed by the Nazis, citing Kaminski's eye witness report as deposition.

In Powiśle on 6 September 1944, the Germans used machine gun fire to conduct a massive murder of incarcerated prisoners as a means of doing away with waste. As a further method of population control, they stormed the three makeshift hospitals, ordering the medical staff to remove the wounded and deposit them near the craters that the bombs from their Stukas created. Again, their machine guns mercilessly shot the victims, after which, the dead bodies were tidily rolled over into the craters as a means of burial.

Chapter Fifty-Three

Despite the repeated attempts by both Monter and Bór to join forces and aim for the defeat of the German presence in Warsaw, the Soviets chose not to respond. After the allied supply drop of 20 September, there was no further aid nor intervention from the other side of the Vistula, even though the recent debacle of Berling's green troops had proved the river to be navigable.

Bór's headquarters on Pious Street was under constant artillery fire. Walking the short distance to meetings on Basket Street had become a death-trap.

The Germans concentrated their efforts on the vicinity of the Polish held positions along the Vistula. They strategically plotted an attack from the bi-lateral positions of both north and south. Emboldened by the lack of Soviet intervention, they marshaled their forces to strike at the western banks of the river, pushing the insurgent militia towards Center City. They utilized all of their heavy fire-power, on the ground while Stukas dropped bombs and strafed the area with machine gun fire. The entire area crumbled, and the blasted buildings literally buried people in the rubble.

SS-Uberführer Rohr was seething. The ongoing German conflict in Warsaw with the unprofessional band of insurgents was raising eyebrows in Berlin. This rebellion had to be quelled. The mighty forces of the Wehrmacht and the Luftwaffe were sorely needed to withstand the intensive territorial seizure that Russia and the Allies were extorting from Germany.

Rohr resented the manner in which his genuinely sincere offer for capitulation was literally scoffed at by the insignificant Bór. He would show the Poles a thing or two about warfare. He would crush them by the end of the month by utilizing the fire power he held under his command and intensifying his military strategy.

Warszawians' morale was at its lowest ebb. Faith in God was at its highest peak. There was no bread or wine, there was no water, communion had become a symbolic gesture, a small cross was used to bless each communicant. Observance of the ritual of mass and receiving the blessing of the cross fortified both the civilian population and the Home Army units. Father Lipinski's varied duties as pastor had taken a serious toll on him; his health was waning, but his willingness to serve his congregation managed to see him through one day at a time.=

Pani Trypka brought his bowl of gruel to the table.

"I had a little trouble with the coffee grinder this morning, Father."

"Not to worry, Zosia, the coffee grinder will outlast us."

The coffee grinder had become the only tool needed in the kitchen. There was no power for cooking; there was no food to cook. Pani Trypka made the three meals a day according to a singular recipe: one handful of wheat, ground together in a half cup of water, it had been nicknamed *Plujka*, spit. Barley left to soften in water overnight was served as coffee. Father hadn't had a bite of bread in weeks.

The nave of the church was filled to capacity during mass on Sunday 24 September. Father had once again delivered an encouraging sermon on the rewards of faith in God against the forces of evil. The mass ended with a fervent prayer to St. Michael, the battling Archangel, whose feast day would occur later that week.

During the exiting of the congregation, Father slipped in an occasional invitation to breakfast in the dining room of the Rectory. In all, he was prepared to receive six guests to enjoy the *kasha* that Pani Trypka had prepared from wheat and barley.

"In the name of the Father, the Son, and the Holy Ghost," Father offered grace, "We appeal to you, dear Father, to guard our hearts and souls, to increase our durability under the onslaught of this horrible conflict. Give us the courage to withstand the inhumanity of these evil oppressors while we acknowledge your divinity in Christ Jesus, Amen."

Heinrich Gruber laid his palms on his knees, straightened up in the chair and offered a doleful smile, "They have captured Czerniaków. I have spoken to an escaped victim of the Berling unit and learned that the bombs and flame throwers have destroyed most of the buildings in town."

Pani Trypka served his bowl of *kasha*. He smiled up at her, *"Dziękuję."* There was silence around the table; Kaminski and Father bowed their heads.

Father looked over at Jerzy. "You and Zygmunt are currently in need of shelter. I'm aware the Belgrade Embassy is being shelled due to radio transmissions that are emanating from under their roof. Our roof is high enough to offer you quarters."

Kaminski smiled and nodded his head in humble acceptance; Jerzy was effusive in his gratitude; he would be able to live with his bride. Irena blushed and lowered her head.

"Michal, that offer goes for you, also. The reason I invited all of you is because I have concern of your living quarters and until the Nazis decide to bomb the church, you should be relatively safe here."

"Thank you, Father, but that would not be convenient for me, much as I would want to be here for Leona. The judiciary committee is meeting on a daily basis. I must remain in Deputy General Monter's headquarters. Also, Jankowski has taken to his bed with a severe case of dysentery. He depends on me to run his messages to and from the CNU meetings. I cannot abandon him."

Leona reached for his hand, "Do what you must to compile the necessary evidence against the Nazi's atrocious acts of barbarism. I will wait for you no matter how long it takes," she blessed herself, "the good Lord willing." There was a softness in her facial expression, an element of the spiritual was evidenced in her attitude. It was as though she had come to an understanding of peace in a world of turmoil.

Sunday, 24 September was the day that General Rohr decided to unleash his fury over Mokotów, one of three strongholds the Poles had managed to maintain. Stukas opened the fray by dive-bombing the area, while the 73rd Infantry artillery swooped over the ground spraying machine gun bullets and setting fire to buildings and citizens with flame throwers. By 27 September only a few rebel units were left. The Mokotów Commander reported that his estimated loss of citizens and soldiers to be at 70 per cent. The highest proportion of losses suffered so far. The Germans had taken Mokotów.

Chapter
Fifty-Four

Bór was overwhelmed by the report he received from Mokotów. Early in the morning, Thursday, the 28th, he called an emergency meeting with Monter and Jankowski. This was a crossroad he never expected to face.

It was obvious that Bór had not slept, he was unshaved, ashen; a dourness draped his countenance. "The morale of the troops is weakening while their determination to keep on fighting is exemplary; however, there is only enough ammunition to cover us for two or three days, and even were the British to perform another drop operation, we have learned that would only benefit the Germans."

Monter nodded in agreement, "There is nothing left of food supplies or medicine; we are in dire straits."

Further conflict was clearly untenable. A crucial moment had arrived for the venerable statesmen who had put their reputations, their very lives, at risk for a cause they sincerely believed would contribute to the ending of the war with Germany. They entered into this fray determined to aid the Russians, who initiated an attack on the enemy at the banks of the Vistula River.

Jankowski, pale and enervated concluded the meeting with the conviction, "We cannot allow the atrocities that occurred in Old Town, Powiśle, Czerniaków, and Mokotów, to be the fate of *Warszawians.*" He resolutely raised his chin, "General von dem Bach has summed up the future of Warsaw. The cultural capital of Poland will become the battleground for the Russians and Germans to fight over."

Bór immediately had his wireless station reach out to Rokossovsky of their immediate plight. He was surprised when he received a confirmation that his message had been received. Would Rokossovsky engage his troops and come to their aid?

A second message was dashed off to London, apprising Churchill of the dire situation confronting *Warszawians* and appealing for Soviet Military aid before October the first. If aid was denied, capitulation would follow. A similar message was delivered to Rokossovsky.

Bór waited twenty-four hours for a response from the Russian sector; their only reply was an overnight delivery of a few bags of ammunition and several sacks of grain, which had split apart on impact with the detritus ruble of the ground below.

Żoliborz was attacked during the early hours of Friday, 29 September. The Germans filled the sky with all of their available aircraft, while the infantry artillery and two Panzer Divisions battered the ground. Bór decided to send an envoy to *SS-Gruppenführer* von dem Bach; surrender was inevitable.

Von dem Bach sent a proposal that all civilians be evacuated from the city, and Home Army soldiers be offered the rights of combatant troops, according to the rules of the Geneva Convention.

The next day, 30 September, Bór called a halt to the battle in Żoliborz; there was no point in subjecting the population to a hopeless cause. The agreement written by von dem Bach for the evacuation for the citizen population was signed by representatives of the Polish Red Cross.

The messages traversing between Warsaw and Berlin had the Third Reich assuming the conflict going on in Warsaw was resolved; the Russians would not intervene, and the Poles were beaten down. Hitler awarded the Knight's Cross of the Iron Cross to SS-Gruppenführer Erich von dem Bach for the conquest of Warsaw, which would be the capital city of Hitler's proposed *Lebensraum*, a habitat or living space. Hitler's master plan for his conquered countries; those fertile farm lands would be inhabited by four to five million Aryans of the Master Race.

Von dem Bach responded with a special report to *Reichsführer* Himmler, lauding the further military accomplishments of the 19th Panzer division on the capture and surrender of Żoliborz.

While Hitler was enjoying visions of his *Lebensraum,* the Government-in-Exile in London was venting fury over the Soviets refusal to offer military aid to the Home Army. There was a faction of the divided staff, who were proponents of the dismissal of the Commander-in-Chief when Stalin first requested it. Sosnkowski was not a humble man. A member of the elite, he looked like an aristocrat, he spoke several languages, and took a lively interest in art, music, politics, and architecture. Stalin had every reason to want him out of the way. During the 1920 Soviet-Polish war, Sosnkowski was instrumental in designing the battle strategy that made Poland victorious.

The Exiled cabinet members were suffering disillusionment and disdain over the loss of a battle that they had ordained. On September 30, 1944, Premier Mikołajczyk confronted Sosnkowski with his immediate dismissal.

After an exhausting day of arbitration, Bór was on his way to his quarters when a wireless came through announcing his appointment of Commander-in-Chief.

When he awoke the next morning, October 1, he had his official confirmation, a wire informing him that as of September 30th, 1944, he was appointed Commander-in-Chief of the Polish Armed Forces.

Chapter Fifty-Five

The cease fire began on the morning of October 1; it was to last for three days while the civilians followed the orders for evacuation. Two barricades were designated as exit points for the evacuation and the hours were fixed for a cease fire at these points for both sides. Rumors had been circulating throughout Warsaw the last few days of September, which only brought confusion to the civilians, until Jankowski sent out printed notices of the dates, times, and departure points for the mandated evacuation. The edict only served to add to their confusion. What would happen to the troops of the Home Army? Almost every citizen had a relative or friend in the military service; many refused to leave the city without the soldiers.

On the first of October, only a small fraction of the population showed up at the checkpoints. The issue came under review at the CNU meeting.

The Block Captains were mandated to appear, there were no longer newspapers circulating to keep the public informed. Monter called the role to be sure that everyone was present, here and there a gap appeared, and the General assigned that block to a neighboring commander.

"It is most imperative that the citizens follow the rules of evacuation during the cease fire. We have no idea what the Nazis will do to anyone found lingering."

The block commander from Buxom Street called out, "General, they've been given the notices and I myself chatted with them to encourage them to leave, but they are more concerned about the Home Army's situation then their own skin."

"It's true!," a Marszałkowska Street commander confirmed the report, "Every one of them has a son or daughter, a relative or a friend fighting in the Home Army. They need to know that they will be safe."

Another voice rang out, "Some of them are more concerned with their bellies. A whole army of *matki* and *babcie* were out on the Mokotówska Racetrack to pillage the potatoes and other vegetables the Germans have planted there, taking advantage of the sentries who are obeying the cease fire."

Monter brushed aside a smile reflex. Sowa responded, "A German official routed them off the field with a bullhorn, warning them that if they didn't leave the field immediately he would order his men to fire. He added that the cease fire agreement would not hold with scavengers on the racetrack."

The General issued an edict, "Relay the information that under the signed agreement, all soldiers will be protected." He reached for a copy of Bór's objectives on the table and adjusted his spectacles, "Let me read you the stipulation, that will be guaranteed, 'Soldiers of the Home Army shall be recognized by a white and red armband or pennons or a Polish eagle, according to the rules of combat under the Geneva Convention dated August 27th, 1929.' "

As a humanitarian gesture, General von dem Bach allocated fifteen horse carts to stand by for those unable to walk the eight miles to the internment camp in Pruszków. There were thousands of people rendered immobile; the injured, the aged, an the physically weakened, who would fit that category. Fifteen carts were a gesture, but not a practicality.

Dysthmus and Kurt took advantage of the cease fire and made straight for the Kamino Forest where the Schultz Sewing Machine truck had been hiding for six weeks. Dysthmus had already reached out to Father Lipinski and Heinrich Gruber with an invitation to join them in Sochaczew. Father would be an aid and a comfort to the aging Father Henryk there and his able assistant, the young Father Chmielewski. Heinrich would disassociate himself from the world of spies and intrigue and begin a new lifestyle by taking on the duties of a peasant farm hand on the Furtak farm.

Bór's message to London regarding possible capitulation was sent by Slota. Bórza stood by and watched the cryptic message being typed out; she laid a heavy hand on his shoulder and gave a soft squeeze.

"We will all wind up dead or in Pruszków. I don't know which is worst," she took a deep breath, "I'll be right back."

Her cot and trunk were all the possessions she had, she sat on the cot and rummaged through her trunk for the gift Virski had given her at the beginning of their relationship. Virski had witnessed many atrocities committed by the Nazis. He knew what went on in Pruszków. She rooted about until she came upon the small ring case. She held the tiny object in her hand and remembered the occasion when Virski gave it to her. She lifted the lid and removed the small capsule that was embedded within the padded crease. She brought the capsule to her lips and bit hard on the shell.

With capitulation just hours away, Bór was involved with matters that must be stipulated in the agreement before signing the document. He and Colonel Kumor put together an agreement from which they would not deviate. There would be no agreement on the condition that the underground movement be considered in the terms of surrender. It was essential that the movement continue operations throughout Poland for the duration of the war. Bór was implicit in his demand that the communist faction, the Armja Ludowa, be granted the same combatant status as the Home Army, and that the members of the Warsaw underground be granted the same evacuation rights as the rest of the citizens.

Kumor, along with Zyndram were the delegates that would meet with Von dem Bach. They arrived at the German barricades at 8 a.m. on the second of October and were promptly escorted to Von dem Bach's headquarters on the Ożarów Estate, six miles outside of Warsaw.

Bach greeted them by announcing his full title, *"Obergruppenführer S.S. und General der Polizei* von dem Bach," The negotiations took place at a round table in the center of the room. Off in a corner, the General's Chief of Staff sat at his desk. Kumor and Zyndram stoically looked on as Bach read Bór's letter authorizing his delegates to discuss and sign an agreement for an armistice.

Bach opened the discussion with a requisite that German forces should immediately occupy the area where the Home Army was centered. He made it clear that this was a guarantee that negotiations for the surrender would not be put off by the Poles if the Soviets sought to intervene on their behalf.

Kumor spoke up. "That is totally not possible," he gruffed "the hostility that both sides have towards one another might spark an offensive act that would set aside any further talks of capitulation."

Bach stood his ground and Zyndram was sent back to Warsaw to convey this message to Bór, who offered a compensatory solution. In order to show good faith, he offered to remove the barricade on Śniadeckich Street that faced the Polytechnic School as a sign that negotiations need not be broken off.

Zyndram returned with the solution and the talks resumed.

Once that issue was resolved, Kumor apprised Bach, "We have a prepared text, written by General Bór-Komorowski on the stipulations of the agreement that cannot be altered." Kumor, a veritable fortress of a man, stared directly into Bach's eyes, which flinched ever so slightly.

Bach and his Chief of Staff were taken aback by this notion, but they agreed to place it under discussion. The proposals were forthright, and the conditions were in the province of military acceptance; there were only a few minor adjustments which were easily employed. All of the Polish proposals were accepted by both sides as a binding agreement.

At 8 p.m. on October 2nd the surrender agreement was signed at Bach's headquarters. A feeling of *déjà vu* came over the unemotional Kumor. Poland's defeat under the blitzkrieg of 1939 also resulted in a document of surrender which was signed 6 October 1939.

Chapter Fifty-Six

The care and protection of government documents was a primary concern within the administrative groups of the Secret State. This contingency had been planned for in the early days of Resistance, during the implementation of the bureaucratic structure that was to be headed by a plenipotentiary.

The street maps of pre-war Poland, had been pilfered from the archives of the City Planning and Development Office under the noses of the German administration. Architect Adam Wiadek, who held an administrative post at the office, had the maps transported to Home Army's Headquarters in the forest where they were safely stored until the end of the war, when Poland would be independent and able to rebuild Warsaw and Old Town. The documents had been commissioned to the care of Colonel Kumor. Kumor, however, was incarcerated, along with General Bór and was considered a prisoner of war.

Zygmunt Kaminski, in his relentless pursuit for items of news, had been a constant irritation for the Colonel. Kumor was a strict administrator with no sense of humor, but his long military experience taught him how to evaluate men. He gauged the metal of Kaminski to be loyal and trustworthy.

Prior to his role in signing the agreement with Von dem Bach, when capitulation was inevitable, Kumor placed the packet of maps and the responsibility that went along with them, into the hands of Kaminski. The Colonel's gut level was satisfied in the knowledge that Kaminski would lay down his life for the documents but also, Kaminski was known to be a sly and innovative individual who could maneuver his way around any situation.

Legality and documents were synonymous entities in the Secret Court. All documents were maintained in triplicate. Judge Peter Butkowski, Advocate Albert Pierski, and Advocate Michal Bednarek held possession of the recriminatory war crimes documentation of the German Third Reich. When, in the future, an International War Crimes Tribunal would be held, these documents would validate the heinous undertakings of the Nazi Party. One of the three participants was sure to make it alive to bring forth the evidence to testify on behalf of the Polish people.

The cease fire began at midnight of 30 September. During those early morning hours, Dysthmus and Kurt had rescued the Schultz Sewing Machine truck and made their way to the rectory to pick up their stow away passengers. Father Lipinski and Heinrich Gruber had their rucksacks packed and ready to go. Father blessed the rescuers with a prayer.

"Father, your Angels have kept watch over these brave men throughout the horrors of the occupation. Now that a rebellion has cost us everything, please command your Angels to guard their hearts and minds, and may we reach Sochaczew safely. In the name of the Father, the Son and the Holy Ghost. Amen."

After the chorus of "Amens," Father placed his hand on Dysthmus shoulder, "Son, will you consider taking Pani Trypka along with us? She has no family, and she has devoted her life in service to God; surely there is a place for her in the country?"

Dysthmus sucked in his lips, let his eyes roam about the room, "Kurt?"

"Of course, Dysthmus! She would be most welcome in any home; she's a good woman and a willing worker."

"Michal, where are Zygmunt and Jerzy? I should like to see them one more time, and bless them."

"Sorry, Father, they are busy folding secret documents into past issues of the Journal. They are in the basement on Pious Street."

"Dysthmus," Michal rose from the table, "I also have vitally important documents that I must keep in my possession, but the carton would be too cumbersome for me to carry through the streets…"

"And how will you get them from Sochaczew?"

"No, no! I need you to drop them off at Pan Świątek's home, he has agreed to transport them along with his priceless antiques to Leśna Podkowa."

Dysthmus chuckled, "Of course! I'd love to say goodbye to the old gent. We'll stop by on our way."

"Leona," Father took her hand, "you are God's child, be strong for your family. Michal and Irena, we have all been in God's hands during these terrible sixty-three days; we are here to tell about it. May God bless your lives so that one day you will live in peace. In the name of the Father, the Son, and the Holy Ghost. Amen."

Heinrich took Michal's hand, "I wish the Bednarek's the same. Have a happy life!"

Heinrich, I shall always be grateful to you for the way you watched over Leona," he gave an extra squeeze to the hand he held, "and for my wonderful son-in-law."

"Okay, okay! Let's get moving," Dysthmus took charge, "Kurt, grab an end of that carton; we'll take care of the legal stuff first."

The Stationery Store on Buxom Street had been leveled; the paper products on the shelves fed the blaze. Kaminski and Jerzy were cautiously treading their way through the debris to reach the basement door. They had all their hopes pinned on St. Anthony to bless them on this mission. There was no door—but the stairway, although not too stable, was available if one chose to trust it.

They looked querulously at one another, engaging in a 'who goes first?'" perspective.

"I'll go." Jerzy resolutely started down the stairs backward, hoping to have the movement of his hands available in the event he would need to cling to something should the stairs fail him.

"I don't know what's holding the banisters in place, but they seem stable enough."

Zygmunt waited until Jerzy was on solid ground before undergoing the descent.

"Now, if only we can get back up."

Jerzy was already on his way to the cement block under the window that had been the repository for insurgent funds. He set his knife into the loosened mortar and pulled the block out, leaving it to fall to the floor. Within the hole was a metal box, "It's all here!'

The houses across the street from the store had been a storage fortress during the Resistance. Ammunition, canned and dry goods, medicine, and money derived from the Allied air flights were hidden in the basements. A goodly sum of money was allocated to provide a stop-over for traveling insurgents.

Out on the street, with crumbled paving under their feet, they were surprised by a German patrol that was cautiously advancing before them. The commanding officer's eyes looking left to right. The cease fire had been established, but there was always the possibility of a foolish sniper attack. The troops marched stiffly, ready to spring into action.

From around the corner, a company of three Home Army soldiers, dressed for battle with helmets on their heads, armlets of red and white, and automatic weapons advanced toward the German patrol.

The German patrol was halted by the officer in charge, who lifted his hand to his cap in salute; the troops slapped the butts of their rifles, and briskly stomped their boots on the ground. The three Home Army soldiers performed a smartly executed 'eyes left' and the mortal enemies honored the cease fire.

The walk to Świątek's house was eerily silent and the scenery grotesquely depressing. Shells of burnt out houses with mounds of debris that contained dead bodies and shattered limbs. Irena clung to her father's arm and tried to keep her eyes forward. Leona looked upon the refuse with a compassionate eye, *God bless those victims and their families.*

Jacob ushered them into the parlor, where they were surprised to see a Lieutenant of the Wehrmacht sitting in one of the arm chairs, his cap on his knee. He rose from the chair, cap in hand; he was fully six foot tall, well built, a square jaw and high cheekbones addressed blue eyes and brown hair. He was young, probably in his thirties.

"Guten Tag," his voice a clear baritone.

"Ah, the Bednareks! Come sit, we've been expecting you." Świątek remained seated.

"This is Officer Gustav Maier. Gustav, may I present Michal, his wife Leona, and their lovely daughter, Irena."

The Bednareks found their seats and Świątek went on with background information. "Pan Bednarek has a double profession; he is an attorney from the Polish Court and earns his living as an accountant now that no Pole is practicing law. His wife, Professor Bednarek, taught University History, and Princess Irena has had her college studies wantonly disrupted."

"How wonderful for you, Pan Bednarek," Maier went on in creditable Polish, "you have your family intact and with you."

"Yes, thank God, we are all in one piece. And your family?"

Michal touched a nerve. Maier took a deep breath, a troubled look accompanied his reply, "My parents were killed during a bombing, my wife and children are living in a basement for shelter. There is not much food, and the hospitals are short-staffed. Pan, things are not much better in Berlin than they are here in Poland." He reached into his back pocket and drew out a small wallet. "These are my children, Adalbert and Gretha, on the other side is my wife, Wilma."

Michal took the wallet; Leona, and Irena looked over his shoulder. The boy appeared to be the younger of the two; both children were very blonde and attractive. The wife, also blonde, had a gentle demeanor.

Leona smiled, "They are beautiful." She looked up. "You have every right to be proud of them."

"How old are they?" Michal asked.

"Gretha is twelve and Adalbert is ten. God bless him, he will never have to fight in a war!" He slipped the wallet back in his hip pocket and sat down. He looked down on the floor, "My father was a Lutheran Minister," he looked up, "I have witnessed unspeakable brutality. I was conscripted in the army with the understanding that unless I served, my family would be placed in jeopardy." He turned the rim of his cap in his hand.

Świątek picked up the story, "Gustav has been like a son to me since he took command of the unit next door," he turned an affectionate glance his way. "I am endowing him with funds to help his family. Leon, his aide, a young man from Munich whose *Liebling* is waiting for him to put a ring on her finger, is also allocated a nest egg."

"I have wired the funds ahead to my wife, in the event…," he quizzically raised his shoulders.

"Now, I too have a picture to show," Świątek reached for a slip of paper that was lying on the coffee table before him, "This is the realtor's copy of a lovely villa in Lesna Podkowa that Gustav has helped me acquire." He handed it to Michal, "It's in a lovely setting outside of town and I hope to spend my remaining days there. Michal, I should like to have you and your family join me there."

Jacob interrupted the scene by ushering in a young soldier, "Leon Koenig is here."

"Ah, Leon, meet the Bednareks, they shall be sharing those benches you have installed in the lorry. Michal, Leona, and Irena." Smiles and head nods went around. "Now, Leon if you and Jacob will help load the Bednarek's belongings on to the lorry, we can be off. Jacob, don't give a thought to tidying up. This stuff will soon be ashes."

Chapter Fifty-Seven

After sixty-three days of continuous bombardment, the city took on the silence of a cemetery at night. In the early hours of 3 October, the residents began the evacuation process. They climbed out of their sheltered basements and barricades, clinging to the scant remnants of their belongings. Men, women, children, all of them emaciated and pale; many of them struggling to put one foot in front of the other. Most of the families were further hampered by having an aged member or member with disabilities that would require transport. Stretchers were not available; hastily put together stretchers made from sheets or crudely improvised wheel chairs were used. Many were carried on the backs of relatives. They had an eight mile march to Pruszków under armed guards that would prod them along.

Zygmunt Kaminski planned his exit around the evacuation time-table. On 5 October, he and Jerzy were waiting on Śniadecki Street to snapshot pictures of Bór, Gregory, and Monter on their way to captivity. Bór and Monter were at the head of the columns as they marched forward with the battalion of insurgents behind them.

German guards, with ready rifles stood by to deal with any incidence that might occur. Poles who were standing by on this cold morning shivered as they waited to bid a last farewell to their vanquished soldiers They sang out with tears in their eyes. The defiant words of their national anthem allowed them to vent their emotions, *"Poland shall never perish as long as we're alive!"*

Kaminski had his eye on one special person during the entire ceremony; he would need to meet with this individual before he left the scene. As the troops marched by, Kaminski elbowed his way through the crowd to approach the Director of the Underground Office for the Recovered Provinces. Władyslaw Czajkowski was responsible for the political future of the provinces after the war, a very influential man.

"Pan Czajkowski, I have, in my rucksack, the maps of the pre-war streets of Warsaw, entrusted to me by Colonel Kumor. I require safe transport."

Czajkowski put forth his hand for a handshake, "Of course, Zygmunt, meet me at the office of the General Welfare Council at three o'clock this afternoon."

There was a stifling air of efficiency at the General Welfare office, conversation was hushed and sparse; the employees were finishing up on last minute details for the evacuation in the morning Zygmunt and Jerzy were directed to Czajkowski's office; he was engaged in conversation with two men. He noticed them standing there and motioned them to enter.

The two men moved aside to clear the doorway and Czajkowski concluded the meeting, "Safe journey, I'll see you when I get to Kraków."

"Zygmunt, let's get you set up. It's a shame I didn't know about the street maps earlier; they could have been included in our documents, which are already on the way to Kraków, our next bastion."

"That certainly would have been a relief. Will we be searched?"

"I don't think the search will be done until Pruszków, but let's get on with your documentation." He reached into a letter basket on his desk, "Here are GWC identity cards and armlets. The truck leaves tomorrow morning at 8 o'clock. There will be two German sentries on board. You may want to consider greasing their palms. The site where the GWC employees will be transported is in Pruszków, but not in the internment camp. If you succeed in making allies of the sentries, they will alert you when to jump off to make your way to the commuter train."

"When would be the best time to confront the sentries?"

"I leave that to you. You're clever, you'll find a way," he shook their hands, "Now, I must be about my business. God be with you."

A German troop truck sat parked outside the offices of General Welfare. The morning was gray and cold, the sky held threatening clouds of rain. The employees of GWC were shivering under their load of personal items as they inched their way in line to board the truck. Guards were standing by to keep the exiting under control. Flanked on each side of the tailgate was a sentry to further control the group once they were inside the truck during the transport.

Zygmunt and Jerzy were approaching the vehicle, Zygmunt reached into his vest pocket, "You stole my watch!"

"You're crazy!"

"You son-of-a-bitch, you stole my watch!"

"Don't call me a son-of-bitch!"

The squabble grew intensely louder, the two men were shouting; the exiting line stood still as the employees gawked at the situation before them. The two sentries ran over to take control.

Zygmunt shoved Jerzy's shoulder, "I saw you messing around with my stuff last night!"

The two of them stood in fight mode as the sentries grabbed them from behind to prevent the next step.

"Bleiben Sie!"

They gave a little struggle, while Zygmunt uttered in perfect German, "How would you men like a few Marks to go shopping with?" The sentry twirled him around, Zygmunt slipped a small wad of bills into his hand. The German gave a quick glance. The other sentry looked over to see the bribe, he loosened his grip on Jerzy, who delivered a like amount to his captor. The boarding was at a brisk pace as the guards continued to prompt the evacuees by poking them with their rifle butts.

"What do you need?"

"We need to jump off the truck before the destination is reached; close enough to the commuter train station in Pruszków."

"It's a short ride."

"Let us know when the time is right."

"Very good."

"What will be our cue?"

"I will ask Mark if he has cigarettes?"

Zygmunt and Jerzy were led to the truck, the dispute having been settled, they were the last passengers to board. They sat on the floor and hung onto the tailgate. The sentries stood guard on the sides of the tailgate.

The Bednareks and Świątek were shifted about on the benches as the lorry slowed down and came to a complete stop. Gustav and Leon were heard chattering as they approached the tailgate. "We are here!" Gustav said in an upbeat tone.

"*Dziękuję Bogu!*" Świątek staggered to his feet, "I need a hot bath and a good lunch."

Michal was surprised, he expected to see an ancient villa, but the property was relatively new. A formal garden, much in need of repair, surrounded the building. A deciduous forest provided a backdrop for the scene.

Everyone was involved with removing items from the truck; Jacob supervised the disposition of the meager furnishings that would be added to the house inventory. There were six bedrooms, each with its own bath. An artist's rendition of Adam and Eve in the garden looked down from the ceiling of the huge sitting room.

"Father would appreciate that," Leona exclaimed. "How beautiful!"

Michal was staggered by the ambiance of the place. The last he saw of Warsaw was a bleakly devastating scene of death and destruction; the contrast was difficult to absorb.

When the last item found its place in the hall, Gustav went to the sitting room, followed by Leon.

"It is time for farewells, Leon and I must return to the unit."

"I was so hoping that you could share bread with us." Świątek's demeanor reflected the sadness he felt.

Gustav offered his hand, but Świątek pulled him close and held him in his arms. Gustav let the tears fall; four years of brutal combat, the loss of his parents, the uncertainty of a future for his family, was vented in that embrace.

Świątek took his toiletry kit up the stairs to his suite to take a bath. Jacob took the Bednareks to their rooms and left them to tidy themselves and unpack while he went downstairs to prepare lunch.

"Mark, have you cigarettes?"

Zygmunt and Jerzy sprung up, swung their legs over the tailgate and dropped to the ground. The sentries fire their guns into the air.

The troop truck moved on, Zygmunt and Jerzy lay on the road until the truck turned a corner; hopefully, the GWC employees would assume they were dead. They dusted themselves off and scanned their environment. They could see the railway station from where they stood, twenty to thirty yards away; they practically ran the distance. They hopped onto the platform, and had not long to wait before the sleek, silver engine approached the station. The doors opened, a conductor in the familiar uniform helped them on board. The car and the seats were clean, the electric lights were burning bright, the passengers were tidily clothed. They settled into their seats grinning at one another. At the next station peddlers were on the platform with carts of bread, cold meats, sweets, and hot tea. They weren't prepared for such a normal enterprising situation and didn't have time to get to their cash.

At the next stop they rushed off the train, Jerzy purchased a *Kiełbasą* sandwich and Zygmunt bought two mugs of tea. It was the first time in weeks that either one of them had bitten into bread. Jerzy tore the sandwich in half, and they chomped and swallowed. Several of the passengers eyed them with reproving glances.

The station, Leśna Podkowa, was their destination stop. When they alighted the train they were astonished. Houses were intact, pedestrians walked the streets and shopped the stores, the store windows displayed a variety of merchandise. Cafes and restaurants were available, just as things had been in Warsaw before the Rising. There was an aura of normalcy all about them.

They arrived in the city a day before their scheduled meeting with the Bednareks. The date was chosen in advance with the consideration that everyone would have safely arrived and found a place to settle. They took a room at the inn to refresh themselves and enjoy a good night's sleep before the reunion at Sunday Mass on the eighth of October 1944.

The only transport available to the Bednarek's were Świątek's two custom made bicycles. "The rails behind the seats should provide adequate passenger space. You only have a four mile ride ahead of you."

Leona offered to stay behind, "I shall wait with Albert, we will say our prayers in the chapel. Go with God."

The church was small. Linden wood carvings of the apostles surrounded the altar and high over the altar was a well-crafted stain glass window with a scene of the nativity. Red cushions covered the pews and the smell of incense hovered over the rafters.

Jerzy and Zygmunt got there early enough to be seated in the third row. They laid their hats on the seats next to them and were surprised when the church members smiled a *"Dzień dobry"* and did not seem annoyed.

Michal and Irena made their entrance just as the priest made his. Quick hugs were exchanged as the congregation stood. The merits of St. Francis of Assisi were extolled in honor of his feast day that was celebrated that week.

At the communion rail, Michal held the divine host on his tongue until it melted before he swallowed. Father Lipinski had run out of substitute grains to replace the depleted bread. Instead, he blessed the communicants with a small crucifix as he muttered, "Body of Christ."

Out on the lawn, the *Warszawians* stood in line to thank the priest for mass and the sermon.

"Welcome, welcome and God Bless you," he was short and portly with a saintly tonsure on the back of his head, "we are delighted that you have escaped the horrors of the Uprising. Please, do not hesitate to ask for anything that we may be able to assist you with; we are at your service."

Jerzy had his arm around Irena and held her close to him. Irena beamed a Mona Lisa smile and clung to the back of his waist as they walked towards the bikes that were slid into racks provided for them.

"Michal, Irena, come, join us at the Inn for breakfast."

"Wonderful idea, Zygmunt," he gave a gentle slap to his back, "We'll be able to test those rear rails on the bikes, to see if they are indeed passenger worthy."

Breakfast was a light fare of eggs, toast, and tea. They had all over indulged on 'real' food as soon as it was available and paid the price.

"Zygmunt, Pan Świątek has offered to house us in his lovely villa, until we are able to fend for ourselves. It's a short distance from town, only four miles. He is most anxious for you to join us as he knows that you are an avid bridge player, and he enjoys your company."

"That is most gracious of the old gent, and I am sorely tempted to accept, but the underground has not disassembled due to the death of Warsaw. Jankowski is recuperating in Kraków, but he will be taking up his post in Piotrków, where the Council of Ministers, the CNU, and *Niedźwiadek,*" the new commander of the Home Army, General Leopold Okulicki, "will take up the Resistance once again. I will be joining them."

Michal's voice was soft and shaky. "Zygmunt, this has such a sense of *déjà vu* about it. Remember the Christmas of '43', when we bid each other farewell, not knowing if we would ever see one another again?" He was openly weeping; he threw his arms around the man who had dragged him into the Resistance.

"That, my friend, is in God's province. The Underground is our domain. We may surrender several more times, but never unconditionally."

"Go with God!"

Epilogue

"When we crush the uprising, Warsaw will get what it deserves: total annihilation."

—Adolf Hitler

"I kneel before the heroes who fought in Warsaw; however, I think that the uprising was the biggest and most reckless catastrophe of Poland."

—General Władysław Anders

Aftermath

General *"Bór"* Tadeusz Bór-Komorowski, Commander of Home Army, March 1943-October 1944. Was interned in Germany at the POW camp, Oflag IV-C located in Langwasser, near Nuremburg. After the war, he resided in England until his death in August of 1966. He was buried in Gunnersbury Cemetery. In July of 1994, his ashes were exhumed and buried in the Powązki Military Cemetery in Warsaw. In 1995 he received the posthumous military award the Order of White Eagle.

SOURCE: Wikipedia

Aftermath

Deputy General *"Monter"* Antoni Chruściel was interned at the German POW camp, Oflag IV-C. He was liberated by American troops in May of 1945. He joined the Polish II Corps in London. Communist Poland denied him citizenship. In 1956, he moved to Washington, D.C. where he continued to work as a translator and lawyer. He died 30 November 1960. He was buried in Our Lady of Częstochowa Church in Doylestown, Pennsylvania. In July of 2004, the sixtieth anniversary of the Uprising, the veterans of the Warsaw Uprising brought his ashes back to Poland and commemorated him in a state funeral in Powązki Military Cemetery. In total, he received fifteen honors, including the Order of Virtuti Military.

SOURCE: Wikipedia

Aftermath

Jan Stanisław Jankowski, Deputy Prime Minister of Poland from February of 1943 - 2 October 1944, continued to engage in the Polish Resistance after the capitulation. He was arrested by the NKVD in March 1945. He was included in the infamous Trial of Sixteen, and falsely accused of collaborating with the Germans, sabotage, and terrorism. He was sentenced to eight years imprisonment. He died March 1953, there is no information on the death and burial, as these facts remained classified by the Soviet Union.

SOURCE: Wikipedia

Aftermath

General Leopold Okulicki, aka *"Niedźwiadek"* or "Bear Cub," and finally, "Cobra," was the last commander of the anti-Nazi Underground. He was arrested after the war by the Soviet NKVD and was part of the "Trial of Sixteen." He died while imprisoned at Butyrka Prison in Moscow.

The *"Trial of the Sixteen"* was a staged trial of 16 leaders of the Polish Underground State, held by Soviet authorities in Moscow in 1945. All captives were kidnapped by the NKVD secret service and falsely accused of various forms of 'illegal activity' against the Red Army.

SOURCE: Wikipedia

References

"RISING 44: The Battle for Warsaw" by Norman Davies, 2004,
Penguin Group, 375 Hudson Street, New York, NY 10014

"NOWAK: Courier from Warsaw" by Jan Nowak, 1982,
Wayne State University Press, Detroit, Michigan, 48202

"THE SECRET ARMY: The memoirs of General Bór-Komorowski"
by Tadeusz Bór-Komorowski, 2011,Pen & Sword, Limited,
47 Church Street, Barnsley, S. Yorkshire 270 2AS

"FIGHTING WARSAW" by Stefan Korbonski, 2004, Hippocrene Books,
171 Madison Avenue, New York, NY 10016

"THE SECOND WORLD WAR: A Complete History" by Martin Gilbert,
1989, Henry Holt and Company, Inc., 115 West 18th Street,
New York, NY 10011

"The Warsaw Airlift—4 August to 28 September 1944". WIKIPEDIA
The Free Encyclopedia, Wikimedia Foundation, Inc.
www.wikipedia.org

Image Attributions

Front Cover Design *by DAMTE Associates Publishing LLC*
Adobe Licensed Image 45667743 Warsaw Uprising Memorial,
Warsaw, Poland by nyiragongo and
Adobe Licensed Image 95900970 Kotwica by lukasdesign over
Public Domain Photo of Warsaw in Ruins 1944

Back Cover Design *by DAMTE Associates Publishing LLC*
Adobe Licensed Image 96163357
Kotwica Over Ruins by lukasdesign

Warsaw in Ruins and all other photo images on pages 302-305 are
Public Domain per Wikimedia Commons
Polish Eagle/Kotwica Design below and throughout
used with permission by PolArt of Michigan

"Rising"
By
Regina McIntyre
Is proudly presented by